mystic pig

a novel by richard katrovas

OLEANDER PRESS

The Oleander Press
16 Orchard Street
Cambridge
CB1 1JT

www.oleanderpress.com

First published in Great Britain in 2008

A CIP catalogue record for the book is available from the British Library.

ISBN: 978-0906672-77-8

Typeset in Centaur and Futura by Hamish Symington • www.hamishsymington.com

Printed in England by Antony Rowe, Chippenham.

The author of eleven books, Richard Katrovas taught for twenty years
at the University of New Orleans, having earlier spent several years
as a waiter in four of the city's premier restaurants. He has been a
professor of English at Western Michigan University since 2003, and
the founding director of the Prague Summer Program since the early
90s. Katrovas's poems, stories and essays have appeared in many of the
leading literary journals and anthologies in America, and he has been
the recipient of numerous grants and awards. Katrovas is the father of
three glorious Czech-American daughters, Ema, Anna, and Ella.

The priest shall offer them up in smoke on the altar as food,
an offering by fire for a soothing aroma; all fat is the LORD'S.

Leviticus 3:16

SECTION ONE

THE KITCHEN SMELLED of the night's greases all soaped over. Someone, probably Chef Michael, had left the door to the walk-in freezer ajar. Nat pressed it shut with the toe of his shoe, and composed in his head the note he would leave Michael after the weekend hustle. Michael, he knew, was plotting to leave anyway, to join the crew at that glitzy new joint on Napoleon; by firing him now Nat would give Michael a while to simmer before the new job started. Otherwise, Michael would screw up nightly and probably rob the restaurant right up to the day he planned to quit, no doubt on that Thursday before Mardi Gras weekend.

> *Michael:*
> *I thank you for three years of splendid service. Clear out your locker and pick up your final check from Peggy. Do not hesitate to list me as a reference.*
> *Sincerely,*
> *Nathan Moore*

Simple. Everything simple, direct. Things get screwed up by elaboration. Every major horror the world had known issued from it. Politicians, of course, were its foul princes: redundancy in the service of obfuscation. Thinking of politicians, Nat always envisioned a microscope slide filmed by translucent minutiae, deadly scum feeding on itself. Nat ran his fingers up under the rim of the first hole of the steam table and winced; it was crusted with flakes of turtle soup and gumbo dried and stuck there he could not know how long, at least since he'd last reamed the hole, two Thursdays ago, as he recalled.

P.S. Scrub under the steam table before you leave or you may not list me as a reference.

He'd worked all his adult life in one restaurant. When Nat was sixteen his father, a law professor at Loyola, had encouraged him to get a job because "work builds character," and was delighted when Newcastle's hired the lanky, fresh-faced white boy to scrub pots. His father had not been delighted when, six years later, graduated from Tulane, Nat was a headwaiter with no intention of going to graduate or professional school of any kind; indeed, with no intention of doing anything but working at Newcastle's, reading books, smoking dope, and having sex with numerous women.

Nat had been the only straight waiter on the floor. All seven of his col-leagues, the other headwaiter Tommy, and the six section waiters – Robby on A, Kenny on B, Teddy C, Danny D, Dougy E, and Ralph in the Bienville Room – were self-proclaimed nelly fags who had worked the floor at Newcastle's since they were pups. All a decade to fifteen years older than Nat, they'd mothered him, collectively, and instructed him well. They'd turned him into a very good waiter, and had voted him second headwaiter over the mild objections of Kent Newcastle. Now Nat was the owner, and three of the Old Queens, as they came to refer to themselves, still haunted to glorious effect the crimson-carpeted main dining room of Newcastle's, and had easily convinced Nat to replace their fallen colleagues (Tommy, Teddy, Dougy and Ralph had died at the height of the AIDS plague) with old friends from other French Quarter restaurants: Mickey, Lonny, Molly and Fu. Nat was very happy with his waiters. They were the best an owner could hope for. The kitchen, however, had always been a huge pain in the ass, and was at present oozingly carbuncular.

He stroked the new silver dishwasher. It was beautiful. He longed to work it one Saturday night, really put it through its paces, but knew that its faithful attendants, Rudy and Bum, mildly retarded twins who'd worked for him five years and loved their jobs, would think he was off his nut if he banged around with them on any night, much less a Saturday. They were the only staff allowed to give him serious lip, besides the Old Queens who just didn't, and they would rag him savagely. They were surprisingly loquacious and what they'd shout over the slamming and humming and grinding of their work and the hissing of the beautiful new machine would only set wobbling Nat's already quavering authority in the kitchen.

Nat read a memo stuck to the corkboard by the time clock:

Mister Moore: Pleez tel Nik stop take his dong out in the kichin. He consent pullin it out and wagin it roun. Makin it talk in that funy voise he do like it was a pupit. He git me so mess up I do my work bad.
Thank
Paul

Well... Paul was new, had only been working the line three weeks.

Nick was a little man with an enormous penis, and was a quite gifted ventriloquist. If he had not been the nephew (or grandson: oddly Mancini referred to Nick by both designations) of Roberto Mancini, for three generations the patriarch of organized crime in New Orleans and the entire Gulf South, Nat would not have tolerated Nick's clearly insane exhibitionism. But weeks, months, had passed and Nick had otherwise been a good busboy, or busman as he insisted, because nobody with a schlong like his, he reasoned often and loudly, should be called a boy-anything.

The Old Queens would each raise an eyebrow when Nick two-fisted his hose and cackled, water witching it in their direction as they stood in stiff repose, elbow to elbow, to load their trays with silver platters from the line and as he returned from dropping a tray of dirty platters and glasses and silver in the scullery; and in response to these nightly occurrences they assured Nick they'd seen bigger, though Nat wasn't entirely certain where they could have, even given their greater access than he to comparative occasions, except perhaps in the Audubon Zoo. Nat wondered, though, if the Old Queens were as impressed as he by how much brighter, wittier, more verbally clever Nick's penis seemed than Nick himself.

Nat had broached the subject of this behavior with Roberto Mancini, who had expressed what seemed genuine sympathy. Nick's mother, Mancini's sister or daughter, had been widowed soon after Nick's birth by "mysterious circumstances," and Mancini had promised to be a surrogate father for the boy, but with four sons of his own, three daughters and dozens of grandchildren, Mancini confessed, in what seemed a mild despair over the phone, that he had allowed Nick to fall through the familial cracks. Mancini had known about the behavior, had even sent Nick to numerous "head doctors" soon after the exhibitionism had begun, even before puberty, but nothing worked; when Nick's talent for ventriloquism became apparent, they'd bought him customized dummies, the best, hoping he'd transfer the complex and quite engaging personality of his penis onto one of the plastic effigies, but nothing worked. And Roberto Mancini was so grateful, so very, very grateful to Nat for employing Nick.

Nat would address the issue yet again at an employee meeting, explain again that the exhibitionism was uncontrollable behavior, a sickness Nick couldn't help. All of them just had to be patient with him, even Fu and Molly, platinum-blond lipstick-lesbians who'd been waiting tables in the Quarter for twelve and fifteen years respectively, the last eighteen months at Newcastle's, and who both looked fabulous in tuxes. When Nat introduced Nick at an employee meeting three months after he'd hired them, Molly and Fu knew immediately whose nephew or grandson "that sick little fuck" was, so cut Nat incredible slack on the issue, and Nat was deeply thankful especially to them and did all he reasonably could to compensate. He even had a slot fashioned into the wall of the foyer connecting the service bar and the kitchen so they and they alone could pick up their orders without stepping into the kitchen. Once again, he would remind everyone just how lucky they were that Nick restricted his behavior to the scullery, employee room, and kitchen.

Nat was suddenly struck with an intuition that not all the prep had gotten done. He hoped he was wrong, but rarely was on such occasions. He jerked open the walk-in, and glanced around. He counted butts, trays, aluminum bowls. He checked the flat pan of bread pudding, and it was full but for a missing wedge. He checked the pot of bisque: a white film covered the bottom. Michael had allowed someone, probably Stinkfinger, to put an almost-empty pot into the walk-in, and there was no bisque for opening tomorrow and it was highly unlikely anyone was scheduled to make it at prep, nor would there be time even if it had been put on the list. Michael had screwed up yet again. Nat put on an apron, sighing.

He pushed twelve ten-ounce bags of spinach into the processor, making sure not to puree. He melted about two and a half pounds of butter in a ten-gallon pot. He added a little more than a cup and a half of flour and stirred the roux smooth and lumpless. He poured in a quart and a half or so of whipping cream, then plopped in three pounds of (real) lump crab, three cans of chicken bouillon, the spinach and its juice. He let it all simmer. Then he melted about two cups of cream cheese, got it smooth, and stirred in five cups of milk and added it to the big pot and let it all cook for about ten minutes. Then he stirred in water until he had it right where he wanted it. He sprayed blue disinfectant on the counter and wiped it down with a paper towel as the bisque cooled, then covered the pot with clear wrap and toted it into the walk-in.

Tonight being no longer tonight, but the next dark morning, Nat poured three fingers of Grand Salute, a wicked indulgence given that it sold for eleven bucks an ounce — only a thirty-eight percent mark-up — from the liquor cart. He sipped and savored as his computer booted up. The previous morning he'd acquired the e-mail address of his birth mother. Nat had known since his mid-teens he'd been adopted at birth, but only in the last few years had felt a growing desire to find and make contact with his birth parents. Mothers, of course, are usually easier in such circumstances than fathers to locate, and it had cost eight thousand four hundred dollars to find Grace Stein.

Though Nat hadn't told anyone in his family, of course Sandra knew he was looking for his birth mother; she'd encouraged him. Sandra lived sumptu-ously and alone on Ursuline in the Quarter. Her home was a beautiful and sprawling space behind iron gates, a verdant courtyard and converted "slave quarters." Sandra's home had been Nat's sanctuary through two marriages, the births of three children, and the deaths of several friends, indeed since he and she were in their early twenties.

Professor Stein:
    Please forgive this intrusion on your life, and if you do not
answer this message I promise not to post another ever again. I am
Nathan Moore. I was raised by two wonderful people I love and
respect, and feel my life has been blessed. I am happy, healthy and
successful, and have three remarkable children by two marriages
to decent, loving people: my first wife who remains my friend, and
my present wife to whom I'm dedicated. I'm writing because I've
discovered that you are my biological mother. I feel no urge to
run to you and throw my arms around your neck and weep. And
I certainly feel no anger. I'm just curious. If you, too, are curious,
please simply ask me what you would like to know, and I will
assume similar license.
    Respectfully,
    Nathan Moore

Nat had a large, soft sofa in his office, a beige-leather blob on which he no longer would even sit since noticing what may have been cum stains on the cushions; Chef Michael, the only employee with a key and permission to occupy the restaurant when it was closed and Nat was not present, prepped on Tuesday and Thursday mornings, and would not be above cleaning his pipe into one of his snuggle-toothed Chalmette honeys on Nat's leather sofa; but both Nat's wife and ex-wife assumed he slept on the thing three nights a week rather than driving all the way uptown, of course a little inebriated after work, in the pre-dawn dark. He turned off the computer, his cell phone, locked the door then the iron gate to the front of the restaurant, set the alarm, and slipped out the back into the alley. In ten minutes at a steady stride he was at Sandra's gate.

He used his key and traversed the courtyard in near total darkness. He ran the fingers of his left hand, as he always did, along the bricks of the twenty-foot wall that separated Sandra's ninety-by-ninety courtyard from one of similar dimensions. The adjacent property belonged to the legendary jazz trumpeter Jimmy "Crawfish" Krews, who lived alone and played his own old records every night, and Nat heard the scratchy strains of "Pontchartrain Pickup", one of Krews' sassiest and most famous records from the forties as he stepped around the magnolia bush he couldn't see but knew was there. He brushed against the voodoo shrine, a genuine artifact from the early nineteenth century, and ran his fingers through the cool, scummy water of the marble fountain that gurgled unceasingly. As he approached the steps he greeted Tucker, Sandra's single-winged, half-blind Snowy Owl who, in the gauzy glow that shadowed his ten-by-ten wire mesh cage, posed upon his Cyprus stump, staring blankly off, a rodent pinned beneath a talon.

No one knew about her. No one, as far as he could tell, suspected that he was even aware of her as anything but a former regular at Newcastle's twenty-three years ago. At first no one but Teddy could wait on her; then after Teddy moved to the banquet room Robby inherited her and the huge tip she always left, fifty dollars on a hundred and fifty dollar check, two-thirds of which usually was for a single bottle of wine.

She was not beautiful, until she moved or spoke. Nat had fallen in love with her, if unshakable obsession determined by an urge to marshal all the world's tenderness (not just the measly store nature allots a single person) against any and all agents of despair, is love.

She'd caught him staring at her across the dining room as she glanced at the check; she was dressed down compared to the other patrons, but splendidly, in black slacks and a blushing pink blouse opened at the neck. She wore a thin gold chain, and a little make-up that showed in the candle flame flickering from each table, and her black hair was gathered and tied back. She caught his stare and did not look away for long seconds, and he could not.

This had happened each time she'd come in for weeks. Nat had barely contained his anticipation and while she'd been present performed his duties as in a trance, and therefore poorly. Her presence became excruciating. Every woman he had sex with became her, and women, especially the friendly regulars, seemed to peg his distraction for what it was, and so, being friends and wishing to remain at least that, began to shun his obviously half-hearted advances. Sherry, with whom he'd gone to school from kindergarten through Tulane, with whom he'd lost his virginity when they were fourteen and with whom he'd continued to have sex, intermittently, right through her marriage seven years later to a rich prick from Hattiesburg, flat out declared she could tell he was goofy over a woman.

But he'd told Sherry nothing about Sandra, nor had he even told Bart Linsey, the best friend of his youth, until much later, and then not everything. And when the object of his desire had phoned him at work on a balmy early November night when "something was brewing in the Gulf," he'd stuttered and blathered but somehow, with shaking hands, scrawled her address on his order pad. She lived only a few blocks from the restaurant so he'd paid a busboy to finish breaking down his station, then thrown his tux jacket into a drawer (where if he was lucky it wouldn't get stolen), undone his bow tie and the top button of his ruffled shirt and had run out the front door, hefty tips still scattered amid corks and crumpled napkins on two deuces in his station.

And he'd been running to her ever since.

SECTION TWO

WILLIE DIDN'T PARTICULARLY like the old white dude, but Bart Linsey had been his Uncle Teddy's best friend, and before he went and slammed his Porsche into an oak in City Park two Christmases back Uncle Teddy had made Willie promise to keep an eye on Bart. Willie hadn't known then what his uncle was talking about but promised anyway, figuring his uncle was just talking funny.

Now the old fart wanted Willie to fetch another quart of booze, so Willie plucked a twenty out of the cookie jar and trotted across St Charles to his mama's store that Uncle Teddy had bought for her. She put the big plastic bottle of vodka into a brown paper bag and glanced around before handing it to Willie. She gave him eight dollars and forty-seven cents change; he pulled down over fifty bucks a week fetching booze for stinky old Bart Linsey.

Bart sat on a couch, a shawl around his shoulders like he was some old grandma. Willie had to twist the top of the bottle for him and Bart's hands shook as he poured the clear stinky stuff into a red plastic glass all the way to the top then chugged about half in one pull. While he was chugging his Adam's apple shuttled up and down and his eyes scrunched shut. Some of the liquor dripped down the sides of his mouth like he was a baby.

Now came the really shitty part. Bart pulled out the pages he'd been scratching on. He started to read out loud, but Willie said, cool it, you've got to pay me first, so Bart stopped and said, oh, yeah, go get a twenty out of the jar, and Willie asked how long it was going to take this time, and Bart said about forty minutes, and Willie told him flat out it was going to cost him forty bucks, and Bart said fine, fine, and so Willie got two twenties out of the cookie jar and then flopped back in the big green chair facing Bart, who seemed like he was nailed to the couch. Then Bart started reading out loud and Willie acted like he was really listening.

Everybody told Willie he was special; teachers and those people who gave him all kinds of weird tests used to talk about how well he could remember stuff and mess with numbers, and he'd been reading since he was three. He was so good at figuring things out, equations and puzzles and stuff, he didn't have to go to school much. He did most of his work with a tutor on e-mail. Mainly he just read books and messed around on his Mac. In the fall they were going to make him take a couple of classes at the University of New Orleans, but he didn't know why. He didn't understand why anyone should have to go anywhere when all a body had to do was just sit at a computer or read books and do almost any damned thing they could do in a classroom. In the fall he'd be thirteen and everybody in the classes would be older and bigger and probably white. Unless he did some serious growing between now and then, he was going to stick out like a sore thumb that's also little and black.

Bart was writing an epic poem and trying to get it done before he died. Which should be any day. An epic poem is a real, real long one usually about a hero who goes on an adventure. Bart's didn't have a hero, though. It was kind of like a TV camera was sucking stuff in and somebody who wasn't a real person talked about God being words and the city being a story and how everybody suffers in their silence.

Willie had always found white people weird. He studied them. He studied them when they were walking around and when they were on TV talking to each other, and he checked out how they talked in books. Willie didn't have anything against most white people. Some had been pretty good to him, especially a couple of teachers he'd had when he was little. Of course some of them were complete assholes and should probably get shot, like that Danny Dork dude, who kept running for this or that office and used to be in the KKK. Somebody should probably have shot him, though some other racist asshole would've just taken his place. Unfortunately, racist assholes were pretty much interchangeable.

And the world's full of them. Willie couldn't walk into any store except his mama's without getting checked out, and he got funny looks from white people all the time. He was used to it, the way his showing up where white people were made them nervous, and nobody can like that feeling of making people nervous just by showing up, though sometimes it was pretty funny, sometimes it made him laugh how white people acted around him, either trying so hard to seem like they were cool with their phony smiles, or trying so hard to ignore him it was like they were taking a shit.

Bart kept going and going. Now his poem was talking about apocalypse, which Willie recalled is when everything goes real bad, and everybody gets bum rushed by Doom. And in Bart's poem everything was burning, flowers were on fire, the sky was on fire, even dreams were on fire.

When Bart finally stopped, he was sucking for air and his head rolled back and bopped the wall. He spread his skinny hand, the one that wasn't holding the pages he'd just read, against his chest, and just rested like that a minute. Then, with his eyes still closed, he asked, like always, what Willie thought of this section of *The Mystic Pig*, and Willie, as usual, told him it's a weird piece of shit and he should just throw it all in the trash. As always, Bart shook his head as if in agreement and seemed satisfied by Willie's judgment, and Willie knew he'd just keep writing and Willie would keep coming to buy him booze, listen to some more of the creepy epic poem, and tell him the same thing until Bart finally got to the end of it or just died.

Before he left, Willie asked Bart why he wanted him to listen to the poem, and though he'd asked before and Bart had just smiled and told him to go away and come back tomorrow, this time Bart smiled and stared out the side window, where the sun was slicing through the green curtains and brightening Bart's white face, the whitest Willie'd ever seen except for clowns, and said Willie was his muse.

This pissed Willie off a little bit because having casually memorized all the cross streets to St Charles he knew who the muses were, and had looked them up in an encyclopedia once. They were girls who gave poets and singers and dancers and such all their ideas. Willie told Bart he knew what a muse was and didn't much like Bart calling him one, and Bart laughed, which was like when you turn on the garbage disposal and don't know a spoon fell in, and said he didn't mean it like in the old-fashioned way, that it's okay for dudes to be muses because Uncle Teddy had been Bart's muse, and this calmed Willie on the subject because if Uncle Teddy could be a muse, it was cool.

Willie shut the door as Bart knocked back the rest of his glass of booze.

He kept his bike behind the store, and ran to tell his mama he was going home to mess around on his Mac. She was dealing with customers, so waved him on, and he ran through the storage hall, tripping a little over a hand truck one of his mama's dumbass workers left lying in the aisle of the path to the door.

He pumped down Broadway and curled onto Zimple, going against the one-way flow of traffic on the narrow street for four blocks. He unlocked the high gate and pushed his bike onto the small patio where his mama grew all kinds of stuff, some you could eat, herbs and stuff, and some you could only look at, flowers mostly. He entered the house through the back door. His mama's cat Reverend Jackson, who was all black except for a big white belly, pretty much hated Willie except when he was opening up a can of tuna or something like that, and then he rubbed all around Willie's legs. Willie gave the Reverend a little kick, not enough to hurt him but just enough to piss him off, then clicked on ESPN for some scores, then caught a little Oprah.

She was looking pretty fine these days, and was talking now to some white dude who actually started crying when Oprah got him taking about the booze problem he used to have. Only a white dude would think it was okay to cry on TV, and that dude was rolling in money, not as much as Oprah but a lot. He could afford a booze problem, just like old Bart who also had a ton of bucks. Only Bart was dying and the actor had a show in the top ten in prime time. Bart should write a TV show instead of that weird epic poem, Willie thought; at least somebody would want to hear what he'd written, because people can stare at and listen to the shittiest stuff on TV, but nobody was going to want to listen to that stupid poem, even for a second, even if they got paid. There had been times Willie had even come close to saying screw it, you old fart. I'm not listening to that stuff for a hundred bucks. But in some weird way it wasn't so bad when he let his mind blow around like a Big Mac wrapper in a gust of wind and Bart's voice became like music in the elevator at Maison Blanche, ridiculous and easy to ignore. When he let Bart's weird words just kind of flow over him it wasn't so bad. And sometimes when he left Bart's apartment having just sat for forty minutes or so just listening to Bart's epic poem as one listens to elevator music, the world looked, sounded, and even smelled a little different. Willie stared a second at the silk roses on the mantle, the ones Uncle Teddy had gotten his mama, and they became a gentle flame, and Willie cracked up for about ten seconds, then slinked into his room and booted up.

SECTION THREE

Nathan:

I like your name. In my only weak moment after learning you were a part of me, I thought of naming you William and calling you Billy, after Billy Eckstein, whose voice sent me into raptures. In fact, you were conceived as 'You Belong To Me' played on the radio of your progenitor's Chrysler. Your father, a seventeen-year-old second-string wide receiver for the Craighton High Yellow Jackets (it was after the big game with Carville; Craighton had won 13 to 10, upping their record to 3–4–1; your father had actually gotten into the game and caught an eight-yard pass), was incidental. It was that voice I wanted, the man from whom it issued. Your father, by the way, was killed in Korea. His first name was Larry, and I swear I'm blanking out on his last name, something like Brighton or Britton... Lord, memory is a quirky mechanism... but I do recall reading in the paper a couple of years later that he'd been killed. I was a virgin; we came together once and rolled, accidentally youthfully stupidly, the genetic dice. You, Nathan Moore, were the winning combination.

My father was a Jewish atheist, my mother a freshly reformed Catholic whose own Jewish mother had been a Christian convert. Dad voted I go down to Mexico and "get it taken care of." Mom shrieked papal fury and won, less on religious or ethical grounds

12

than simply because I was scared to go to Mexico. One heard horror stories about those Mexican butcher shops, and I actually knew a girl who'd almost died in one. You should understand, though, that it was a close call. My dad arranged for the adoption, and I spent the last three weeks of the pregnancy in New Orleans. I never saw you. They put me under and did a C-section. I never even heard you cry.

I was sixteen, and the truth is I was relieved that you were out of me. Something was definitely missing; I felt a loss, but not one for which I was compelled to mourn. I wish I could tell you that I have felt the loss ever since, but I haven't. It bled away in a few weeks. I'd managed to keep my condition from everyone, even my closest chums. I've two very dear friends from that time, women in whose company I grew up, am growing old, and they don't know you exist. I won't tell you why, at least not yet. I suppose, though, the short answer is that after some point, perhaps that period in our lives when we most needed one another (when husbands were changing into monsters or eunuchs or both, issues of family and career began to make a racket over our lives, and parents started dropping like the beloved and infirm house pets they'd all in some sense become to our over-achieving, death-denying hearts), I was just too damned embarrassed that I'd gone that long without telling my soul mates such an intimate detail. (How do you bear up knowing now that you're an Intimate Detail?). Then there's guilt, but that's the part I don't want to talk about yet, and is the chief component of the long answer.

Anyway, I emerged at the beginning of senior year, shielded by the story that I'd spent the previous spring and summer in New York with my father's dying sister. I lied outrageously, and artfully for a teenager possessing, as yet, little experience at duplicity. And suddenly everything was normal.

What is your relation to truth, Nathan Moore? Let's be pen pals for awhile. Maybe we'll decide to meet for a couple of drinks sometime, maybe not. I'll not feign affection for someone I've never met. The only reason I'm writing back is that I liked the tone of your letter, especially the part where you indicated that you're not sentimental, and because, like you, I'm frankly curious.

And like you, oddly, I've only been curious the last few years. I'd never have tracked you down, though; it would have been wholly inappropriate. But I have to say I'm mildly pleased that you found me. Well, more than mildly, but how much more I'm not sure yet.

What kind of adult are you? Do you have control of your life? Do you have many friends? You said you're still friends with your first wife, and things are going great guns with your "present" wife? On the first score, allow me to opine that men who remain buddies with exes are usually doing them no favors. It often means they've found some way to compel the woman to repress rage and loathing she has every right to feel and loudly express, and that the magic by which this is achieved is simply the same mechanism of control (call it charm, but whatever it is it's a lie in the service of power) as had by turns sustained and destroyed the union in the first place. On the second score: give me a break, kid. "Present wife"? You're screwing around, right? Tell me about it. I personally don't believe in marriage except as a contract for raising children. But if someone comes into a marriage vowing fidelity, well, a contract's a contract.

Of course it ain't that simple. I've never met an honest man.

Have you?

Grace

Nat read the printout of the letter from his new e-pal by candlelight on his sofa (over which he'd draped a lightly spattered drop cloth from the supply room). He smoked a Cuban, one he'd been saving, and sipped Remy from a chipped mug.

He'd found three of her books in the Tulane library, and perused them. Though ostensibly on different subjects, all three seemed mainly concerned with marriage. The books were written for an audience of specialists in her field and other academics in related fields, so they were hard going. Arguments between intellectual positions he didn't know existed, regarding issues he'd never heard articulated, dominated, but here and there a little rhetorical sunshine burst through the jargon — which she seemed to "deploy" lightly, though he realized he wasn't qualified to judge — and something he believed was an idea he understood glimmered awhile.

Marriage as economic structure was an idea he understood. Marriage as a power relation he understood. Marriage as the cornerstone of "patriarchal oppression" he understood. Indeed, patriarchal oppression he understood. Leftist feminist critiques of classic Marxist paradigms he didn't understand so well. He only vaguely got how the concept of paradigm – some guy named Coon or Klune or Keen… something about changes in scientific thinking – was being used. When she started in with the base and superstructure stuff, Nat vaguely recalled a poli sci course he'd dozed through over twenty years ago. He had to admit that some of Grace's writing might as well have been in a foreign language: "Fixed signs of biological sex difference," "that gender and sexuality are analytic coordinates men conceive as distinct," "new hypotheses and new paradigmatic clusters in the tradition of cross-gender renderings…" and facile references to French theorists, especially a Frog named Foucault, made the reading an enormous chore. A twenty-year-old General Studies degree hardly prepared him for such difficult stuff. But he found it all quite fascinating, and wanted to understand what Grace was talking about in her books, even as he strongly intuited that one purpose of her explorations was to "discover and marshal strategies" by which most men, including himself, would get their nuts snipped.

He knew that a lot of intellectuals took that lefty stuff pretty much for granted, especially feminists, and most especially feminists in universities. When he was younger and actually thought positive social change was humanly possible, he'd assumed, vaguely, that "some form of socialism," as he used to phrase it, was how the world needed to organize itself. He'd remained vaguely liberal on social issues and crisply conservative on fiscal ones thorough his adult life, realizing that such a configuration represented an unresolvable contradiction; but he lacked the will, and probably the intelligence, the raw smarts and sufficient points of intellectual reference to reconfigure his sense of social reality, to assume a vision of the world that was in good faith. His entire adult life he'd been comfortable with muddle.

As were most people. The ideologues who shouted at each other on Sunday morning current affairs TV shows were the exceptions, as were Christian conservatives and their spiritual brethren, those creeps who blew up government buildings and wanted to kill all dark children. In fact, as far as Nat could see, everyone with a clear political vision had, by extension, a clear agenda, and every political agenda by its very nature existed to obliterate something, and even when what it existed to obliterate seemed evil or sick or irrelevant and therefore an obstruction to happiness as someone or some group had clearly defined that most desired state, other stuff, perfectly good human stuff, always, always, got obliterated, too. Nat accepted that he was a political idiot, but considered the alternative a miserable one.

Nat waited until he got home, and the girls and Lou were in the deepest phase of sleep, to answer Grace.

Grace:

Thanks for getting back to me quickly. Yeah, let's be e-pals for awhile.

My relation to the truth? I'm in my forties, faithless in a religious (though not necessarily "spiritual") sense, and have little faith in human nature. I think I'm a skeptic, but I'm not book-smart enough to know if that's an accurate description of how I look at things. I lie, indeed live a lie. You're sharp about how I characterized my marriages, but only half right.

I suppose you should know that the reason my first marriage – failed isn't the right word – dissipated was simply that my spouse fell in love with someone else. Well, her falling in love was, at least, the final reason. Bridget had thought of herself as bisexual most of her life, and had never hidden that part of her nature from me. I'd always accepted it as a condition of our friendship. We conceived a beautiful child, our son Nestor, and lived, if not always happily usually contentedly, for eight years under the same roof. Then she met Katie and fell deeply in love. She was never duplicitous, never "unfaithful." She just told me how she felt. I thought a long time, weeks about her revelation of feeling, and suggested we separate and that she act upon her longings. For months I returned to my home to take care of Nestor only those evenings Bridget was going out with Katie.

Katie moved in; Bridget and I divorced. Nestor loves his mother and is deeply fond of her companion, whom he's lived with now for a decade, and he and I get along as well as any father and teen son I know of. So put that in your feminist pipe and smoke it, Professor Stein.

I have to say, though, that I do wince to think that I referred to Lou as my "present wife." And yes that slip does speak volumes, though the story therein is quite different than the one, I bet, you expect.

You are far away, and hardly in a position, and certainly could not feel much inclination, to pass on to anyone who would care what I'm about to tell you: for twenty-two years I've loved exclusively the same woman. I'd have married her, but she would not marry. I'd have lived with her, but she'd not live with me under the same roof knowing how much I wanted children and that she could never conceive.

She insisted that I marry someone else. She even made my marrying someone else a condition of our relationship. Please understand: my marriages have not been shams. Genuine affection underpins both relationships. I am a good companion and a very good father. I am attentive, even indulgent toward my families. Perhaps something of me is subtracted from their lives by my secret life with Sandra, but I don't know what. I believe it is even possible I'm a better father, better companion, precisely because I keep a part of my life wholly to myself and enthralled by Sandra's essence; that within the haven of my secret love I'm able to heal myself as others cannot. What peace I know I can't imagine achieving by any other means, and of course it is Sandra's will, I've always assumed, her unvarnished need, that determines the circumstance of that peace.

This is the first time in over twenty years I've put into words the deepest circumstance of my life. Sandra and I don't talk about what we are, and as far as I know, and I'm quite certain, absolutely no one knows about our relationship. Are all secrets lies? May one have such a secret as mine and be an honest man? Of course not. May a fundamentally dishonest man such as I be decent? I do ask myself various forms of this question often, and usually convince myself that I am decent.

I'm now tapping this out on my home unit rather than in my office where I usually conduct my correspondence. It's twenty minutes until midnight; Marti, my eleven year old, balanced on the lip of puberty and tough as any boy, athletic and savagely honest and bright and passionately just in her dealings with peers, I hear snoring lightly; Edie, my five year old, Buddha-like and otherworldly, shockingly introspective for her age yet quick to laugh and make small mischief, has crawled in bed with Lou, who is a gorgeous earth mother redhead whose body turns heads and whose face arrests them. My "present" wife is bright and funny, dreamy and intuitive;

she lives in novels – she goes through three romances or detective novels a week, but also serious stuff from time to time – and operates a vintage clothes store with a friend; we've argued seven times in ten years, and none of those spats was memorable except that it was framed by long periods of contented calm. Lou's nestled into her motherness, and will, I suspect, remain so well into midlife; twelve years younger than I, she probably could have done better, but seems contented, I think even quite happy, with her lot.

I will now call a cab, walk the tiny wretched creature that is Lou's dog (it was full-grown and evil when I met her, and grows more evil as it creeps toward extinction, an event I shall celebrate silently in my heart), then go to Sandra's. I'll return at dawn, do some cooking for the day, take my oldest to school, then sleep until three, at which time I'll rise, walk my youngest to the park where we will feed ducks dried bread. I'll arrive at my restaurant, Newcastle's, by five-thirty. We will begin seating by six. My restaurant is one of the finest in New Orleans. Perhaps someday you will see it. Perhaps someday you will meet your grandchildren.

So I'm Jewish; when I learned your name, I considered the possibility with some wonder. When I began my quest for you I didn't expect that kind of revelation. I rather like it. I feel connected now to something monumental, and yet also feel shame for presuming that connection. Tell me more about the family history, or don't. I really want to hear about you. I tried to read your books. You're very smart and know how to talk in a special language only other smart initiates fully understand. I think, though, that I understand some of what you write about. I'll keep trying.

Nat

Artimus was waiting at the corner. Nat climbed in the cab. Artimus, as always, said nothing, just smiled, revealing a single snaggled tooth plugged into otherwise unencumbered gums. He was a man in his sixties so ugly he'd fallen through the aesthetic realm and reentered the world grotesquely beautiful. All Nat had ever gotten out of him was his name, that he'd been married to the same woman for forty years, had nine children and twenty-seven grandchildren, and had never in his life been out of New Orleans except once to Memphis, and twice to Baton Rouge. The dash of the cab was covered with garish Sacred Hearts, saints, Marys and Jesuses. Once, out of nowhere, Artimus had volunteered that he'd never been robbed, and Nat was certain Artimus believed his good fortune nothing less than the collective goodwill of that crowd on his dash.

Nat had been thinking a lot lately about killing himself, and he wasn't sure why. He considered himself happy, yet increasingly he felt a deep, slow unvarying current for which no word he knew seemed adequate. None of those smug French terms even came close. It contained, yet was not, a yearning for not sleep but cessation.

Of course he couldn't end his life. He could not abandon his children. Yet he thought increasingly about how he might achieve extinction, and figured pills the right way for him. Was it normal for such a man as Nathan Moore, a happy man grounded in success and familial affection, to think so often of death? To fear and welcome it in equal measure?

As Artimus cruised down St Charles, Nat tried to see all that was numbingly familiar as though it was not, and as they passed Morgan Heights, where he had attended school and where Marti now attended, he recalled Dr Reed Sanger, one of only two PhDs then on the faculty of that venerable private school during the sixties and seventies. He'd stood barely five feet tall, been plump and effeminate, and dressed exclusively in fine tweeds and linen. His black shoes shined, always, conspicuously bright. Dr Sanger relished reading poetry aloud and compelled Nat's senior-year classmates to do likewise for the duration of most class periods. He encouraged histrionic, even parodic oral interpretations, so even the boys who otherwise thought poetry the stuff of girls, sissies, and other sensitive sorts, could indulge in lugubrious interpretations of "Annabel Lee" or some of Dickinson's weird little ditties and get a kick out of hamming it up primarily for the other guys in the class. Dr Sanger enlivened a subject otherwise forbiddingly boring, and toward the end of the school year hammy performances became more subdued, serious. The weird stuff began to sink in, take hold. Even talk of iambs, trochees and the like became interesting, and the class as a whole too late realized it had been collectively seduced by a natty gnome with a foreign accent (he'd grown up in Boston, they later learned from the obituary).

The weekend of the penultimate week of school, he gassed himself in his oven. The chilling news had resonated even more eerily for the fact that that Friday he'd introduced the class to several poems by Sylvia Plath, one of which, "Lady Lazarus," was explicitly about suicide. The last thing Dr Sanger had said to the class was that he believed Plath, one of those rare odd souls in love with death, stayed alive only as long as she had something to say.

Nat himself had nothing else to say, he figured, but having nothing to say had never been an issue. He'd done a little writing at Tulane, had even been encouraged to continue by a professor not known to give encouragement frivolously. Nat'd knocked out a couple of stories, a few poems in a mildly cadenced free verse, but had never been flooded with literary ambition. He'd mainly wanted to have his own business and raise kids. He enjoyed reading and going to decent movies, and though he couldn't claim to be an aficionado he loved jazz. Sandra occupied the space making art might otherwise. The story of her was the artifice of his life.

And this was the story he fashioned: the only time he'd ever feared losing her was when he wasn't married. He'd met Bridget during a trial separation Sandra had insisted upon. He'd been pressing Sandra to marry him, and she'd resisted mightily. Finally, she'd calmly insisted that they stay away from one another for awhile. She'd claimed, convincingly, that it had nothing to do with her requiring intimacy with anyone else; she'd simply needed to be alone for a little while. She'd also insisted that he feel free to "shop around," as she'd put it. He did. He met Bridget at the Pontchartrain Beach Amusement Park in a crowd of recently graduated school buddies. She was a nurse at Charity. She'd grown up in the Ninth Ward. She was pretty and funny. She became pregnant. As Nat chose to recall, Sandra insisted that he marry Bridget, that his being married would change nothing between him and her. But it did change things. It made things better. The pattern repeated after the divorce.

Having settled into his twenty-plus-year illicit relationship with a sense of finality he'd never felt in marriage, except that his marriage to someone else was clearly a condition of his happiness with Sandra, Nat rarely anymore ran his mind along the contours of their intimacy's undeniably odd configuration. An interesting twist is that she'd discovered in her teens that she'd never conceive, and had been deeply affected by the revelation, though by the time Nat met her she'd come, it seemed, wholly to terms with the fact that she would never give birth. The fact that he so clearly did desire to have children had not been the sole reason she insisted that he marry. Her own need for privacy, Nat had learned early, bordered on the pathological. Whenever they came together, at whatever odd pre-dawn hour or stolen weekend afternoon, always seemed an occasion for celebration. In over twenty years, though, she had never complained of his leaving, indeed, seemed to require that he leave her before she slept.

Early on they'd discussed why this was so, why it was they could not be together through the night, and Nat had even, sheepishly, on one occasion suggested "counseling." Sandra had laughed at him, then consented at least to discuss the matter openly. They were only a few months into their relationship and were testing their verbal intimacy; one of the ironies of their generation, Nat later realized, was that emotional intimacy lagged behind physical expression, the opposite of what had been more generally true for earlier generations, at least in the middle classes. Fucking soulfully before they learned how to spell one another's last names, so many people experienced shyness only after coitus.

He recalled what she'd intimated to him one cool late November night, regarding a particular afternoon not that long ago. She and a guy had been driving to Lake Charles to visit friends. The car had broken down. A pick-up carrying two middle-aged white men and a black man in his early twenties had stopped and offered to take them to a gas station just up the highway. She and the other person had climbed into the bed of the truck and after a couple miles it'd pulled off the main highway onto a dirt road flanked by a bayou and a thick stand of trees. The men had tied up and gagged her companion. Then they'd raped her brutally and repeatedly. They did humiliating things, the two older men taking particular delight in just standing and witnessing, cheering on the younger one's more vigorous physicality. Their goal, she'd realized even as they were achieving it, was to humiliate her and her companion utterly. As Nat recalled the story, just before dark they simply got in the truck and left.

Nat recalled weeping upon hearing this. She'd asked if knowing what had happened made him want to leave her. And without hesitating he'd answered no, no, no. But he'd insisted that she "get help." She'd asked why she should. She said that she felt no distress, at least none she was aware of. What happened had happened. It had changed her, certainly, but she wasn't sure she needed to transform into something she would have been had she not been violated. She'd told him she was actually fine with what she was, even if what she was, partially at least, resulted from being brutalized. Her loathing, her deep and abiding hatred of those men, was as much a part of her as her love for Nat.

But so much of that time was a blur. He couldn't trust his memory except as an agent of protection.

"Artimus, pull over for a second, right here," he said.

"We ain't there yet, Mr Moore," the old cabby said even as he slowed and drifted to the curb.

"Wait here," Nat said, and unfolded himself from the vehicle. It was dark. The street lamps were dim or busted in the block. They'd stopped in front of a little white-fenced brick house whose yard was a neat and busy garden. A prolific rose bush flamed with blooms and tight, red buds, and Nat reached across the waist-high fence and pinched a blossom a foot down its thorny stem, and worked it back and forth until it snapped off. He did it again, and again, and a dog inside the house began to yelp, at first sporadically, then continually, and lights popped on inside the house as he snapped off two more buds. He reached into his left pocket and worked a twenty out of his clip, folded it twice and stuck it onto a long thorn. Then he ran back to the cab, his right hand bleeding.

SECTION FOUR

WILLIE SOAKED THE beans in cold water for about an hour and a half, then sorted out a few little rocks and a couple of rotten looking beans. He drained the cold water, using a dish to hold in the beans as he tipped the pot over the sink. He filled the pot back up about two-thirds with hot water and cranked up the gas flame all the way; he blew on the blue blossom and made it shiver and sound like tiny thunder because two of the petals didn't catch right away.

When the water started to boil, he turned the flame way down, like it was one of those FM stations his mama listened to. He dumped in the chopped onions and garlic (his grandma wouldn't like him putting in so much garlic, but she'd been dead since he was eight so he figured why not) and chopped up ham bits and a couple of hocks. He salted and peppered, sprinkled in some cayenne and about a quarter of a bottle of the green Tabasco, and two bouillon cubes. Then he did something that surely would set the bones of his old grandma spinning. He plopped in two fistfuls of chopped cilantro. Sorry, Grandma, he said in his head, covered the pot and made sure the flame was as low as he could tweak it.

He ran out to the patio, dragged the cans through the gate to the curb, walked his bike out, locked the gate.

He made a lazy turn onto Broadway and some asshole honked and yelled to Willie to watch out and called him a stupid little nigger. Willie in no way had gotten in the dude's way, and he'd not done anything dangerous or illegal.

So he took both hands off his handlebars and shot a double-barreled fuck you. The red car screeched to zero twenty yards in front of Willie, and two big white dudes jumped out and ran hard at him. He jerked his bike around and tore off against the flow of southbound traffic.

Those first few pumps are the hardest. You feel like slow motion, in a dream. Living for speed, pumping to live, trying to max out, and because two huge white assholes want to hurt you, the pain is throttled by fear. Willie, terrified, thought about his beans. If these two shit-for-brains caught him, he definitely wouldn't make it back in time to turn them off. Maybe they'd burn and somehow start a fire in the kitchen and the whole house would go up. His Mac would be destroyed, all his stuff and all his mama's stuff.

He pumped so hard he pissed his pants and didn't give a damn. He hated this. He hated the flapping of their feet against the asphalt and their heavy breaths. He hated their hate and stupidity. He hated how big they were, and determined. One huffed that he's going to kill the little spook, and Willie wondered why. Because he'd flipped them off with both hands? A black dude definitely would not jump out of his car and chase you if you flipped him off. He might stop long enough to shoot you, but he definitely would not run after a bike. It's just too goddamned undignified! Why were these two dudes making themselves look so stupid, especially now that he was really smoking and they'd never catch up?

A thumb-sized rock whizzed by head-high and skimmed across the asphalt, just missing a Culligan Man van, and then another struck by his outside pedal and ricocheted at a twenty-degree angle against the curb. Then the pop and burn behind his left ear but he didn't stop. He turned left and circled back to his house.

He stood with his back to the closet door mirror and held up his mama's round little mirror that had two sides and one magnified. He dabbed at the bloody place, cleaned it, then screwed up his face to get ready for the sting and dabbed the iodine. It stung like hell and he got tears in his eyes but he wasn't crying, not officially, because when you've got tears in your eyes from pain and don't make any crying noise it isn't crying. He didn't know what to call it, but he wouldn't call it crying.

He worked a Spiderman Band-Aid over the wound, checked the beans, added some water, then ran back out and jumped on the bike. DM5835 was on the Alabama license plate, and the car was a '97 red Mitsubishi. There was a Tulane parking sticker in the lower left–hand corner of the rear windshield. They were big guys – could they play for Tulane? Two white guys on the same team? Then he remembered the bumper sticker: ALPHA PHI GUYS ARE WELL then a picture of a noose. He didn't know what it meant, exactly, but he knew where the Alpha Phi house was. He passed it on Broadway every day, and on Friday afternoons through the weekend the place was usually packed with Tulane students getting drunk and hanging on each other real clumsy like white people seem to do when they're acting like they don't care how they look.

Willie spotted the car parked a third of the way up the last block of Oak just before it hit Broadway and the Tulane campus. The Alpha Phi house was half a block to the right on Broadway.

It took him maybe three minutes to collect roughly three pounds of dog shit, some fresh, most in various stages of decomposition. He scooped up the piles with a flattened Roamer Milk carton he found in the gutter, and heaped it by the passenger door. He applied the dog shit with a stick slowly, carefully: EAT THIS BAMA.

The few cars that slid past didn't figure out what he was doing, or didn't care. And a couple of Tulane students strolling by paid no attention, but the kind of mood Willie was in meant he didn't give a damn. The writing took about half a pound, being that he laid it on pretty thick, but most of it was still left. So Willie smashed in the passenger-side window with half of a cinder block that was propped against a fence, and with three flicks of the flattened carton splattered the inside.

The alarm shrieked and Willie pedaled away. He circled and waited in the bushes half a block down. The two Alabama chumps made it out pretty fast, maybe seven minutes, and Willie was thrilled at their anger and despair. They knew he did it. They couldn't believe it, but they knew. Willie couldn't believe they were actually going to call the police. He almost cracked up laughing. The cops were going to get a kick out of the whole thing.

Willie peddled to Bart's. Instead of taking his bike to the store he jerked it through the gate and up the steps and propped it in the hall.

First he fetched the booze. Then he listened to the poem for about twenty minutes. This piece was about angels with rotting teeth and whales that swim up on the beach to die. It was also about a man who drives a car into a tree to kill himself, which reminded Willie of Uncle Teddy. It finished with a razor blade belonging to a dude named Occam slitting the sun, and blood coming out.

Again, Bart asked what Willie thought, and, again, Willie told him to burn it, burn all of it. Then Willie got the money and left. He glanced at the sun, and thought about his beans.

SECTION FIVE

I N THIS DREAM, the children on the other side of the wall are in torment, and Nat lifts the huge sledge hammer as though it weighs nothing, but when he raises it to smash the wall, it grows so heavy it falls upon his head. He touches his hair and it is wet and hot, but when he looks at his hand he sees no blood. So he lifts the sledge again, for now the children are howling his name, and some are calling him daddy, and he knows that the ones who scream his name died in a bus crash on River Road when he was nine, and that the ones who scream for daddy are the children he and Sandra never had, and this time when the hammer grows heavy over his head he directs its weight toward the wall, which gives like an eggshell, but on the other side are no children, just filthy cats covered with sores, the very ones he saw in Mexico City years ago, their eyes oozing pus, tabbies and blacks and whites, but the children's voices are louder now, on the other side of still another wall, and Nat runs to it and punches and it gives like brittle tile, crashing around him, and there is only darkness in this room, but the children's voices, their torment beyond measure, are louder still, and Nat steps into the darkness, and follows a prick of light that appears on a far wall, and when Nat touches it his fingers burn with cold, for he touches thick ice, he then pounds but cannot break through, and a light begins to grow in the room on the other side of the wall of ice, and Nat can see small bodies writhing and beating themselves, though the agent of their misery is invisible, and one child rises from the floor and presses her face to the ice, and she is beautiful and her pain is all-consuming, and Nat squats to her level and sees her lips move and hears her tiny muffled voice beg him to take her away, hears her imploring through tears, her face contorted, asking why he does not take her away from this. The ice clarifies and the girl is Sandra.

In all of his dreams over the past eighteen months or so, Nat tried to rescue children and failed. Sometimes they were his own, sometimes children he'd heard about on the news. In this case, they were children whose deaths in a school bus accident had haunted him as a child. Always they were in terrible pain. Though the dreams were lucid, there were always elements Nat couldn't recall upon waking. This time he remembered that the children called him daddy but were not Nestor, Marti, or Edie, and that there was a little girl calling to him through ice.

He didn't dwell on the dreams. Especially since he'd become a nightly drinker, he'd not recalled too much of his dreams. As a young man he'd had a remarkable couple of months in which almost every night he'd dreamed he'd left his body and flown about, and the dreams had been so lucid that Nat had not been entirely certain he'd not somehow left his body. He would even test himself, fly somewhere and try to memorize everything in that space and then look at it the next morning, and as far as he could tell what he observed in the dream corresponded to what he surveyed the next day: a newspaper folded just so on a table, dishes stacked just so in the sink, once even a dead fly on a windowsill.

He'd sometimes even left the house, flown over roofs to Audubon Park, skimmed the pond, the grass of the golf course. Once he'd seen a dead squirrel draped over the root bulge of an oak near the brick bridge between the golf course and the asphalt promenade encircling the entire park, and hurried the next day to see if it was where he'd seen it, but figured that when it was not where he'd seen it by moonlight, its absence proved nothing; a dog could have moved it, a kid with a stick and nothing else to do.

Nat didn't really think he'd ever astral projected; he did, however, think that the numerous acid trips he'd taken between the ages of fourteen and twenty likely rewired his dream machinery such that even at mid-life that whole aspect of his existence was probably whacked out beyond his own reckoning. And he supposed it didn't much matter. The dreams, though frequent and distressing, were at least interesting. He wished, though, he could salvage upon waking all the details of at least one.

Poon lay shaking on the white shag throw rug on Lou's side of the bed, and had not stopped shaking since Nat and Lou had married. Poon, short for Poontang, a name affixed to the beast by a former boyfriend of Lou's, was an unholy mix of Yorkshire and Chihuahua, though Nat sometimes half-joked that not far up the family tree there was probably a nutria sprawled contentedly on a limb. Nat as a rule was massively indifferent to all animals, except those whose parts lay broiled before him on a platter. But Poon he'd always loathed, through the bug-eyed ratty little creature's decade-long death throes, and thousands of dollars of vet bills, Nat tolerated Poon as one tolerates all the nastier bits of the human condition over which human will exerts no authority, and Poon had simply condescended to Nat from the very beginning.

Stepping into his running shorts, pulling on a tank top and slipping into some sandals, Nat scooped Poon up and took him to the front door, clipped the leash onto the ridiculous mauve collar circled with fake diamonds Lou insisted the dog wear, and walked it, slowly, so slowly, for Poon walked as though each tiny step were an act of heroic doggy will, from the porch to the sidewalk, where, squatting, as always, as though for the last time, haunches trembling in a fit of deathward-plunging palsy, Poon managed to excrete a meager watery turd Nat retrieved dutifully with tissue and dropped into a baggie. Back inside, he opened a can of special diet dog food one could purchase only from a vet, and which cost three times as much as good canned tuna. He forked the fragrant contents (like a rack of lamb; there even seemed a hint of mint jelly) into Poon's dish, and watched the creature become almost animated consuming its meal.

"Marti, get your butt up, babe," he yelled, and was answered by a prepubescent groan. "You know what we've got to do today," he added, and stripped for his shower.

As he straightened his tie in the mirror, he glanced over his right shoulder and saw shadows of Marti's feet moving through the streak of light below the door of the other bathroom, the "girls' bathroom," which he dare not ever enter, more for his own sense of well-being than theirs.

When she emerged, Marti wore the uniform of Morgan Heights: white blouse and navy blue pleated skirt and blazer.

"Nat, would you do this?" she said and thrust a brush at him and then turned away. He started at the bottom and worked up slowly, untangling the fine strands so much like her mother's in texture, though dark brown like his.

"Baby, why don't you tie it back or something before you go to bed," he mumbled as he worked at a particularly complicated knot.

"Sure," she said.

"Got your bag ready?"

"Sure," she said.

"Want frog guts for breakfast?" he asked.

"What?" she squeaked.

"Said, want some grits and grillades for breakfast?"

"That's not what you said."

"Then what'd I say, drift?"

"I'm not a drift."

"Yeah, and the Pope's not Catholic."

"That's lame, Nat."

He seasoned and floured the slices of beef round and fried them in his favorite iron skillet. Then he removed the meat and added about three tablespoons of finely diced garlic, a palmful of finely diced red onion and red pepper, and sautéed. Then he put the meat back in with some tomato and a little bit of water. He sipped Lou's terrible coffee from yesterday as the food simmered, and Marti fiddled with school stuff. He made about three cups of instant grits. He put three strips of the beef on a bed of grits, and ladled on some of the gravy.

"Eat up, Chump Change, and let's go over everything before we get there," he said as she sopped a chunk of beef in the gravy. "You clobbered him because he lifted up your dress, right?"

"Yep."

"First you slapped his hand, then he banged you on the head with a social studies book, to which your response was a right cross to his jaw."

"Roger that."

"Then when he went down you jumped on him and pounded him."

"Well, that's the part that's fuzzy. I was pissed, Daddy. Guy's been messing with me since second grade. You've heard me talking about him."

"For three years, almost every night. If I didn't know better I'd think you actually liked him."

"Yeah, well, you do know better. Tony's a creep. His brother Kent's a creep. His sister Mel's a mega-creep. Even the parents look like super-rich creeps. But creeps are creeps. Tony didn't just lift up my dress, he put his hand under. He touched my drawers, Daddy!"

"You didn't tell me he touched your drawers."

"I was embarrassed. How would you feel if somebody touched your drawers?"

"That would entirely depend..."

"Daddy!"

"Okay, I get your point," Nat said. "But you didn't just put him on Queer

Street, babe, you busted his front tooth. You sat on his chest and wailed on him."

"Not that long."

"Until a volleyball coach and two history teachers peeled you off. And you're a repeat offender. You'll likely be the first female tossed out of Morgan Heights for brutality."

"You proud?"

"Yeah, a little," he grinned. "But jeez," he added, turning grim, "you know how much Morgan Heights costs? Your mother and I already have a hell of an investment in that place. What are you going to do if they toss you? Go to a Catholic school?"

"Eeeeeeeeew," she said, puckering at the prospect.

"Public school? Jesus Christ, Marti, you want to end up in public school?"

"You wouldn't dare," she breathed, coolly.

"Don't be so sure," he said, though he knew she was right.

It's good to see you again, Mr Moore, though I wish it were under more pleasant circumstances," Dr Francis Johnston said, smiling thinly as she shook Nat's hand.

"Indeed, Dr Johnston. I'm sure this is not your favorite duty," Nat replied. Marti was already seated on Nat's right, across from Morgan Heights' headmistress; a big, busy but orderly desk separated Johnston from Marti and Nat.

"You've got a hell of a kid there, Mr Moore," Johnston said, and smiled wryly. Nat and Marti glanced at each other. Francis Johnston was sixty-ish, from one of the oldest, most venerable black Creole families in New Orleans. She'd gotten the job three years ago, much to the surprise of everyone not associated with the search for a new headmaster after Max Kelly dropped dead at a pep rally. Rather than as had been the case with old Mad Max, her advanced degree was not DEd from LSU, but a PhD in history from Brown, and though a strong believer in multiculturalism, she favored a brand of it that centered on Great Books. Numerous such delightful contradictions, passionately and brilliantly argued at the interview, backed up by a splendid resume, so dazzled the committee, on which Lou had been one of the parent representatives, that Johnston had been the only candidate of forty seriously considered.

"Please call me Nat," Nat finally said.

"I'm Fran," she shot back. "She's a hell of a kid, and we're going to hate to lose her," the headmistress finished.

"So you're kicking me out?" Marti asked, a quaver in her voice.

"Missy, what I'd like to do is what my mama did to me – take your precocious little rear to the backyard, pull up your dress, and whip you good for five solid minutes. Make you cry for shame and mercy! Now, you listen to me," Johnston was clearly warming to her task. "You are smart, you are strong, you are spirited, and Marti Moore, you've got a heart big as a house. I probably shouldn't tell you this, but it makes me happy to know there are some little girls today who'll give as good as they get, but if you're going to fight like a boy, then you've got to play by the rules. No boy would've done what you did. He'd have made an appointment. You know what I mean, Missy?"

Marti clearly didn't.

"I think she means the etiquette in these matters is to say you'll meet the guy after school, somewhere off the school grounds," Nat clarified.

"That's right. You sucker punched that boy, Marti. I wish I'd seen it. I'd love to have seen it, in fact. The pretentious little twit deserved to get his clock cleaned. But if you think you're tough enough to fight the boys, then you play by the rules: no sucker punching, and no kicking in the private parts, and definitely no biting. And you don't take them on in these halls, on this school ground. You understand? If a boy had done what you did people would be calling him a coward. Sucker punching is cowardly!"

"Excuse me, Fran," Nat said sheepishly. "Did you know the boy touched her drawers?"

"Say what? He touched your what?" Johnston said, screwing up her face at Marti.

"Yeah," Marti whispered.

"Yeah what, child?"

"He lifted up my dress two times, and I told him to stop or I'd pop him, then he reached under and put his fingers inside the top of my underwear," she finished, her voice trailing.

"Why didn't you mention this before? No, don't bother," she sighed. "Sweetie, you have my permission to whack any boy anywhere in this school who treats you like that. But I'll tell you what; I'm going to suspend you for the rest of the week. And I'm putting another little frowny face next to your name in my special book. You've already got three. One more, Marti, and I'm going to use the white-out, and you'll only be a memory here. You understand?"

"No, I don't," Marti replied. "If I have permission to pop a guy who treats me that way, why are you throwing the book at me?"

Nat glanced at her. "Throwing the book at you?"

"TV," Johnston interrupted, "they all talk like that," and then to Marti said, "two reasons: first, I asked you point blank what happened after the fight and you lied to me. Your reasons may have been noble, but you shouldn't have lied. Second, well, it's a matter of degree. Bopping a guy who puts his hands where he shouldn't is one thing, squatting on his chest and busting him is quite another. Marti, stay cool, okay? From this moment on, if you have problems with anyone, you bypass everybody else, even your teacher, even Ms Tully, come straight to me okay?"

"Yes, Dr Johnston," Marti said, sounding genuinely contrite.

"And Nat, while I've got you here, will you tell me how the kid got this way?"

"What do you mean?"

"I mean, how did she learn to fight? I've met your wife. I'm quite sure Lou didn't teach her."

Nat grinned despite himself. "I've been giving her boxing lessons since she was four. She's actually got some talent. Sometimes at holidays we have box-offs when she and all her boy cousins about her age on Lou's side, there are about nine of 'em, put on headgear and sixteen-ounce gloves and go at it. She usually takes the trophy."

Johnston smiled a second, then got serious. "Thanks for coming in, Nat." She stood, extending her hand. He shook her hand, then took Marti's instinctively like when she was small, and at first she seemed to welcome his grip, but then wiggled away.

When Nat got home from the park with Edie, the water man, *Percy* in red letters over his right shirt pocket, was shouldering two plastic jugs of spring water into the house by the back door; Nat nodded to him, held the screen door with his foot as Percy exited with four empty containers, the fingers of each large, dark hand negotiating two ten-gallon jugs; he grunted thanks to Nat, but did not look at him.

"Hi, Percy!" Edie shrieked.

"How you doin' little lady?" Percy answered without looking back.

Lou was packing for their weekend trip to the condo in Destin. They'd leave at five tomorrow morning, but she had a lot to do for the rest of the day, so she was getting everything ready now. "You want me to pack Dudley?" Lou asked.

Nat grinned, "Why are you asking me that?" Dudley was Nat's favorite sweatshirt, and had been for over twenty years. He had never traveled anywhere without it.

"Yeah," Lou breathed. "What about shoes? Which running shoes?"

"I'll take care of that stuff, Red. I'll pack that little blue duffel when I get back from the restaurant. You just get yourself and the girls. Need some help? Where's Marti?"

"No, and on the computer."

"Want me to make lunch?"

"You've got to get over to Rubyfruit Jungle, remember?"

"I wish you wouldn't call it that. It used to be my home," Nat protested, but with a weary smile.

"You gonna invite Nestor?"

"Yeah, but he won't come."

"Of course he won't, but you've got to invite him. I wish he still liked me," she said, trying to unknot one of Edie's shoestrings with her teeth. "When did he stop liking me?" She said, a Buster Brown in her face.

"When he hit puberty and noticed you're stacked like a warehouse. He just doesn't know how to deal with being sexually attracted to you."

"I don't buy it," she said as she did each time Nat made the argument.

"Fine, don't. You sure you don't want me to make lunch?"

"Mama, Poon peed!" Edie yelled from the kitchen.

"Nah, that's fine. I'll give the girls some noodles from last night, and I'll grab something while I'm at the shop."

"Why do you have to go in today? I thought Peg had things covered until Tuesday."

"We got a call from a movie company! They want to come in and see what we've got. They're doing a flick set in New Orleans in the forties, and Peg told them we have scads of forties stuff, which of course we don't, but there's a place…"

"Gotcha, Red," Nat interrupted. "You want me to take Marti with me?"

"She wants me to drop her at the library and pick her up later."

"That's fine. Did she tell you about our meeting with Johnston?"

"Yeah, some. Give me the low-down in the morning. So you're gonna sleep on the couch tonight?"

"Yeah, I think so. Some folks are coming in who like me to sit and drink with them. So I'll get back here probably right about when we want to leave. You'll have the van packed. I'll just jump in the shower then crash in the back with the girls. You don't mind driving?"

"If you drive coming back," she said.

"Mama, Poon peed!" Edie yelled again.

"Deal," Nat said, took two quick steps and bit her neck lightly, then pivoted and left the house.

As it turned out, he was a bit late getting to Bridget's, so as he cruised down State Street toward Magazine, he dialed the house.

"Yeah?" Katie answered.

"It's me, Katie, how's things?"

"Everything's razzle-dazzle in this movie. How's yours?"

"I wouldn't mind leaving a few frames on the cutting room floor. Nestor there?"

"Yeah, sure. Come here, champ!" she yelled, "your ol' man's on the phone."

"Dad?"

"Yeah, pal, I'll be there in ten, okay? Sorry I'm late."

"No problem. I was gonna wait seven more minutes then slit my wrists."

"Patience you got from your mother," Nat said. "See you in ten."

Pulling into the driveway of his old house was always a little spooky. The large down payment had been a wedding gift from his parents, and Nat had gotten it paid off in six years. Never very handy, he'd nonetheless labored, even several years into his second marriage, many weekends over the years on the numerous projects a large house generates. He'd touched every inch of the place, painting the interior twice, the exterior once entirely by himself. Bridget recently had had siding installed, and it didn't look too bad, though he'd resisted having it done over a decade earlier when she'd first suggested it. That house was the only home Nestor had ever known.

His son was a skinny, long, blue-eyed boy with straight brown hair down to his shoulders and a cameo face like his mother's. A bright kid who made mediocre grades all his life, he was a chess whiz. Unfortunately, chess seemed his only abiding interest, and as he progressed through his teens, Nat and Bridget, and even Katie, were growing concerned about what he would do with his life.

Katie's white Chevy truck was pulled all the way up to the garage door, and Nestor's new bluish-silver Corolla, the graduation present Bridget and Nat had gone halves on, was beside it, blocking the front door. Graduated just last December, having schlepped through a couple of laid back summer school sessions precisely so he could finish early, Nestor had requested that he be allowed to take off not only the spring, but the entire following school year as well before enrolling in college. Happy that at least he seemed to envision a misty future in which he would indeed matriculate somewhere, Nat and Bridget had warily assented to his wishes. He had a part-time job at Computer Land, and when he wasn't working was stationed in his room playing chess online, or pouring over books of chess strategy. How many people in the world make a living playing chess? Nat wondered. Probably not very many, but of course what Nat and Bridget kept their parental fingers crossed for was the day Nestor's knack for the game spilled over into one or another "practical" realms. Surely the ability to hold complex strategies in one's head and patiently deploy them had practical applications. Perhaps Nestor would become a financial planner or a politician or a university administrator or a novelist or an architect, though Nat would be happy even if suddenly Nestor showed an interest in pipefitting or waste management, anything other than the black and white squares of a chess board.

But he was a great kid. Before and after the divorce, Nat and he had spent long hours together just talking. Nat would read the books his son read, mostly science fiction, so they could talk about them when they went to City Park on Sundays. Nestor's was a gentle soul, and an old one, as folks used to say. At the ages of five and six he'd been one of those children who seemed an oracle of radical innocent wisdom. He never cried much, always avoided conflicts, got along with everyone.

Katie — tiny, pert, indefatigable, big butt crammed into faded jeans, wearing the sweatshirt Nat had gotten her for Christmas six or seven years ago, RUG MUNCHER in rainbow letters across her ample breasts — gave Nat a quick hug, grabbing the cheeks of his ass as she did so. Bridget had met her twelve years ago at Oschner's where they both were nurses. Nine years younger than Bridget and Nat, she seemed, like Lou, to proceed from a different generational perspective, one unsullied by mid-life melancholy. Emotionally solid and loyal, she also projected a cheerful vacuity, which seemed a perfect antidote to Bridget's tendency to flirt with despair, and, most importantly to Nat, Katie and Nestor were great buddies. They liked a lot of the same music, and she'd even gotten him to express a small interest in sports, particularly basketball, something Nat had always failed to do.

"You know where he is," Katie said as she padded into the den.

Nestor had the board set up. This time he would begin the game without one of his bishops and both of his knights. Since he was ten or so, he'd been able to spot Nat a few pieces to make the game interesting. Forty minutes later, Nat was in check, and conceded.

"You've still got some moves, Nathan," Nestor said.

"How many?"

"Either five or twelve, depending."

"On what?"

"How long you want to postpone the inevitable."

"I conceded," Nat repeated.

"That's probably been your best move," Nestor grinned.

"When you figure out a way to get rich and famous playing chess, will you take care of me?"

"Father," his son began, a melodramatic tinge to his voice, "you deserted me when I was a child! My mother's a dyke! I'm just a kiss away from hard drugs and unsafe sex! I'll be lucky to see twenty! So burden your other children with oppressive dreams of unearned riches!"

"Twit," Nat said, and plucked his ear. "So, what's it gonna be? MIT? Harvard? Cal Poly? What are you going to do with your life?"

"I thought I'd get my Associate Degree at Delgado first," Nestor responded mischievously. "I've got my eye on their restaurant management program."

"Don't be an asshole. Give me a straight answer."

"I swear I don't know. Did you?"

Oddly, this was the first time Nestor had ever posed the question. Nat told him yeah, in a way, that he'd known he wanted to be a waiter and read books and be with lots of girls; he also told his son that what kind of spooked him was that though he himself had no special talent, he thought he did indeed understand what Nestor was going through being good at something nobody would ever pay him to do.

Nat envied his son for being good at something, for having a gift, and told him so often. As he glanced around the room, the only one his son had ever occupied other than a few motel rooms and bedrooms of friends on the occasions of adolescent sleepovers, Nat considered how similarly cosy his own childhood had been, how secure and grounded. He himself had never left New Orleans except for brief jaunts; he'd seen the world, which is to say numerous faraway spots outside the Crescent City, but never occupied it. Nat's boyhood globe, an antique that had belonged to his own father and his father and his, had perched on the rear-left corner of Nestor's desk since grammar school, and was now covered with green, red, blue and yellow flag pendants marking a vast network of internet chess chums from Bismark's Prussia and czarist Russia to the Wild West and across the whale-teeming Pacific to the inscrutable Orient. Nat had never commented upon Nestor's defacing of a family heirloom worth many thousands of dollars because he knew the act was utterly innocent, and he'd never liked the damned thing anyway.

In fact he was lying to his son; he, Nathan Moore, had never in his life known what he truly wanted to do with that life. He rolled from the desk chair to Nestor's bed and lay back, his forearm across his brow, shoes dangling off the end, and gazed at the plastic stars stuck to the ceiling soaking up daylight to glow in the dark. "Yeah, well, most people never really know what they want to do. They settle. And what's sad, kid, is that the time's coming when you're going to have to settle on something, even something you may grow to hate."

"I'm okay with that, Dad. Really. I could hand you and Mom a lot of horseshit and get you off my backs, but I haven't wanted to do that."

"And we both appreciate it," Nat said, sighing involuntarily.

"But I really haven't known what I want to do besides play chess. I mean, just blindly jumping into something and then finding out later that you hate it doesn't seem too smart," he offered, and Nat nodded. "Look, I'm going to tell you something, but I don't really want to get into it with you until I'm sure where it's going. You know Bax? The guy I work with?" Nat nodded again. "Well, he's pretty hot with computers. He can design programs and stuff. We're working on something, maybe something big."

"What is it?"

"You wouldn't understand. I'm sorry to put it that way. But until we think it out a little bit more, I don't think I could explain it so it would make much sense to you."

"Sounds entrepreneurial," Nat said, heartened.

"Yeah, well, it is. Internet."

"If it takes off, will you still go to college?"

"Nathan, if this takes off, I'll buy one," Nestor said, not smiling.

Bridget's black Land Rover hummed to a stop at the curb; Nat realized he'd blocked her from turning onto the sloped driveway and felt a small pinch of the old domestic guilt. It was the sort of thing that had occurred all the time in their marriage, so many days of which had seemed littered with tiny inconsiderate gestures bespeaking boredom and dwindling affection. He drank milk from the carton; she read in bed until three in the morning. Standard stuff.

She entered clutching grocery bags. "Nat," she didn't quite yell.

"Sorry," he didn't quite yell back.

"You never learn," she scolded, more to tease than castigate.

He joined her in the kitchen, reached into a bag and pulled out a jar of green olives. As she unpacked the bags, the two paper sacks she'd carried in and the several plastic bags Nestor and Katie had fetched, Nat unscrewed the top off the jar and popped two tart little ovals in his mouth.

Always pretty, Bridget had grown beautiful with age; that is, she seemed to Nat a more attractive forty-three year old than she had a twenty-five year old. At twenty-five she'd been merely pretty; in her forties, she was striking. The creases in her facial skin, the shadowed grooves under her eyes deepened her features, made them somehow more worth gazing upon for the sole consideration of their composite beauty. He popped another olive in his mouth, then screwed the top on the jar and placed it in the door of the refrigerator which Bridget was squatting before, rearranging condiments.

"I'm taking Lou and the girls to Destin in the morning," he casually announced.

"You staying in the time-share?"

"Yeah."

She chuckled as she remained intent upon her task of ordering the condiments. "Hate it, don't you? Lou's tightening the screws. You don't have a chance," she grinned as she rose, turned to the counter for a half-gallon of milk and wedged it onto the shelf behind an almost half-empty milk container before shutting the fridge door.

"Yeah," he agreed, "I don't have a chance. The girls love it. There's a fishing pier. And Lou's best friends have already bought in."

"Tom and Jerry?"

"Ben and Harry, wiseass," he corrected, referring to the men who had been a solid couple for over twenty-five years, and who had been Lou's best friends since she was in her teens. Unfortunately, they'd never much liked Nat, though they wore brave, if transparent, faces regarding his marriage to Lou. They would arrive on Sunday, a couple hours before Nat, Lou and the girls would leave, and brunch for all was a vague goal.

"You let that woman jerk you around," Bridget said.

"And you didn't jerk me?" he shot back.

"Watch it, buster. I stood up for my rights. I never manipulated."

"I thought you liked Lou," he said.

"I do. You know I do. I've always thought she was decent, and she's certainly a good mother," Bridget opined beginning to set the table. "Grab the cheese board, would ya?" Katie had already made the lunch and put it on the counter; Bridget was now transferring everything to the table. "I just think she's manipulative. How many times have I told you that? It's not even that I think she always knows what she's doing. Some people don't. It's just second nature," she finished, tossing the salad. "Come on, guys," she called to Katie and Nestor. "I think she takes you for granted, a little, anyway. And I think your busty white trash darling's made a pretty good little life for herself."

Nestor laughed as he entered and heard the last remark.

"Ouch! That's gotta hurt, Nat!"

"I didn't come over here to have my wife's character abused," he said lamely.

Katie slapped him on the back from behind, "Truth hurts, huh, sweetie?"

"A couple of RN's with working-class daddies calling Lou white trash?"

"Working-class ain't automatically white trash, bud!" Katie yelled.

"Come on, Nat, you know her family. You even try to hold down their contact with the girls," Bridget said as everyone sat down to dig in, and Nat poured iced tea in everyone's glasses.

"Lou went to college. She's a reader. She's bright."

"And all her cousins are eleven-fingered sister fuckers," Katie chimed, and she and Nestor cracked up.

"That's a bit over the top, sweets," Bridget scolded mildly, suppressing a smile. Even Nat had to work to keep a straight face.

"Not all of them," he said finally, and he and Bridget cracked up, too. "But seriously, gang, I think you guys are too tough on her. You used to like her, Nestor."

"I still like her okay."

"Then why don't you come over anymore? The girls miss you."

"Bring 'em over here," Nestor suggested.

"I do, sometimes. But you're evading."

"I'm just not comfortable over there. I honestly can't say why. It's no big deal."

"So I guess that means you won't come to Destin with us," Nat pressed.

"No, that's not what it means, but you're right that I won't come. I've really got stuff to do, and I've got to get in to work for at least three hours on Saturday. Sorry, Dad."

"So you're not coming with your mom and me to Biloxi?" Katie asked.

"Nope, can't. Besides, I hate those casinos. They're too much like churches."

"How's that?" Bridget asked.

"They seem like places people go to be unhappy," Nestor said matter-of-factly.

"But they're exciting!" Katie bubbled.

"You can be excited and unhappy," Nestor responded, and Nat appreciated the observation, nodding.

"But they make me happy!" Katie insisted.

"What doesn't?" Nestor asked, coolly, and Katie actually paused to consider the question. Nat chuckled.

"Well, a little optimism never hurt anybody," Katie finally said. "Bridget and I'll cruise the Redneck Riviera and drop two or three hundred bucks, right babe?"

Bridget rolled her eyes, a signal that she was being dragged along yet again to realize one of Katie's swell ideas for having fun.

"You always act like that and you always end up loving it!" Katie enthused. "We can wiggle into muumuus and goof on the cool dudes wearing gold chains. Besides, I wanna catch a fight at the Hour Glass," she exclaimed, referring to the Mississippi casino in Gulfport that was becoming an increasingly popular venue for boxing. Nat and Katie shared a passion for the sport that he was much more self-conscious about than she. Katie loved boxing unreservedly, he with a twinge of guilt. She'd encouraged him to teach Marti to box, as her father had taught her. Was Nat raising a dyke? He didn't think so, but didn't much care, either. He and Katie had gone to a couple of local smokers together, and had had great fun. If Marti could live as happily as Katie, Nat didn't care if she did so as a diesel dyke or a ballerina, or both.

"You know who I saw at Whole Food?" Bridget blurted, just recalling.

"Why do people ask those kinds of questions?" Nestor responded.

"I was talking to your father," she said with mock haughtiness.

"Why do people ask those kinds of questions?" Nat echoed.

"No, dammit, I'm going to sit here until somebody guesses!" She said, playing along.

"Amelia Earhart!" Katie shouted.

"Bobby Fischer," said Nestor.

"Jimmy Hoffa," said Nat.

"You're the closest," Bridget informed Nat.

"How's that?" he asked.

"I saw Roberto Mancini. He was with a girl just a few years older than Marti. They were buying salmon."

"One of his grandkids," Nat said.

"No way. This creature was not dressed like anybody's granddaughter, and she had legs to her neck. And the old gangster didn't act like gramps. Had his paws all over her tight little ass."

"Mother, please," Nestor said.

"Right there in Whole Food. You'd think he'd worry about his wife finding out," she continued.

"He'd probably just have her whacked," Katie suggested, and everybody chuckled.

"No, from what I hear, the guy's a pretty solid family man," Nat said. "He just doesn't have to worry. No one's going to tell Roberto Mancini's family anything he doesn't want them to know. It's as simple as that. It's the arrogance of power."

"I thought you kind of liked him," Katie said. "Didn't you hire one of his kids?"

"His nephew, or grandson," Nat sighed. "And yeah, I like ol' Mancini just fine. And so do you, if you're going out to gamble this weekend. Nobody wants to give him credit publicly, but the guy pretty much single-handedly developed the industry. And he's been almost legit for over twenty years, if we accept the court's decision on that last indictment and I think we've got to. He's an old-fashioned gentleman. But he's also still somebody you don't want to piss off."

"That's why you hired his nephew?" Nestor asked.

"Yeah, pretty much."

Roberto Mancini, every New Orleans citizen knew, was about as legit as Confederate currency, which is to say no less legitimate than Louisiana politics generally, at whose soft underbelly Mancini had always managed to procure the most prolific tit. Mancini had survived that last indictment even as a former governor, two state legislators, and an insurance commissioner all ended up doing eighteen to thirty-six months in federal facilities. Somehow Mancini's bevy of honey-tongued bayou lawyers had convinced not only the grand juries, but the corruption-numbed citizens of Louisiana, in Baton Rouge courthouses and then from the solemn steps of those buildings each day before the cameras, that Mancini was just a businessman trying to achieve the advantage any successful businessman must. The public officials were influence sluts, and Mancini's just a guy trying to get an honest massage. In effect, Mancini's lawyers had convinced everyone that it was at least possible Mancini had walked into a massage parlor not realizing it was really a whorehouse. Yes, he sought help to build a giant casino in New Orleans East, one that would rival that monstrosity snuggling up to the French Quarter; yes, Mancini made no bones about his desire to transform hapless New Orleans East into "the Las Vegas of the South" as he touted it in the press; yes, he believed that the problem was not that the gambling industry was saturating the region but that it was a mere garden hose attempting to irrigate a sprawling desert of possibility. Yes, indeed, Mancini in his youth had been a murderer from a family of murderers, none of whom had ever been brought to justice. But he was also one hell of a civic-minded guy, a real local hero, a visionary, and most importantly in Louisiana, he was a Colorful Character.

"Did you ever cheat on me?" Bridget blurted.

Nat was startled, but tried desperately not to seem so.

"Where the hell did that come from?" Katie asked, and Nat was grateful.

"How can you ask such a question?" Nat said, trying hard to project as much indignation as he could fake.

"And why would it matter?" Katie asked, slicing a block of cheddar.

"Well, of course it shouldn't. But I think I'd want to cut your balls off if I ever found out that you had. Isn't that weird?" she wrinkled her nose at her own rhetorical question, and Nat was thankful that the actual question no longer hung before him, but that the conversation had turned to pure subjunctive.

"It's not like you want to sleep with him again," Nestor said matter-of-factly.

"Of course not!" Bridget affirmed.

"I kind of understand," Katie said. "If you found out he was bonking other women, it would change how you have to think about that whole time."

Nat quickly took the opening: "I can say categorically that I never slept with another woman while we were together." Was he lying? He wasn't certain if he was lying.

"That's nice, Bridget said rather dreamily, but in such a way as to suggest that the matter was not closed. She chewed a stalk of celery, stared off. Nat realized he was still married to her, a little bit, anyway, and shivered.

———————————

On the way to the Quarter, Nat mulled over that prospect. He had in fact felt somehow more married to her than he now felt married to Lou, though it was much easier being married to his "present" wife than being married to Bridget had ever been. Bridget had always been intensely focused; Lou always seemed slightly sedated, though never inattentive, distracted. It was as though Lou was on a really good drug, always, one that allowed her to function normally. Prozac? No, surely she would have told him, and as far as he knew the effects of that were not what he observed to be the essence of Lou's calm.

Because Bridget had gotten pregnant before they married, she'd been fixed to the hearth from the very beginning. Nat had certainly done a lot of his share of parenting (has any woman ever truly thought a man was doing his fair share? he wondered), spending almost as much time alone with Nestor as Bridget did, but the fact that when he was away from home meant that Bridget would be with the child allowed Nat space for his secret life; and of course he needed space for it, disconnectedness.

In his heart, Sandra, in fact, much preferred Bridget. She liked Lou just fine, but felt she had more in common with Bridget, and certainly she did, beginning with the fact that they were close to the same age, similarly intelligent, even temperamentally similar, though Bridget had a quicker wit, and Sandra probably the overall quicker mind. They even had similar body types.

As Nat conceived his secret life, Sandra had never met either of his wives or any of his children, yet felt she knew them all intimately, and certainly, through Nat, did, in great detail. As Nat imagined it, after sex they would talk for hours before he'd leave, or rather Nat would talk, talk through the details of his day, his concern for his children, for his wives, and for his business, usually in that order. Would his marriage to Bridget have lasted, or lasted longer, if he'd met her before falling in love with Sandra, if he'd never met Sandra? If he'd been more attentive, would Bridget still have fallen in love with Katie or another woman or man? That he could not answer those questions definitively bothered him now. He did not want to be a little married still to Bridget, or he thought he did not, or wasn't certain, didn't know, couldn't say.

For the first time since he met her he suddenly loved Bridget, or for a moment his love for Sandra migrated to Bridget before he could yank it back to its proper place. As he drove down St Charles he considered the moment that had just passed as he'd crossed Napoleon, half a block behind him now, and recalled awakening once before dawn as a child and forgetting that he and his mother were visiting his father's sister, Aunt Mimi, in Oxford, Mississippi; he'd walked into a closet and pissed all over his aunt's Bissel, and when he'd realized he was not pissing into his own toilet, and could not recall where he was, had howled and screeched and could not stop, could not exit that terror for much of an hour, even as his mother held and rocked him.

Such a terror raced through his veins but dissipated quickly. As he raced around Lee Circle his breathing steadied, and in the wake of that terror lingered a sadness that remained snagged to his blood even as he glided into the Quarter, from the Rampart side, down St Ann.

Michael had found the letter in his cubbyhole in the Employee Room. "What the fuck is this?" he asked evenly as Nat sauntered in through the alley door to the scullery, then the kitchen.

"It's a letter," Nat said.

"You're firing me?"

"Yep."

"Why, Nat?"

"Because we both know you're getting ready to bolt. And because I don't like you fucking on my couch."

"Who said I'm getting ready to bolt?"

"Think I'm stupid? Cornelius is opening his glitz palace on Napoleon in, what, three weeks? Four? Now look me in the eye and tell me your own fucking brother hasn't asked you to run his kitchen. You know, Michael, if you'd come to me and said you were leaving we could have done this professionally. You should have done it right. You should have given me notice, and I'd have honored it. It's that sneaky shit I hate. Every goddamned kitchen employee I've ever known was a sneaky son-of-a-bitch."

Michael acted stunned. Nat figured he probably was.

"Yeah, well, sure, Corny asked me."

"And you said no? Don't fuck with me, Michael. Don't treat me like you treat my couch. You were going to hang here until the last minute, then split, and leave me dangling, you prick."

"You're sticking a knife in my heart," Michael whined. "I've always been loyal to you."

Nat laughed.

"I've done good work," Michael added.

"To that I agree. You've been a good kitchen manager, but you're a lousy chef. You've got no imagination. You think because you can carve ice into swans you're some kind of artist, but everything on the menu was on it before you got here. We're serving the exact same high-priced slop I was slinging as a waiter here over twenty years ago, and it happens to be the same slop the place was serving before the war. I never asked for wholesale changes, but when I hired you we talked about 'evolving'," Nat made quotation marks in the air, "the menu. Remember? But nothing's changed. Not a single goddamned thing."

"This is one of the most successful restaurants in New Orleans, the whole friggin' South. Why would you want to change anything?" Michael asked.

"Because we're successful like a... like a fucking mausoleum. I feel like I'm selling tickets to Lenin's corpse."

"Heh?"

Nat gathered himself. "Michael, I don't feel like this restaurant is even mine. I feel like a caretaker. Nothing's changed in the place over the twenty years I've been here, and there's every indication nothing changed over the twenty years before that. I need to find a way to keep Newcastle's character intact even as I make it something else."

"I really don't know what you're talking about," Michael sighed.

"And that, my friend, is why you're gone. Let me be perfectly up front with you. I was going to let you go after Mardi Gras anyway. Give you proper notice, and let you walk."

"I didn't know you were such a cold bastard," Michael said.

"It's just business, pal. Just business."

45

SECTION SIX

Nat:

Okay, I smoked it, and it tasted like rationalization, but that's fine. What makes me a little happy is that you seem decent, or at least as though you want to be. This mistress of yours sounds like an interesting woman who's got your wang in a vice. Good for her, except that it all sounds a little sick. You've been living this "secret life" (goodness, what melodrama) for so many years you can't even see that it's sick, or you've grown numb to the sickness, as sick people do. Pain can sometimes become just life. Too bad joy can't.

I'm not trying to play Big Mama here, or Professor Woman, or any other female archetype you, I suppose necessarily, must attach to me. I'm simply stating an all-too-human truth, the kind mommies do indeed impart quite early and often: lies eventually hurt the liar. As long as you continue your "secret life" real intimacy will never be possible, not even with your Secret Love. You think you have intimacy with her, but you don't. No woman could insist upon the wacko arrangement you guys've managed without building a wall inside herself. There's something behind that wall she's never let you touch, and intends, obviously, never to let you touch. And so the artifice of your relationship with her may be beautiful, but it is only artifice. And as long as you require that particular, I would guess vacuous beauty, intimacy with others, with the exception maybe of your children, will be impossible, though I bet that when your kids reach a certain age they too will become inaccessible, or rather you will become inaccessible to them.

You have a sister, Martha. She's thirty-one, pretty, smart, good to the core, a pediatrician here in Austin. We're extremely close. She's had five more or less serious relationships, and has grown tough in her heart, has scars on her soul from the Romance Wars. She's been involved with a married man for the past two years. It's been very convenient, in the short run liberating. But she told me the other day how the relationship has taken a toll on her lover. I know it's not the same kind of deal you've got, yours being more interesting, much sicker, more unique, but what she told me certainly corroborated what I, too, have experienced: for the woman who decides to reap the benefits of such an arrangement, who decides therefore that she's not in competition with wifey, what becomes freedom punctuated with passion, passion puffed up with illicitness, must bear witness over time to the diminution not of the passion, but of the soul who sparks it. I cannot guess what your Secret Life has whittled you down to, though from the tone of your writing I'd guess something with a fine point. Well, that's all I've got to say about this. Martha dumped Hubby With Kids last week; she's in a funk, but now at least she'll have a shot at finding someone who wants to combine his gene pool with hers.

Listen, I would like to meet you and the kids. I'll be in New Orleans, believe it or not, this coming Ash Wednesday. I'm giving lectures at Loyola and Xavier that Thursday and Friday. Why don't you pick me up from the airport? I'm coming in on Southwest 1180, 2:20 PM. I'd love to meet the kids, but I don't want to meet any of your women. I don't want to get dragged into your lie. Forgive my bluntness, but when you found me, you found that.

Grace

Ms Showalter wasn't at the counter when Willie bought the pile of books he wanted to check out. Where's Ms Showalter, he asked, and the skinny sad-looking white dude in the real ugly brown suit standing where Ms Showalter usually did said she was sick but that he'd be glad to help Willie. Willie told him he didn't need any help, except to check out this stack of books. The man started to stamp and deactivate the bar codes on the books but then stopped and stared at the titles. He went through the stack of seven thick hardbacks, glancing down at Willie several times. Before the dude could say anything Willie shoved a note at him across the counter; it was written by Willie's mama, and said Willie had permission to check out and read books about this kind of stuff. Sad Eyes said he'd let Willie check out those books even without the note; he'd just never known of a kid as young as Willie reading about Nazis and the Holocaust, and Willie said he heard people talk about it all the time all over the place, even heard Oprah talking about it, so he read a book about World War Two, and now he was going to read some books about the Nazis and the Holocaust, especially since that Danny Dork dude baked a birthday cake for Hitler every year, or at least that's what somebody said on TV. Besides, Willie told Sad Eyes, he was twelve, just small for his age.

Sad Eyes had a strange look on his face, like he was deciding to laugh or get mad, and he just stood there for a minute, then looked at Willie and smiled, and the puzzlement in his eyes just hung there, and Willie tried to think why this skinny white dude was acting so strange, and so he asked him.

The dude stared off a second then finished stamping the books. He didn't answer. Willie clamped his chin over the top book, after Sad Eyes slid the stack toward him, and got a good grip under the bottom one. The dude still didn't say anything, just smiled with shiny, sad eyes, so Willie shrugged, shifted his stack, clamped down hard again with his chin, and turned to the door.

When he got to Bart's, nine long blocks away, his arms were burning from the weight of the books and he dropped the stack by the door. He knew nobody was going to mess with them there, so he pushed into the apartment. Bart was scribbling away with the grungy yellow shawl around his shoulders. The dude smelled really funky, but Willie'd gotten used to it. Bart was mumbling under his breath as he scribbled. Willie just headed for the cookie jar and got a twenty, then scooted across the street for the booze.

This time Bart's poem talked about a golden pig, a girl who wept diamonds, and a family sitting around a supper table munching on their king. This shit just gets weirder and weirder, Willie thought, and then in the poem millions of naked people were lined up and given numbers, and blue men wearing blue uniforms started picking numbers out of holes in their helmets, and every time a number was called out a person who had it started to scream and cry and got carried away by the blue men. The ones who got carried away were the winners, and the losers just kept standing in the line staring at their numbers and waiting

48

for blue men to call out more winners.

Bart never stopped shaking, though the shakes were so small and quick one after the other it was more quivering than shaking. Willie glanced at the bigass sound system by the left window, huge speakers that reached almost to the ceiling. Willie had never heard music in that room unless his mama was playing it. The CDs, mostly Uncle Teddy's, were covered with dust. Why didn't Bart listen to music? Willie's mama would put on Ella doing Gershwin when she cleaned up, and Bart would sit there scribbling like he couldn't hear Ella Fitzgerald doing what she did with songs, like all he could hear was inside his own head.

Even that sillyass cookie jar had been Uncle Teddy's. His uncle had kept it in his kitchen just for Willie, and his Uncle Teddy could whip up some damned good cookies. Now old Bart used it like a wallet.

In fact, almost everything in that apartment had been his Uncle Teddy's, even the pictures on the wall and some little statues from Africa. Bart'd gotten rid of his stuff and just kept some of Uncle Teddy's when he'd moved out of that big house on Lowerline where he and Uncle Teddy'd been roommates. And as Bart started coughing so hard his white face turned red and tears poured out of his eyes, Willie wondered why he always seemed to fall apart just when he was finishing what he was reading to Willie.

Again, Willie shook his head and told Bart just to burn it and start writing something for TV or the movies, because nobody who wasn't getting paid would listen to that weird crap. Bart thanked him, and Willie ran to pluck his money from the cookie jar, then without another word closed the door behind him, and collected his stack of books.

When Willie pushed into the store, an old woman, real little and black like his grandma was, was buying a lottery ticket from his mama, and he thought about the line of naked people and the blue men, and his mama shouted after him to be careful riding home, not to mess up any of the books.

Three of them he was able to get into the little basket on the handlebars, so it wasn't so hard riding. He steered with one hand, and held the other four books balanced against his chest.

When he passed the Alpha Phi house that red Mitsubishi was parked right out in front, with a new window, and Willie decided that second if those two chumps spotted him he was going to drop the books and haul ass, but nobody came out of the house, so Willie just cruised.

Grace:

It's five a.m.; Lou and the girls will sleep until seven. I'm sitting on a terrace overlooking a gulf beach, sipping chicory coffee, which I dislike but it's the only kind Lou will drink. That woody aftertaste is but one example of the little compromises a successful marriage requires. A tiny fog bank is slipping across the edge of the water, about fifty yards from my condo tower, and a red light is blinking on the water maybe five miles out, though I'm no good at judging distances. The moon's big, and there are plenty of stars. The wind, slight but sustained, a little damp, is what I would like to feel as I lay dying.

Blunt? Like a fucking hammer to the temple. But that's okay. Better that than watery politeness, under the circumstances. It's funny: I've been dreaming about walls and screaming children behind them, but a wall inside Sandra? Maybe, but how can you, of all people, condemn that? She keeps a part of herself wholly to herself, and yes, our intimacy is an artifice and therefore a lie, but isn't it the case that artifice, even as it lies, tells a greater truth? Isn't there truth in beauty? Forgive me. I've only read a few scraps of big ideas here and there, but I've always sort of liked the idea of beauty being some kind of truth, like in that poem by Keats, though I don't see the formality of my relationship with Sandra as something to display, to be regarded by others. The secret of what we are I think has become the essence of what we are. Vacuous? Well, you're only guessing, and perhaps projecting, I don't know. Whatever we have is substantial. You can take my word for it, so piss off. Sick? What artifice doesn't issue from the sickness we feel at the prospect of life being random? What attempt to make something beautiful doesn't occur in the throes of such sickness? What you call sick in another context would be called evil. People like you have become the new moralists, the new priests shouldering a new orthodoxy, one more slippery than the old, but ultimately no less self-referential. (I think that's the term I want; see Mom, you're teaching me a new language with your books!) For you, nothing is evil; everything's sick.

And that sickness has a name, just like evil had a name. Satan, meet patriarchy! Shake hands, fellas!

I'm a father, a dull, phallic signifier (how am I doing with the lingo?) in that odd Hell of unsteady yet enduring patriarchal determinants. But you know what? I'm also a night goblin, rousting about in the shadows while others sleep. I'm a silly monster my kids are not only not frightened of, but regard more in the spirit of a large pet who comes and goes, more or less protecting the hearth, than of a gray wall of intractable laws and their enforcement. Hey, I'm just looking at myself, like everyone else, trying to figure out who I am. Maybe we never stop being sixteen. Isn't that really when it starts? Right about then? Isn't that when suddenly you realize that the child you recently were, so sure of itself, so sure of who and what it was, is a foreigner trapped inside you? It will always be there, must always be accounted for, even as you have become someone else. And there is no single moment marking the birth of that rattled self, that self wholly aware of how ordinary it is in most respects, but also feeling a uniqueness that would allow it to occupy the entire fucking universe all by itself, allow it to be God.

So you're fourteen or fifteen or sixteen and you could be God if the universe would let you, but it won't, so you have to be human and account almost daily for the child you recently had been, a child who will always be there and who will be the only immutable fact of consciousness unto death. But there's something else. An itch. A compulsion maybe? No, I prefer it to be an itch, one that never can be scratched or balmed. A sense that there is something of you, maybe the part that could be God, maybe not, that is knowable and that you should try to know. Why? No fucking reason. No fucking reason at all. There's just that itch. In my secret life, in those brief moments I indulge in that artifice, and yes I admit freely cheerfully unambiguously that it is an indulgence, the itch ceases.

My mother was born in a little village outside of Prague, and speaks with a beautiful, lilting accent. When I was a child, she told me Czech fairy tales. My favorite was about Otesanek, a child who grew out of an oddly shaped root a farmer found in his field. The farmer and his wife were childless, and joyfully accepted the weird babe into their home. But it kept growing and growing, and eating and eating, and eventually ate everything, all the farm animals, and even its adopted parents. Finally, a babicka (there's a little hook over the c that makes it ch) a grandmother, came along and with a hatchet hacked the giant child and freed everything and everyone from its belly.

Where the hell does a story like that come from? And why as a child did I delight in it? When I ate a lot of dinner, requesting seconds or thirds, my mother would joke, when my father was around, "Watch out, Tata, it's Otesanek!" And all three of us would laugh. When I was fourteen, one day I remarked offhandedly how little I looked like either of my parents, and they took my observation as the occasion to enlighten me as to why precisely it was I resembled neither of them by any physical feature. To break the tense silence that followed the revelation, I announced, "So, I am Otesanek, after all!" And my mother wept as she laughed.

Someone's walking on the beach carrying a lot of stuff I can't make out, though obviously one of the things he's carrying, a long, arcing pole, indicates his mission. Now he's opening a little chair; now he's casting a line out to the water. Now he's sitting down in the little chair, and there's a white bucket, it looks like a bucket, beside him.

The sky's darkened and the moon's rolled off under some clouds. Dawn's coming. Listen, if I'd had my way I'd have been with Sandra from the beginning, openly and exclusively. But something happened, and it's not something I can tell anyone, even you. Sometimes a person is hurt so deeply that to continue living the small joys that stave off suicide he has to find a place or condition so private nothing may trespass. I think you know what I mean, at least in the abstract.

Christ, yeah, I'll pick you up, though that caveat about not meeting my "women" pisses me off a little. Since I'd have a hard time explaining why my birth mother doesn't want to meet my wife, I'll leave the kids out of this for now. We'll meet face-to-face and figure out where we'll go from there.

Nat hit SEND, got offline, closed his laptop.

Edie had a bad dream, and Nat rocked her for twenty minutes. She babbled about a tiger and a space monster and Miss Piggy and he just shushed and rocked her until she drifted off. She drooled a little on his arm.

52

He climbed into his running stuff, laced his shoes.

Nat settled into a loose jog over the damp lip of the waterline, where the beach sloped as much as thirty degrees in places, causing greater tension on his right ankle as he headed east toward the pier, then on the left as he headed back toward the condo tower. He knocked out, he figured, about two and a half miles, then did a hundred sit ups in two sets of fifty, then seventy-three push ups to exhaustion. He hadn't been to his gym in a couple of weeks, which was unusual. He regularly went four times a week, forty to fifty minutes a session, before heading out to the restaurant. The push ups made his shoulders ache a little. At six feet, two-twenty, Nat was well built, especially in his upper body, and could bench press two-seventy on a good day. He was definitely feeling his age, though, and wondered how long it would be before he'd have to change his workouts, now consisting of fifteen sets of twelve to fifteen pretty heavy reps. He'd ask his doctor whom, of course, he dreaded seeing, but was scheduled to visit for a routine check-up early in April.

All three were still asleep, so he began to sing loudly. He sang, 'Put on a Happy Face', and danced through the apartment. He continued to sing, loudly and badly, as he made more coffee and got breakfast ready. Edie ran out and leapt into his arms. She rested there, head on his shoulder, as he continued to putter in the little kitchen then howled, "Toooooooons!" and shimmied down and raced to the television. "Toons! Toons! Toons!" She chanted, until he walked around the kitchen counter, picked up the remote and tapped it on. The roadrunner kicked up white clouds as the coyote, yet again, not only failed to catch and eat the goofy bird but got thoroughly reamed and crunched in the process. Edie squealed, "Beepbeep!" and frolicked with laughter. Then she grew suddenly serious.

"I wish he'd catch him, just once," she sighed.

Nat put a bowl of something tropically colored and loaded with sugar on the table and poured non fat milk over it. "Eat, Cheeks," he said to Edie, and without taking her eyes off the screen she back-pedaled to the table, plopped down, and spooned her cereal into her mouth.

Lou entered next, yawning and scratching her breasts through her vanilla nightgown. Over a decade younger than Nat, she could pass for being twenty years younger; she was a striking svelte redhead with faint freckles all over her Celtic-pretty face. He handed her a cup of the foul chicory blend she loved, and she put it down and threw her arms around his neck. He hugged her back, with genuine affection, and of course Edie popped up and ran over to throw herself at them, wrapping a little arm around a leg of each. She was not to be excluded from any demonstration of familial affection.

Lou released, then Edie. Lou fell back onto the couch; Edie went back to her cereal and cartoons. "Feed me!" Lou roared.

Nat toasted a couple of bagels, and put out cream cheese and smoked salmon. Lou ate vigorously. As she did, Nat entered the larger bedroom. Both girls had crawled into bed with them in the middle of the night, and Marti still luxuriated amid the clutter of sheets and pillows. He lay beside her and blew in her ear. Then he tickled her behind her neck. She tried to act as though she were still sleeping, puckered up to force back a smile that threatened to explode. Then he lifted her pajama shirt and blew a loud, wet fart on her belly. She shrieked and wrestled him hard, fizzing with giggles. How much longer would such play with her be appropriate? He hoped at least a little longer. Edie ran in and heaved herself into the action, and as the three shrieked and wrestled on the bed, Lou stood in the door. Holding an imaginary microphone, she did color commentary. "Yes, ladies and gentlemen, he was the champ, but he's met his match in the team of Marvelous Marti and Amazing Edie! Now he's down, he's out of the ring, now he's pinned! One, two, three, it's over! It's over! The champ has fallen! The champ has fallen! The champ has fallen!" Marti and Edie raced around the room, arms raised in victory, as he lay utterly defeated, splayed on the floor beside the bed.

It was warm for the season, high seventies, very nice. The sky was cloudless, the breezes small and occasional. They'd found fishing stuff in the closet, and Nat bought bait in the little shop at the end of the pier. Having grown up in a "Sportsman's Paradise" as the Louisiana license plate proudly proclaimed, he'd nonetheless done little fishing and absolutely no hunting over the course of his life. He actually spied on other fishers near him to see how they baited their hooks. He finally got his line in the water then helped Marti get hers in.

Lou sat in a folding chair, her fair skin protected by a large umbrella whose shadow bathed her, absorbed in a trashy novel the glossy scarlet cover of which flashed in the strong late-morning sunlight when she turned a page. Edie, fair and freckled like her mother, and smeared with white sun block, presided over a village she constructed from the damp sand at the water's edge. When Nat felt a tug on his line he jerked once and started reeling. "Edie!" he shouted, "I've got one!" She dropped her blue spade and raced for the pier. Marti looked on excitedly. He reeled slowly, trying to time it such that Edie would arrive to witness the whole event. It was big and strong, whatever it was, and the more Nat fought the more excited Marti became. As Edie skidded to a halt at the railing, squealing and chattering, Nat's excitement became amazement. The thing was fighting mightily, and the other fishers nearest him gazed upon his good fortune, and no doubt critiqued to themselves how he was reeling it in.

When the thing finally broke the surface, Nat wasn't at first sure what he'd hooked, but as he reeled it up he realized he'd acquired an approximately eighteen-inch baby shark.

Nat flopped it onto the bluish-gray weathered planks of the pier, and the three of them marveled for several seconds as the tiny predator flapped about. Nat wasn't certain what to do. Should he throw it back? Should he try to cook it later? He looked up for a clue from the other fishers, but they were already back to their own lines stretched out into the water. Nat wasn't even sure how to get the hook out of its mouth. He could see the jagged pointed teeth, the unmediated passion for existence in its eyes.

"He looks pretty mean, Daddy," Edie commented.

"Of course she's mean, she's a shark," Marti contributed.

"How do you know it's a girl?" Edie asked.

"How do you know it's a boy?" Marti responded.

"I guess you're right. I don't see no tail," Edie agreed.

"A," Nat corrected, transfixed by the creature.

"A what?" Edie asked.

"A tail. You don't see a tail, or the tail," he mumbled, staring without blinking at the sleek little beast. Edie called Nat's and Poon's penises tails. Poon had two.

Finally, he picked up his pole and, dangling the little shark over the railing, cut the line six inches from its mouth. It splashed, and Nat observed it pause a long few seconds then dart away. He felt bad to have left the hook in, but he'd been frightened of getting too close to its mouth. Swimming around with a hook in its mouth would be better than drowning in air.

"Why'd you let her go?" Marti asked.

"Yeah, why, Dad?" Edie echoed.

"Because it's cowardly to kill something you're scared of if you don't have to," he answered without thinking of what he was saying, but it was a satisfactory explanation for the girls, who didn't press, though upon further reflection Nat wondered if Ahab had been a coward, or had simply been trying to kill his own cowardice. He laughed at himself for making such an incredibly silly connection, but considering his own cowardice always evoked the silliest abstract reflection.

Of course there are different kinds of fear; something having the potential to kill you is not the same as its having the potential to become something that could kill you. And of course that little shark had done Nat no harm; if it bit one of his kids, he'd not be magnanimous. But that little animal's desire to continue existing, as it had gagged silently in the sun, Nat conceived in sharp contrast to his own sudden desire to cease. And as he fumbled with his line, trying to re-hook and re-bait his rig, as he listened to the chatter of his beautiful children, Nat felt more deeply than he ever had the simple unvarnished desire to be dead.

Then it passed, as it always did, but this time it left a residue, a smear of gray pollen on his otherwise life-loving heart.

And this was a secret even Sandra did not know, that at odd moments (most of his life at distant intervals but lately with greater frequency) Nat wanted, deeply and desperately, to be dead. But the desire would pass, and from the midst of a love of life he would regard that fleeting desire (sometimes it even seemed a *need*) to be annihilated, and marvel at it as though it were a dormant bulb that sprouted and blossomed furiously and briefly only to sleep again. He'd always assumed that such "attacks," as he thought of them, were common to all people, but had come to realize they were not, that he was a member of a very exclusive club. Some such as he pined for death more often than not, and found the courage to act upon their need to cease. Others, like himself, would feel the desire to die, to be dead, just occasionally. Only since the attacks had become more frequent had he thought much about them. This one had lasted all of ten seconds, and if his girls had not been standing near he'd have followed the little shark, fallen the twenty feet off the end of the pier and welcomed into his lungs the warm gulf saltwater. As he fumbled with his line Marti's grew taut and bent; Edie squealed delight and Marti reeled, gave a little line, reeled some more; in five or six minutes Nat was helping her haul a nice-sized snapper over the railing of the pier.

Early evening, they drove to a nearby restaurant. It was on the water and featured an all-you-can-eat buffet. From every corner hung a TV, each blaring a different sports event. It was filled with families, and Edie quickly found a tribe of five to eight year olds to run around with. The place reminded Nat of the wonderfully tacky joints in Bucktown near Lake Pontchartrain, except that it strained mightily at having a decor, something few of the Bucktown restaurants, to their credit, bothered with, and as a consequence achieved the marvelous anti-decor that was their charm. There was cork and netting all over, and innumerable stuffed fish on plaques. The place was called Davy Jones Locker, with no apostrophe, and the waitresses dressed vaguely like pirates, in black pedal-pushers and white blouses that had thick red horizontal stripes. In the corner of their name tags was a smiling parrot wearing a patch over an eye, an earring and a red bandana. All of the waitresses, too, wore red bandanas.

Nat, whose cholesterol was quite low, generally avoided fried foods he himself didn't cook, but decided to throw care to the gulf breezes and get the all-you-can-eat, none of which wasn't fried. Lou ordered it too, as did Marti. Edie wanted waffles, but settled, after much negotiating, on a fish burger. The Moore family bellied up to the buffet with a dozen other white people, all casually dressed, thirties and forties, a little overweight, and piled the deep-fried bounty of the Gulf onto their platters.

As he ate heartily and sipped his frosty mug of beer, Nat watched a fight on one of the TVs. A slick black welterweight was tattooing a plodding Asian kid. Nat didn't recognize either fighter, and was surprised he didn't recognize the black kid because the kid was really good, and Nat kept up with the game.

Nat had boxed a couple years in his teens, and had thoroughly enjoyed hitting guys, an activity for which he'd shown some talent; he'd have cheerfully continued in the sport, especially given that he'd possessed good power in both hands, had several of his opponents not hit him back quite so hard. The first time he'd gotten really clocked, he'd quit.

The black kid finally got his out-classed opposite into a corner and worked him over until the ref wedged between them and mercifully stopped the fight.

"That guy's good. Quick," Marti said.

"Yeah," Nat agreed.

Marti was becoming something of an aficionado herself, and was thrilled that women had begun to box professionally. Even Ali's daughter was getting in the ring! She'd seen a couple of female bouts on undercards of HBO and Show-time "championship" fights (even she was frustrated by the absurdity of so many "champions" in each division); Nat taped them, and he and Marti would watch them on Sunday mornings before he dropped off to sleep.

"I wanna do that," Marti said.

"Never," Lou said evenly.

"It hurts," Nat added, lamely.

"I know, but I still wanna do it."

"Never," Lou repeated.

"Maybe," Nat said, draining his beer. Lou didn't approve of his encouraging Marti to box the cousins, giving her lessons, buying her gloves and a speed bag that hung in the corner of her room, and which she worked over almost an hour a day.

"No daughter of mine will ever do such a thing," Lou said evenly.

"Would you say that if I was a boy?" Marti asked.

"No, I'd say no son of mine will ever do that," Lou responded. "I'd be especially against it if you were a boy. Your chances of getting hurt would be greater. Only poor kids box. It's outrageous exploitation."

Nat agreed with her and said so. Lou was usually dreamily apolitical, but on two or three issues — auto safety, violence in sports, and animal rights — could be ferocious.

"So why do you watch it?" She asked.

How many times had they had this conversation? Even Marti rolled her eyes. She didn't want to hear it all again.

Edie's fish burger was barely nibbled, and her milk was not even half drunk. She was shrieking around the restaurant with her tribe, and Nat wanted her to eat. He glanced behind him in the direction of the shrieks, which were interlaced with crowd noise and color commentary of a basketball game. He stared, searched for his daughter. He scanned the room once, twice, three times, and again.

"Where's Edie?" he said.

He rose and walked around the room. He pushed into the bathrooms, the Men's and the Women's, then he pushed the swinging door into the kitchen. A large black cook turned from dropping a fry basket into sizzling oil and stared at Nat, a cigarette hanging from his lips. "Did a little girl, a redhead, come in here?" Nat shouted over the crackle of frying and crackle of radio music. The cook shrugged.

Now Lou and Marti were looking under tables. Edie wasn't in the dining room, Marti yelled to her father.

Nat knocked through a crowd that frowned at him as he shoved toward the door. He asked the hostess if she'd seen a little red-haired girl go out the door. She said she wasn't sure, but a guy just left with a little girl who was crying. The hostess couldn't recall the child's hair color.

Nat tore through the door. A white Mustang with temporary tags and tinted windows crunched over the gravel of the parking lot and pulled onto the main road. Nat ran full-tilt to the van, fumbled with his keys, finally got in and scattered pebbles and crushed shells as he spun his tires ripping out of the lot.

He pounded his horn and pushed it as hard as he could with the heel of his hand, as though the harder he pushed the louder it would sound his fury. Bumper to bumper with the Mustang, he could not ram it for fear of injuring his baby, but he would not back off, he would die behind the wheel of that van before letting that car leave his sight. There were long lines of traffic going in both directions; the Mustang could not go any faster, was trapped, and Nat pulled beside it, forcing traffic from the other direction to arc around him, and the Doppler slide of their horns as each alarmed the air were nothing to do with him; he could not see through the tinted glass, so could not know if the driver glanced up at him, but Nat pointed again and again, showing his teeth, for the Mustang to pull onto the sandy shoulder of the two-lane road running parallel with the beach, and it finally did, and Nat angled the van forty-five degrees in front of the white car and leaped out. It was twilight; the disturbed traffic in both directions normalized; the two long lines sparkled on their opposite courses.

He was shaking. His eyes were filled with tears. His hands were fisted. He was ready to die.

The black window came down six inches. "What the fuck you on, man?" a voice squeaked.

"Get out of the fucking car!" Nat roared. "Give me my baby!"

The door flew open and a skinny kid with long greasy blond hair edged out waving his steering wheel lock like a weapon over his head. "What's your fucking problem, dude?"

"Give me my kid, cocksucker!" Nat blurted.

"I ain't got no kid!" the boy, maybe seventeen, pimples blazing across his face, shouted back, cowering, waving the wheel lock.

Nat ran at him, the boy jerked back; Nat scanned the inside of the car then screamed for the boy to open the trunk.

The boy opened the trunk. "See, man? I ain't got no kid!"

Nat had prayed, actually prayed for Edie to be in the Mustang. He sprinted to the van and spun it around through a chorus of car horns and screeching rubber.

As he ripped into the restaurant parking lot, he saw Lou, Marti, and Edie sitting on the steps. He slammed the brakes and sat in the van and wept for a full minute. Then he dried his eyes with a McDonald's napkin that had been wadded and stuffed where the windshield curved into the dash.

Grace:

It's the next morning. If you're like me, you don't read your emails on the weekends, and so will likely read this fast on the heels of the last one. I have something important to say to you, and I need right now to say it because I'm feeling each ticking second leave its shavings on the floor of eternity, and whatever it is that's whittling my life proceeds not toward some design, but brute extinction. All my adult life I've had moments, triggered by nothing I wish to define, in which I deeply desire to be dead, though dead isn't quite it, to be nothing, but that isn't quite it either, never to have been is more like it, though in those moments I seek death, which is the only substitute for never having been, though it's a poor one. Yesterday, I had such a feeling more intensely than ever before. As always it passed, but not completely.

Then later, for six minutes, I thought my youngest had been abducted by someone committed to defiling then murdering her, and as I drove back toward my wife and other daughter, I felt no hope that circumstances could be otherwise. Then I saw her, with her sister and mother, from a distance of fifty yards, and she smiled at me. The setting sun was in her face and she smiled and waved, and I realized earthly paradise is the mere postponement of inevitable disasters. I saw in her face the men who would someday win her trust and affection then desert her, and I saw the terrifying loneliness of her old age. I saw how little happiness lay beyond the happy childhood her mother and I are contriving for her, and I felt what a terrible offense against Nature it was to have conceived her, for Nature surely doesn't require any of us, and we therefore are superfluous, and all that is superfluous in Nature is an offense against It.

But fuck Nature. When Edie threw her arms around my neck and said, "Daddy, I'm sooooooo sorry! I was playing like I was a shark and laid down under the 'quarium so I could hunt the little fishes," Nature was superfluous to me, to my heart – partly a thing of nature, partly a thing contrived, like a garden – and I did not doubt my joy was worth all subsequent sorrows.

What I need to tell you is thanks for not going to Mexico.

"Who you writing at this hour?" Lou asked as he hit SEND then got offline, turned off his laptop.

"Just stuff," he mumbled, as he closed the lid. "How you feelin'?"

"Good," she said, "pretty rested." They'd fallen asleep around nine-thirty.

"Well, I got seven good hours. Been up about an hour."

She kneaded his shoulders then rubbed his temples. Then she bent over and kissed him. She tasted of morning, and he could smell her vagina.

He followed her into the kids' room, the smaller bedroom, because Marti and Edie had hustled over and crawled into the big bed at around midnight. First he touched her the way only she wanted to be touched, which was similar in terms of timing and pressure to how Sandra wanted to be touched, but nothing like what Bridget required. Bridget liked to be touched hard then fucked gently, but Sandra and Lou liked to be touched gently for a long time, then fucked hard and long. She came four times as he touched her, and as she made the little hiccup sounds she'd begun to make when Marti had gotten old enough that repressing loud moans was necessary, Nat thought of Sandra, her shrieks and grunts, her dirty talk, her hands in his hair, and when he entered Lou he thought of Bridget's perfect cunt, how it had seemed made for him, and Sandra's cunt, which was not perfect except that it seemed like eternity's cunt, or God's, or the only one that he required, but he never tired of his wife's, or hardly ever, and he fucked her for a long time, as sex time goes.

Afterwards, they lay together and spoke softly. They talked a little about Newcastle's, about Bridget, Katie, and Nestor, and Lou asked again why Nat's son, who'd known her much of his life and even at one time called her Aunt Lou, recently had seemed to dislike her so much. "It's only been the last two or three years. Remember how it was the first couple years of our marriage? He and I were pals."

"I've told you what I think. He wants to fuck you, and he's ashamed that he does."

Lou didn't deny the possibility. It even made sense. "But don't all boys want to screw their mothers? They don't all act like they hate them."

"You're not his mother. You're Lou, the sexy woman with big tits who lives with his father, and he's already kicked my ass in that ol' Oedipal thing, anyway, in a manner of speaking."

Do you think there's anything I can do?" She asked earnestly.

"Besides offer to give him a blowjob?" She smacked him on the stomach and they laughed. "Don't worry about it. He'll go to college and start getting laid and his perspective will change considerably."

"Will Marti go to college and start getting laid?"

"Let's hope so," he said. "Let's hope she starts when she's seventeen or eighteen, though we'll be lucky if she waits that long. Let's hope she's into serial monogamy, and doesn't get knocked up until she's secure in her career and relationships. But yeah, let's hope she gets laid as much as she wants, and that she likes it all her life."

"What if she's into women?"

"It seems a distinct possibility, heh? I certainly don't have any problem with that. The world will kick her ass a little for it. But Katie and Bridget manage fine. You know, I really think our little spitfires's gonna get femmed by puberty. She's always going to be a tough cookie, I think. I have a feeling she's destined to do good stuff," he predicted.

"What kind of good stuff? She's bright and does well in all her subjects, but she doesn't really shine at any one thing," Lou observed.

"But she shines, anyway," he said with pride. "She really shines."

And they talked about their children in hushed voices past dawn.

SECTION SEVEN

I T WAS THREE forty-seven in the morning, and somebody was messing with Willie's window. He knew it was the one somebody'd try to get through because it was the only one that didn't have bars.

He ran to tell his mama but she wasn't there, and he remembered through the fogginess of just waking up that she'd told him she'd stay overnight at Lamont's but would get back before Willie got up at about seven.

Whoever it was had gotten the screen off and was doing something to the window. Willie dialed 911 and told the operator someone was trying to break in and he couldn't talk long but send the police quick. He jumped into his jeans and pulled on his Georgetown sweatshirt. The dude'd given up jimmying the window and just smashed in one of the panes and fiddled around for the latch. Willie ran to the kitchen and snatched up the cleaver and hustled back and jumped up on the bed and hacked at the bulge in the curtain. He hit meat on the first whack and heard a shrieking howl and "shit" then three pops and window glass shattered in upon his bedding and he yelled "shit" and ran for the front door and crouched, listened. He heard someone gallop through the weeds on the side of the house then clang over the low, white fence. He waited.

Then he unlocked the door, peeked, switched off the porch light and walked outside, through the little gate of the white fence he and his mama painted together last spring, and stood, barefoot, staring down Zimple, shaking.

The white Ford Taurus came flashing up from the east and two white cops got out aiming flashlights at him. Hold it there, son, one of them said, and Willie said if I was your son I wouldn't be so black and the other shined his light right into Willie's eyes and said what are you doing out at this hour, wiseass, and Willie put his hand up to shield his eyes and said he was the one called for the cops and was just waiting. The one blinding him asked for identification and the other asked where his mama was, and Willie said what will it be, ID or Mama, and the one shining the light in his eyes told him to watch his mouth and Willie pushed back through the gate to get in the house and fetch his birth certificate from the Important Stuff Drawer in the kitchen, and the cop standing behind the one shining the powerful light directly into Willie's eyes said hold it, did we tell you to go, and Willie said he was going to get his birth certificate, and the cop said get your mama out here, and Willie said his mama wasn't in there right now because she went running. She's a marathon runner and gets up to run at three and goes until about seven.

He could tell by their silence that the cops were thinking that over, and while they did, Willie asked, real nice, if he could go in and get his birth certificate so he could get around to telling them why he called for the cops in the first place.

Just come here and tell us what happened, one of them said, and he couldn't even tell who because now they both were aiming lights into his eyes, and he blinked, squinted, shielded his eyes and told them. Then he led them in, flipping on lights, showed them his room. There was blood on the curtain and on the sill, and a few drops on the bedspread. There were three bullet holes pretty close together in the wall opposite the window, and three in the big framed photo of his grandma in the hall on the other side of the wall, and three in the opposite wall.

The chubby red one said it looked like Willie whacked him pretty good, and checked out the sill. Then he looked around the room, checked out Willie's Mac, the posters of Dr King, Bryant Gumble, and Ted "Mad Dog" Singer, the great linebacker who'd recently driven his car into a tree. So your mama's jogging, the blond one said, and Willie said no, not just jogging, she's a marathoner, and she's real good, and she'll be back at around seven, and Willie just hoped these dudes would be gone by then because she wasn't going to look like she'd been out running but like she'd been to a fancy party all night.

They asked him questions about what happened and wrote stuff down on notepads. Then the red one noticed a book with a swastika on the cover on Willie's desk and asked what's a kid like Willie reading a book like that for, and Willie asked what's a kid like him, and what kind of kid would he expect to be reading a book like that, anyway. Besides, Willie continued before Red could answer, what's his book got to do with some asshole shooting up his house, and Blondie got mean looking for a second and said well, little buddy, that mean ol' bogeyman knows where you live and you don't know jack shit about him, what he looks like or anything except that one of his hands or arms is wounded. Red added that the guy was probably pretty miffed right now at this house and everybody in it, so maybe Willie had better be a little extra careful from now on, and both of them got nasty little smiles when he said this, and then Blondie added that maybe Willie's marathon mama had better be careful, too. Then they headed for the front door, all their police stuff creaking and squeaking from their huge black belts as they strode across the carpet, Red laying down little prints from the fresh dog shit crusting the grids of his right boot heel.

At the door they asked again if Willie'd seen the guy's face, and Willie again said no, he hadn't seen anything, just heard the dude yell when Willie whacked him. Then Blondie said they'd make sure a police unit passed the house every few hours for a few days, and that if Willie saw or heard anything suspicious to call 911 again. Then Red said that if the police ever came at this hour again and Willie's mama wasn't home, it wouldn't matter if she was out running or whatever, Willie's going to be in a world of trouble. Red said Willie's mama should call the police when she gets back. They'd cruise around the neighborhood meanwhile, and pass by the house a couple of times over the next hour. Then Red said to Blondie like Willie wasn't even standing there that he didn't think they could just leave a minor alone like that, and Willie thought, oh shit, now what, then said he could knock on Mrs Smyth's door in back, on Cherokee; she was old and never slept, just watched old movies all night. He could stay with her until his mama got back from running.

Both cops would rather not have been dealing with him, he could see in their faces, and Red said okay go check if she'll take you. Willie ran around to the Cherokee side of the house and on back to Mrs Smyth's little cottage, and sure enough he heard the TV. He knocked on the door, then after half a minute, so long because she was so old, he saw her white head poke up to the glass of the door, and when she saw him, then the cops standing on the sidewalk behind him, she unlocked the door. Willie quickly explained what happened, but instead of saying his mama's out running, just said she'd be back before seven and can he stay with her for a couple of hours. She said yes of course, and Willie said he'll be right back, and sprinted back to his house, grabbed a book and his keys, then wrote a note for his mama not to worry because he's at

Mrs Smyth's and to come get him; he'll explain later. And as Willie dashed back around the corner after locking the front door, and as he saw the police looking bored just standing there, he realized he had to get a gun.

At the Friday afternoon employee meeting, everyone was sprawled in chairs in the banquet room in their civvies; the twins, Rudy and Bum, wore overalls with no shirts, and their fleshy dark shoulders were covered with tattoos no one could really make out because the ink was not much darker than their skin. Molly and Fu, who were good friends but involved with other women, looked smashing; Fu wore tight pants and a pink blouse that showed nice cleavage, Molly a simply-cut black dress with slightly puffed sleeves. Paul, Dude, Puddin' Head and Stinkfinger (he'd worked the fish station for eight years, and the nickname came with the job; Nat could not recall his actual name), all wore jeans and T-shirts sporting a variety of symbols and sentiments. The Old Queens – Robby, Kenny and Danny – wore slacks, sport shirts and tasteful ties; the New Queens – Mickey and Lonny – did not wear ties. Nick wore running shorts and a tank-top, and sat at the back, his legs sprawled out, his hands clasped over his lap.

Nat sat at the head of the banquet table, jacket off, tie loosened, reading glasses on his nose. He read through the weekend VIP reservations and who would get whom and whatever special conditions applied. Then he paused.

"I suppose you've heard about Michael," he said.

"What?" Fu blurted, and everyone else looked clueless, too. Nat was surprised no one had heard.

"He's no longer employed here," Nat said.

"Why not?" asked Stinkfinger. He and Michael were buds. Why hadn't Michael at least told Stinkfinger? Nat had worked a deal with Michael so that Nat could take the girls to Destin; he'd paid Michael triple for the two days Nat was gone, and Nat had been sure Michael would take the opportunity to put his own spin on why he was leaving, make it appear it was indeed his idea. Nat had considered such an arrangement the tactful, professional way to deal with the situation. He never sought to humiliate anyone. But Michael had blown the opportunity.

"Because I fired him."

Stinkfinger was the only one in the restaurant who actually liked Michael, but everyone squirmed a little at the prospect of anyone getting fired.

"What'd he do?" Puddin' Head – sauces and desserts as well as the grill – asked.

"It's not what he did. It's what he didn't do. Look, you guys don't worry. Everybody's secure here, okay? But we need a real chef."

"Michael may be a weasel, but he is a real chef, Mr Moore," Lonny said, his brow wrinkled.

"Yeah, he was trained as a chef. He got good training. He knows how to manage a kitchen, how to do things by the book. But, I don't know about you guys, especially you guys," he looked at the Old Queens, his old friends and mentors to let them know they were the second "you guys," but I'm tired of the same old shit. I don't want to make so many changes that we lose our MO, I just want to tweak the menu, get a real chef, an artist in here who'll build on what we have. We've got to reinvent ourselves," he finished, the Old Queens, concern stitched into their brows, staring back at him.

"You have somebody in mind, Nat?" Danny asked; it was understood that only the Old Queens could call him by his first name.

"Yep. Already hired her."

"Her?" Molly said, her face lighting up.

"Yeah," I've hired Terry Birdsong," he announced.

"Terry Birdsong? From Pascal's? She's famous," Dude, the prep cook and backup broilerman, said. "I worked with her for about a month over at Beju's a couple years ago."

"You like her?" Nat asked.

"Like to fuck her," he said, and Fu balled up a napkin and hit him in the face with it, and Nick sniggered.

"Like to fuck her!" Nick parroted, grinning like an actual idiot.

"Now cut it out, Nick," Nat said.

"Mr Moore," Jack's tinny soprano inquired, "Does she know about me?"

"I've told you before, Nick, I refuse to talk to your dick," Nat scolded. "Now put it back."

"Yeah, but Jack's got a point," Molly said. "Does Birdsong know about the little fuck?"

"Yeah, I explained about Nick," Nat assured her.

"You told her about me?" Jack squeaked.

"Yes, I told…" Nat stopped. There he was, talking to Nick's dick again. "Nick, put it back, right now, or I swear I'll fire you."

"You wouldn't do that, Mr Moore," Jack said as Nick indeed reeled him back in. "Everybody loves Jack!" came the squeaky voice as through a wall. He definitely wasn't loved, but everyone did marvel at Nick's talent for controlling that voice, shading and muffling it. He was brilliant.

"Nice work," even Fu had to admit.

And of course Jack was right. Nat wouldn't fire Nick.

"You told her straight about this guy?" Molly asked, a little incredulous.

"Yeah, sure, as best I could. But you've got to admit that someone has to experience it to understand it," Nat said.

"Look, she knows there's a guy here who's a relative of an old friend of the restaurant (at this Jack's muffled voice could be heard doing a soprano James Cagney "You Dirty Rat" followed by rat-a-tat-tat machine-gun fire) and that he's got a serious psychological problem (now he did Jackson Browne singing "Doctor my eyes have seen the years...") that manifests in exhibitionism (Ed Sullivan on *Nick at Nite*: "We've got a reeely big shooo for you tonight..."). I tried to explain... well, shall we say, the magnitude of the problem (at this there were sniggers all around, and Jack said, "What shall I do? Why sir, I shall praise it!" which Nat was pretty sure was a snip of dialogue from *Moby Dick*.)

"Isn't that from *Moby Dick*?" Robby inquired, turning in his chair to look back at Nick.

"Don't know. Never heard of 'em," Nick answered.

"Them? What do you mean you've never heard of them? It's a novel," Kenny said.

"I thought it was a rock group," Nick said placidly.

"Yeah, me too," said Dude ("Thar she blows!" squeaked Jack, as though from inside a clothes hamper. "Quick, Queegquah, grab a napkin!").

"So Birdsong's gonna shake things up?" Dude asked.

"That's not the point. I just want the restaurant to evolve," Nat said ("But Jim, what about the Prime Directive? These beings may not be ready for this!").

"But how? Into what? We all make pretty good money here," Fu said, "I worry about changing too much." ("Smells like a mid-life crisis to ol' Jack-a-doodle-do!" and at this everyone glanced at one another.)

Nat smiled. "Maybe that's it, gang, but it's not all, I promise. With gambling coming in more and more, I'm betting that over the next couple of years fewer locals are going to venture into the Quarter to dine. We thrive on a local clientele, as you know, people who come in out of habit a couple times a month.

We're a part of the rhythm of their lives. But we're located smack dab in the middle of the largest concentration of tourists, some of whom come in because the restaurant's rep spreads pretty far. But as the casino starts to kick in, if it does, and especially if other forms of gaming pop up in the Quarter, two things could happen: our regulars will begin to feel less inclined to hassle with parking, *et cetera*, and fewer of the kinds of folks who'll dine at Newcastle's will be coming to the Quarter from out of town. I'm talking a couple, three years down the road, and I admit I don't have the fucking foggiest how we should change. I just want to have someone running the kitchen who's more than a caretaker. I'm not saying we stop serving Oysters Rockefeller or Oysters Bienville, or Pompano en Papillot, or Veal Newcastle's, or Shrimp Toulouse and Crabmeat Rector, or anything else we're known for. I just think we should try to do what we're good at even better, and try to add some stuff. Birdsong's a pro. One of the best around. Let's welcome her tonight, show her the ropes."

"Lady needs a rope?" Nick rasped.

"No!" several voices shouted back.

"Forgive my monkey, he knows not what he says," Jack squeaked.

"Don't talk to him. Don't ever talk to him," Nat insisted to his crew, even as he realized, as did everyone else, that he was referring to Jack.

Terry Birdsong was an affable, mid-thirties Ninth Ward girl who'd been doing service work in the Quarter since she was eight and bussed tables on weekends in her parents' little joint on Rampart. While other pretty young females wore short skirts and served cocktails, she went straight to the kitchen. She rose to sous chef at Bejoy's in the Royal Sonata through the mid-eighties, apprenticing to the brilliant Chef Renee Borjailie, who helped her get a scholarship to study at the state school in Geneva for a year.

Birdsong had a solid reputation in the underworld of New Orleans' gypsy service workers, many of whom would work one establishment for a few years, another for a few more, yet another a few more, only to end up again in the first as though they'd never left; most greeted one another by asking, "Where you working now?"

She had a reputation for running a tight kitchen, for getting in her people's faces when they fucked up, and of course everyone knew she was biding time until she could open her own place. Nat figured he'd be able to keep her maybe a year, but that that might be long enough.

They'd met at Snug Harbor on Frenchman to discuss the prospect of her taking over the kitchen at Newcastle's. It had been six-thirty in the afternoon, a bit early for Nat to drink, so he'd ordered coffee. She did, too, and a double shot of Bushmills. Nat had liked her immediately.

"Nat," she'd told him, having not asked permission to call him by his first name. "I grew up in Bywater, in half a shotgun next door to a bakery where you could get the best dope in town to go along with your donuts. I stayed in school just long enough to piss off every teacher I ran into and fuck the defensive line of the JV, first and second string. I didn't even make it to the varsity before the school told my parents I was... what'd they call it? Incourag... Incouraging..."

"Incorrigible," Nat had suggested.

"Yeah, that's it. They told my parents I needed professional help. Well, I'd been working on weekends in the old Birdsong Cafe all my life. You ever go in there?"

Nat had told her that the Birdsong and Buster Holmes were his only two sources of sustenance for much of the seventies.

"Then you probably remember a skinny little girl hauling those plastic tubs of dirty dishes to the kitchen. That was me."

Nat hadn't remembered, but nodded and smiled.

"I can't explain it Nat. But I knew when I was eight, even younger, that I was going to be a chef." She'd knocked back the Irish whiskey, and chased it with rapid sips of the coffee.

"My mom was a crappy cook, and Dad, bless his heart, could work the grill on a Saturday night when the Birdsong got packed with every flavor of queen. He worked it like one of those maestros, but that ain't cooking, Nat, and I knew it even then. I watched all the cooking shows on TV, always with a pad and pencil, and I collected cookbooks the way other girls collected Barbies. My first job was at Bremming's. I was the only female in the kitchen, and I had to give the owner's son a blowjob to get there. I was the only girl in a kitchen packed with the ugliest, fattest, most pissed off black men you ever seen, but they pumped out some damned good food, and they were so good they didn't have to take shit from nobody, not the waiters, not even the owner. Those fat, black motherfuckers became my heroes, and I haven't looked back."

She was a pretty, ball-busting chick who wore too much make-up and her hair in a ridiculous frosted curly-girlie perm that cascaded to her shoulders. "I love what I do," she finished, and signaled for the cocktail waitress.

Nat had hired her on the spot.

The first couple of nights, she'd hung back, said almost nothing, watched, listened. On the job she wore no make-up, and Nat was shocked by how much

70

prettier she was without the thick shellacking she'd had the first time he'd met her. She wore her own white smock and chef's hat. Over her heart was her name in red letters, and on the pocket the crest, Nat assumed, of the school in Geneva where she'd trained for a year. On her third night in the kitchen at Newcastle's she clearly decided that the operation was now hers. She'd met Jack the first night, had stared placidly at him, shook her head and said, in a low voice, "You poor thing," with absolutely no irony, as far as Nat could tell from the door of his office.

Jack, and Nick, had seemed genuinely disarmed. Jack had made a couple more appearances, but evoked nothing but sad, pitying glances from the new chef, and seemed as a consequence a little deflated of his usual robust cheer.

That third night, when Terry Birdsong decided it was time to take over, a Friday for which the reservation book was all but filled, Jack appeared from around the steam table; Nick, five foot three or four, was mostly hidden behind the chrome wall. As Nat chattered with Terry behind the line, going over some changes she wanted to make immediately in how the line coordinated, to be followed, she made clear, by more dramatic changes in the structure of relations in the kitchen, Jack appeared, semi-erect as always, wearing a tiny pink sombrero Nat recognized as one taken from the cap of the cheapest supermarket tequila, singing "Babalooa."

"Jesus, that makes me sad," Terry breathed.

"It doesn't bother you?" Nat asked.

"A nice stiff leg never bothered me, Nat," she assured him. "But that poor baby's in a world of hurt."

"What do you mean?" Nat pressed, even as he admired Jack's Spanish.

"Well, I think it's sad that a man Nick's age is still a virgin," she said matter-of-factly.

The singing stopped. Everyone in the kitchen froze. The humming of the walk-in freezer suddenly seemed like a jumbo jet taking off.

Jack went from semi-erect to roughly two feet of dark dangling skin. Nick stuffed Jack back and ran to the employee room. "Everybody back to work," Terry Birdsong shouted, and the clatter and din of preparation for a long night blended again with the humming of the walk-in.

It made sense. How many women would have tolerated Nick and/or Jack on any level? Of course for every male on the planet, every nose-picking, unwashed, farting, thoughtless slob it seemed there were at least forty-seven perfectly decent females prepared to accommodate his unique blend of petty perversions, and myopic assumptions regarding his natural right to exploit them, but Nick had to be one of the grand exceptions. Could Nat imagine Nick asking a woman out on a date, especially given that Jack would probably do the asking? Certainly. But could he imagine the woman who would indeed agree to date the two of them? He realized there were probably many women who would agree to a three-way with Nick and Jack, even understanding that the greater love in the configuration would always be Nick's for Jack, and possibly Jack's for Nick (though it seemed Jack was less taken with Nick than Nick with him); Nat simply couldn't imagine such a woman.

"Sorry about that," Terry said.

"Why are you sorry?" Nat asked.

"You think he's gonna be in any shape to bus tonight?"

"JesusJosephandMary... you're right."

"He can't be your only busboy."

He's the only one we can get our hands on tonight," Nat moaned. "I'm going in there to try to perk him up a bit. But tell me how you knew."

"It's pretty obvious," she said, checking the refrigerated chrome drawers where the various meats in their various cuts were stored for the night ahead. "We look a little short on veal. Hey, Stinkfinger, while you're in there pull out about a dozen more medallions, wouldja?"

"I guess it seems obvious when you point it out, but you seemed to know from the get go," Nat pressed.

Terry Birdsong told Puddin' Head to change the grease in the fryer, which pissed him off even as he began the messy, slightly dangerous task. "Those things come in standard sizes, just like clothes off the rack. You got your small, your regular, your large, your XL, and your XXL. That thing's off the scale. Even a size queen like me's got her limits." She chopped chives in an expert blur. "But if he was just a little dude with a monster schlong and a sunny disposition, he'd still see plenty of action. Plenty of girls out there who just live for the ol' skin stump who'd take him on just to say they tried. I mean, like they say..." She separated yolks and whites with a rapidity that dazzled... "the female equipment being designed to pass babies, and being there ain't ever been no dick big as one, at least as thick, ain't too many big ol' healthy girls couldn't take a fair chunk of a monster pecker like Jack if they worked at it. So the fact that he's a deformed freak ain't why he's never been laid..." She smelled a tin of reduced cream and slung it into the plastic bucket under the fish oven. "...pussy fear's why," she concluded, as she rubbed a pumice stone over the grill.

72

"Pussy fear?" Nat echoed.

"Oh, yeah, it's a serious condition," she assured him.

"You mean, he's gay?"

"Lord, no! Most queers love women and hate pussy; some fear it, but most just hate it. No, no, it's straight dudes that fear it, get truly terrified of the ol' hair pie," she asserted, reducing butter for the Bearnaise. "Ain't nothing more debilitating to a man than pussy fear," she asserted again with a clinical certainty.

"How do you think a guy gets like that?" Nat asked earnestly as Terry Birdsong gently brushed him aside. He was getting in her way as she moved swiftly and surely in the narrow space between the cooking and serving stations.

"Ask his mama," she breathed, wholly absorbed now in her preparations for the evening.

SECTION EIGHT

Nat:

There are parts of the world, conditions of life, to which we stand as gaudy little gods because we can afford to center our "emotional lives" (something abstracted from creature existence), on "moral" and "ethical" concerns alien, even a little absurd, to the destitute many.

The tone of your last e-mails was pathetic and cute, and quite alarming, really. Frankly, picturing a middle-aged restaurateur contemplating good and evil as he gazes into a pre-dawn beach fog makes me want to suck a lemon. Not that I would sour for you such a deliciously melancholy reverie. Goodness gracious, my not-so-young Werther! How did you get to be so Germanly romantic? Don't bother answering that; I'm being a bitch-mama now, but I'm allowing myself to play that role precisely because I feel a necessary condition of this correspondence is that we are unflinching in our criticism of one another, to the extent that in our letters we reveal our lives, and not just in slickly edited, and therefore idealized, forms. I will not allow a gram of sentimentality, not a pinch, to go unchallenged. If you wish to blast me as hard-hearted, lock and load.

A private life is a bourgeois perk. A secret life is a luxury. For example, I don't begrudge you your mistress any more than I begrudge you the Lexus or Town Car you may drive. It's a "lifestyle choice." Let us simply acknowledge that not everyone is born into circumstances such that she or he may make lifestyle choices.

And don't think I'm condescending to you. I, too, live well, am often ridiculous, which is to say I have my ridiculous requirements. The other day the hot water shut off in my condo and I went ballistic. I was in the building supervisor's face wheezing fury. He was a little Hispanic fellow, sixty-something, chubby, big black mustache; he was the sort you've seen wearing the funny suit with mirrors stitched all over it and a huge-rimmed hat, strumming an over-sized guitar (pernicious stereotypes have their homely uses!). I was in his face screaming about hot water, red-cheeked and whining about my personal hygiene. He stood there and took it. I glanced over his shoulder and saw on the wall a huge blue sacred heart; it was wrapped in thorns and dripping holy blood. Beneath the blessed organ, on a wooden table in the foyer, were a dozen or more photographs of children. The aroma of the same seven things cooked again and again wafted on air-conditioned currents around him, and I ranted on about my hygiene, and even as I stomped and yelled I felt my own absurdity in that man's eyes, and the border crossing of his distant youth was revealed in those sad eyes, and to say such a thing is of course to indulge in my own kind of sentimentality, but I stood ranting in the face of that little sad dark man and what I read there in his eyes, in the margins of my own absurdity, was not hopelessness but something akin to it, a passive acceptance of the power of others to humiliate him, and the knowledge that that acceptance was the price he paid for small creature comforts.

Look, thoughts of suicide, that is, considering it seriously, even for a few seconds, ain't normal for someone leading your kind of life. Depression can be chemical; ninety percent of the world's romantics occupying the Misty Flats of their Souls are simply victims of their own weird chemistry. I'll leave that little (quite tired) analogy you drew in your penultimate e-mail alone, except to say that I do indeed see more sickness than evil, but you're wrong to suggest that I don't accept evil as a valid category; I just think it has a structure, that that structure can be known, that anything knowable, understandable, can be changed. For example, I accept

that Germans were Hitler's "willing executioners;" I also think that
Germany is now a thriving democracy (to the extent democracies
may thrive in the throes of market imperatives) containing some
of the more enlightened citizens of the world. All the old folkish
evil bubbles below the surface, but powerful counter forces,
life-affirming forces, have been set against that evil. As long as
Germans are German that evil will be potential; keeping it only that
is the new heroic task of the German people.

Evil is when, say, the sickness of nationalism reaches such a
magnitude that even those who are not afflicted have no choice
but to manifest its symptoms. When otherwise decent people have
only the choice of perishing by resisting, or continuing to live by
co-operating in horrors, a condition of evil exists. The individual?
Mengele? Pol Pot? He – yes, almost always "he" – may be sick to
the core; we may want to call him evil, but to do so will distract us
from the fact, the incontrovertible fact, that for every monster who
is such by virtue of his personal volition, there are countless others
who would be monsters if circumstances allowed. Most monsters
are cowards; they require very particular circumstances, like delicate
flora. Don't doubt that this country of ours is crawling with men who
would willingly, cheerfully, joyfully build, administer and participate
in the daily maintenance of factories for exterminating large
numbers of their fellow citizens.

Nat, I'll not feign maternal concern, but I am feeling something
for you; I just don't know what to call it yet. I am concerned that
someone who, on the one hand, seems so pleased with the life
Fate and late capitalism have bestowed upon him can seem, on the
other hand, so incredibly troubled. You're probably past due for the
ol' mid-life theatrics most men stumble through so hilariously, but
the dissonant undertones of the sentiments you express, how you
express them, are more than troubling. Have you sought any kind
of counseling before? Most men, especially, hate the idea, but they
shouldn't. Don't think there is any substitute for real professional help,
not these communications between you and me, not the arms of
your Love or the love of your children. You need to talk to someone,
I think, who can be dispassionate. Maybe you drink too much and
need some kind of mood pills. I don't know; I'm not a pro.

I'm so glad your kid is well. I once couldn't find my baby for two full hours when she was seven. I was terrified, and have known no such terror since, so I understand, in my maternal bones I understand, what you experienced. And I'm glad, too, that girl I was didn't have the nerve to go South of the Border.

I've got tons of work: seminar papers to read and grade (or in some cases, because they are entirely unreadable, just grade), lectures to prepare, absurd committee work to take seriously, etc.

Grace

The children are silent, but he sees them as through a backlit membrane, in silhouette but more distinct than shadow. They huddle, stamp their feet, each hugging herself, pressing into the knot of others. Their chins are on their chests; they shiver.

Nat runs toward the wall and it is Mardi Gras, and he is little, lost in a crowd that is roaring and laughing and spilling, and a hooded person on a black float that is absorbed into the night throws an entire rack of fat white beads at Nat's head, but they turn into sparrows, scatter, and another hooded figure picks up a small naked boy who's been lying amid the beads and bobbles to be thrown from the float, balances the child on one palm above his head, and heaves the boy and Nat tries to catch the child who is bigger than Nat, and grows larger as he floats towards Nat's head and the crowd moves away, but now the children are wailing like cats, and are fighting on the other side of the wall, as one small voice cries his name, for she has been set upon by the others. There are eighty-one of them, and eighty have set upon the one small girl. But they all drop dead, and she rises from amidst their bodies, and steps over some and walks over the sprawled torsos of others then stands, a shadowed aura, behind the membrane, then tears through it and –

This time Nat remembered his entire dream, and wept silently in a cold sweat, convulsed beside Lou who had her leg thrown over snoring Edie. He rose, washed his face, padded into the kitchen. It was four-twenty, still dark. He poured four fingers of Old Crow, dropped in a couple of cubes. He sat at the kitchen table, drank, tried to compose himself.

He basically thought Grace was full of shit, especially about "professional help"; he knew people more fucked up than he who spent at least a grand a month on professional help and seemed more wacky now than when they started the whole self-revelatory process; the main difference was that now they could talk openly about what pathetic creatures they were, and of course the problem with that is no one wants to listen to such crap who isn't getting paid to. Nat didn't just assume so – was certain, the way the religious are certain – that though one may gain insight into the human condition reading Freud et al, therapy only fucked a person up. Drugs he believed in, though, and thought that it might be wise to drink less and find some good pills, preferably, but not necessarily, prescribed by a licensed physician.

Nat walked Poon, fed him, toyed with killing him. The last vet bill, three weeks ago, had been eight hundred and forty four dollars. Nat made good money from the restaurant, and had a modest trust fund that augmented his income quite nicely. Neither he nor his family would likely ever want. But keeping that rodent alive was costing almost as much as Marti's tuition at Morgan Heights. He once calculated how many Third World children he could sponsor through the Christian Children's Fund with what he paid out for Lou's pet in just one year, and had presented his calculations to his wife, who had not been amused.

At six he called his mother. He knew she'd have been up since five-ish. "Maminka," he said.

"Hello, darling."

"Mama, I need to talk to you about something, but not over the phone."

"Well, I'm always here, Nathan, and you're always welcome. You're just so busy. I never get to see my grandchildren."

"You know where we live! You never visit us..."

"Let's not have that argument so early in the morning."

"Look, I'll bring the girls and Nes over tonight for dinner. I've got a new crackerjack chef, and tonight'll be a slow one, so I'll just go in for a couple hours then pick the girls up and bring them over. Nestor can drive, and after dinner he can take Marti and Edie home so I can hang around and talk to you for awhile, okay? Is this too little notice?"

"No, no it will be fine. I'm very glad. I'll make svickova!"

"Great. About seven?"

"I'll see you then, dear," she finished.

Nat was suddenly terrified of seeing her, getting through dinner and then telling her that he'd found his birth mother.

When he was very young, too young to speak and then later when he could, and spoke the baby Czech and baby English both, she'd wept nights holding him, chanting in a whisper, "Jarka, Jarka... Jarko, Teta ma rada..." *Your aunty loves you*, and though she began speaking beyond him, as he drifted toward sleep, she would be speaking as if to him, as if he were Jarka, a little girl, and she were his aunt.

And his father once heard her call him Jarka; Nat'd been swinging in the big tire his father had hung from a rope and tied to the strongest limb of the oak in their backyard, and his mother had called, "Jarko," for Nat to come in for lunch, and it had been the only time Nat had heard his father raise his voice to Mama. His tata had yelled, "Are you crazy?" and had asked the question several times at the top of his voice; his tata's fists had been balled and he'd seemed to strain against hitting Mama.

Then Mama had wept, and so had Tata, and Nat had hugged them both and wept, too, though he hadn't understood why except that it had to do with Jarka, who sometimes Mama thought he was and that she was his teta, his aunt. Though she never again uttered the name. Years later Nat's father had told him about Jarka, the doll of a girl who'd perished in Auschwitz, his mother's best girlhood friend. His mother had not been able to utter her friend's name or refer to her except through the doll.

The little girl in his dreams was sometimes Sandra, sometimes Jarka, really both, and Jarka was somehow also a part of him. He felt so deeply he could not deny that Jarka was a part of him, Jarka the doll of a murdered child, and the murdered child.

His parents had spoken in lowered voices to other adults about previous life, about his father finding his mother when his father was an Army Intelligence officer in England after the war, how she and her own mother had gotten there by the good graces of an uncle who had been rich before the war, and had gotten even richer during the "Protectorate" period, collaborating with the Nazis, but funneling much of his new wealth out of the country. Uncle Jiri had actually worked secretly, Nat was told years later, for the underground, channeling valuable information to Benes in London. There had even been talk of his uncle enabling the assassination of Heydrich.

But there had actually been little talk of the war in Nat's presence; when Czech relatives visited from Chicago and the little Czech towns in Texas serious conversations hushed as he entered rooms, even though his mother had stopped speaking to him in Czech when he was not yet four, and so he had not been able to understand most of what the Czechs had said to one another at the table in the kitchen over strong "Turkish" coffee and Mama's kolaci. There had been a great sadness in which they, especially his mama, had not wished to include him.

It was late morning now; Marti was off to school, Lou and Edie had driven to the shop almost an hour ago, and he wanted to go outside. He walked into the park, crossed the little stone bridge over the lagoon, lay down by the chunk of meteorite on the edge of the golf course, and did not mind the looks he got from the paunchy hackers who whooshed by in electric carts. He lay in the shadow of the inexplicable six-by-six wad of metal from beyond the sky, and spoke to Sandra as though she were there, beside him, on the grass.

Willie rode his bike into the projects a little after dark. His cousin Luther's step daddy was sitting on the back steps sipping a King Cobra Malt Liquor, staring at the traffic. He'd just gotten out of Angola, so he was taking it easy, getting used to things. Willie trotted by him and the old dude grunted when Willie asked how he was doing.

Aunt Sally was frying catfish and asked Willie if he wanted some, and Willie said that's okay, he just needed to talk to Luther about something. Aunt Sally's friend from three doors down, a skinny woman with a lot of gold in her gums wearing white shorts so short you could see up where it's not even leg, sipped a strawberry Big Shot and slapped her knee laughing about some big old red dude who asked her for a date.

Luther was watching *Babylon 5*, and one of those lizard dudes was scream-ing at the dude with clown hair who talked like a vampire. Luther was spread out on the floor and Luther's little sister Lorella, about Willie's age, lay on the couch painting her nails and watching TV. The new couch and the TV they'd just gotten from those funny guys on TV with the commercial where the old one shouts Let 'em Have It! even though nobody's got any money or job or anything.

Willie told Luther he's got to talk to him outside, and Luther said wait until the commercial, and one came pretty fast. Luther, all six feet five inches of his sixteen-year-old body, stood up and followed Willie out the front door.

Willie checked things out all around, then stooped and pulled a wad of fives and ones and a couple tens and some twenties out of his sock. Luther counted the money, then told Willie to wait a second and slouched back in. He brought back a crinkled brown paper bag wrapped around something and told Willie he'd better be careful with it, and Willie told him again it's just to protect the house, and Luther said cool, just be careful. Willie tried to stick the bag into his pants, but it was too bulky. He finally just held it under his shirt.

When Aunt Sally's skinny friend said what you got under your shirt, boy? when he had to pass them to get back to where he left his bike, he just blew by and said he's got black under his shirt, what's she got under hers, and while Skinny was cracking up she said he's a sassy little peckerwood, which didn't make any sense because he always thought a peckerwood was a really stupid white dude from the country, but he figured some people might just like saying peckerwood, whether it makes any sense or not. Skinny seemed like the type who'd do that. But when Luther's stepdaddy asked Willie what he had up under his shirt Willie took out the bag and said he's got a pair of pants Luther's too big for, and grumpy old Just Out Of Angola said shit, if Willie can wear it Luther must have outgrown it about ten years ago. And Willie smiled and said, Yeah, that sounds about right, and got his bike going on the dead grass and packed dirt and jumped on, holding the bag between his left hand and the handlebar, then put it in the basket when he got rolling smoothly on the sidewalk.

Willie took a long way home, staying off of Napoleon and St Charles, hitting all the dinky streets and keeping an eye out for cops. All he needed was to get pulled over holding a gun. They'd treat him like he was a nightmare.

When he got to Plum, he really had to pee, so he went in the alley and peed on a garage door but a dog jumped at the fence next to the garage and made him pee a little on his shoe, and he wanted to shoot the dog, but knew he could never do that because he liked dogs, even white people's dogs that get trained to attack black kids. This one was a German Shepherd, and he wanted to eat Willie's face, but the fence was strong and high, so Willie just finished peeing and smiled at the dog.

As he pushed his bike through the back gate, he smelled collards and cornbread, and they are two things that smell so much better together than alone. When he got through the back door he gave the Reverend a little kick while his mama still had her back turned, and put the bag on the counter by the big spoon she used to test what she was cooking.

She asked what was in the bag, and he said she'd better look.

Willie'd been popped up 'side his head before, but this time she did it with a lot of leverage. She started her hand somewhere near the sink, and by the time it got to his head it was sweet with velocity, and knocked him up against the refrigerator.

Well, he'd kind of been expecting that, so it brought tears to his eyes but he wasn't exactly crying. She always felt real bad real quick after laying a good smack up 'side his head, so he waited a few seconds and sure enough she started crying, just like he figured she would. She hugged him and blubbered about a little boy having to think of such things, then rose, got butched up as she called it, which meant she stopped the blubbering and got kind of hard, then took the gun and clips through the dining room and living room, which weren't really different rooms just one long space divided up, into her bedroom.

She returned and told him it's between the mattress and the box springs on her side, which meant her favorite side, the right side closest to the closet; when he was little, Willie'd sometimes slept on the left side, his head close to the radio. She said he's not to touch it unless he knows there's immediate danger and she's not there. She told him that means somebody's got to be coming through the window again; he's got to be sure he's in danger. He said cool. But then she lost it a little again, cried without making noise, shut her eyes tight, pressed both her hands against her forehead. She whispered this ain't right... this ain't right... this ain't... and Willie said he won't touch that gun no matter what. It'll be her gun. He said he doesn't think he could deal with it, anyway, that if some dude tried to come through the window again Willie'd just run out the front door. He promised his mama that that was her gun, and that he wouldn't mess with it no matter what, and she was all over him again hugging and blubbering, and then she whispered that Mad Dog would be proud of him, and this made Willie proud, and it also made him feel a little silly for feeling proud, because he hadn't gotten that gun to make anybody proud; he'd just gotten it for his mama.

Then he told her he'd promised Bart he'd come by. His mama told him to be careful, and to check if Bart needed her to come over and do anything. He trotted out through the kitchen onto the patio, clamped the flashlight onto the handlebars, and scooted out into the young night. Before peddling onto Cherokee, he checked out his window on the side of the house to make sure the plastic his mama put over it looked okay, and it did.

This time the poem was about how love obliterates the self, a kind of suicide then resurrection. Perhaps because it was dark outside and only one dim bulb burned, in a lamp covered by a dark red shade with gold frills by the couch, the mood was different than usual, and Willie found himself listening with more interest, and stared at the long shadows all over the walls as Bart spoke in that funny voice, the poem voice. There were sad people swimming in each other's skins awhile, floating in each other's secrets and obsessions. Willie knew he wasn't really getting it, but he didn't care, the sadness he got, and the loneliness. Bart was one sad and lonely dude, and Bart didn't forget for a single second that he was dying, that any day, any hour, any minute, from the looks of him, he could fall right over and stop. In a way, Willie was looking forward to Bart checking out so he wouldn't have to listen to this crap anymore. And now the poem was talking about a garden where all a person's lies about love were rotting fruit and where a person's truth about love was good ripe fruit, and how in that garden filled with the smell of rot there was only one piece of fruit that wasn't rotten, a lemon.

After Willie grabbed his muse money from the cookie jar, Bart asked him what he thought of the new section, and Willie said the whole thing really sucked, but that the part about the garden was pretty funny. Maybe Bart should burn everything but the garden part, but on second thought, Willie said, Bart should probably burn that part, too, because if it were all by itself it probably wouldn't be that funny.

SECTION NINE

I T WAS ONLY three-twenty; Birdsong wouldn't arrive until four, and Stink-finger and the other stove jockeys until four-thirty. Paul was on prep this week, and had been in from seven to eleven with Birdsong, getting everything set up for the next several nights, at least through Thursday.

So how'd he get in? Nick was on the floor in the Bienville Room, knees to his chest, his face pressed into the far corner by the bus station. His fingers were spread and his palms seemed glued to the walls.

Two nights ago, he'd worked, stone-faced, mute. It had been pleasant, but sad, too. No one said anything about what had happened, about Birdsong outing Nick as a virgin suffering from pussy fear, but everyone seemed to feel the same thing by the end of the night: Jack was missed. Nat could tell that even Molly and Fu missed him a little ("Damn... now we've got to start coming all the way into the kitchen," Molly had sighed). At the end of the night, Nick had broken down his station, done his cleanup, changed silently into his civvies and left through the scullery. Nat had heard the twins, as Bum hauled out the garbage and Rudy polished the glorious machine, say goodnight to Nick and Jack, but neither had answered.

Nat suddenly realized that Peggy, who did the books from ten to one-ish, had probably let Nick in; she knew who he was, and that Nat wouldn't mind. But why had he come? What was he doing?

"Nick?" Nat said softly.

Nothing.

"Nick?" he said a little louder.

Nothing.

"Hey, big guy, you sleeping?" he said in his normal speaking voice. Of course he wasn't sleeping, sitting scrunched up against the wall in the corner like that. Nat walked over to him, reached down and shook his shoulder.

Nothing.

"Nick, what you doing, fella? You okay?" Of course he wasn't okay. He was out of his mind, had never not been out of his mind. Call it nuts, crazy, off the ol' noodle or psychotic, whether caused by pussy fear or some complex tangle of pathologies leading back to his mother's tit, Nick was cuckoo. He was also the nephew or grandson of someone Nat not only didn't want to piss off, but indeed wished to ingratiate himself with. Roberto Mancini was grateful to Nat for giving Nick a legitimate job, and therefore purpose to Nick's life or lives, as the case may be. "Hey, Nicky boy! You want to work the banquet tonight? I'll let you be Danny's back, how about that? Danny can start training you to wait tables! How about that, pal?"

Nothing.

This was getting creepy. He shook Nick hard with both hands and shouted his name three times. Nothing.

Nat pulled a chair from the banquet table, sat in it backwards, arms draped over the chair back. He stared at Nick's muscular, catatonic little body. Nick wore jeans, a black T-shirt with Kid Rock's most recent tour dates stenciled in white, good black boots. A thick silver chain ran from a belt loop to the big wallet sticking out of his back pocket. He was any young guy pissed off and scared, pissed off for being so scared and particularly scared that anyone else should ever know how much fear lay quivering in his heart. Nat was suddenly recalling when Nestor was three and would hide in the closet when Nat had buddies over to play poker. The little boy'd been too shy, at first, to visit with the men, but wanted to be near his father, so he'd sit for as long as half an hour in a nest of old clothes, in the dark of the closet with the door closed to a slit, until finally he'd creep out and put his head in Nat's lap for awhile as Nat continued to fiddle with the cards and chips and chatter with his buddies.

"Jack?" Nat said softly, and waited.

"Jack?" He said again.

"You rang, boss?" came the small, muffled voice.

"What's wrong with Nick?"

"Don't know, but he's got me worried," Jack said.

"Is there anything we can do?" Nat said, uttering the pronoun with an involuntary shiver.

"Don't know. 'S got me stumped."

Nat was stumped, too. "Well, like can you…" he'd started talking before he knew what he was going to say.

"Can I what?" Jack pressed.

Nick didn't move. He seemed not even to be breathing.

"I don't know… like, take over?" Nat said, surprising himself with his own words.

"What you mean?" Jack squeaked.

"I'm not sure, Jack. But what's happening here can't be good for either one of you," he said.

"You're telling me… I'm choked up against his leg…"

"Yeah, well," Nat interrupted, "be that as it may, could you, like, take over? Take charge? I mean, you're the one everybody likes," he blurted. He didn't know where he was going with this, but he pushed on: "Nick's kind of an idiot," he said. "You're the smart one. Why don't you just…" Just what? What was he counseling?

"Why don't I just what? I'm not following you, boss."

"Switch," Nat said.

"Say what?"

"Why don't you just switch?"

"What you mean, switch?"

"I mean trade places. You take over, take charge. Put that chump Nick in the pecker, and kick yourself upstairs. Consider it a promotion. What the hell, I'll do it! I'm the boss, right? Nick, you're fired. Jack, you're hired. You're the man!"

There was a long silence. Then Nick's hands moved, slid down from the wall where they'd seemed stuck. His face, slowly, turned from the right angle wedge where each cheek had pressed against a wall. He rose to his feet, surveyed his own body as though he were seeing it for the first time. Then he looked at Nat, and a broad smile took over his face.

"Jack?"

"Hot damn! Beam me up, Scotty, cuz I've got miles to go before I sleep!" Jack roared.

"How you feeling?" Nat asked, amazed. The phone at the entrance had been ringing, and he could now hear his own recorded voice imparting vital information.

"Like I just blew out of Plato's cave, and ain't nothing going to make me go back in, dig? Ol' Jackadoodledoo's here to stay, boss!" He slapped Nat on the back as he bounced out of the Bienville Room, whistling, Nat was pretty sure, something by Vivaldi.

"Help! Help!" Nat heard a small, desperate soprano shouting, and it seemed, miraculously, to do so from the midst of the Vivaldian melody.

"Shut up, monkey," Jack sneered then continued whistling.

Willie finished his trig and history homework and e-mailed it to his tutor who popped back that Willie still owed her an essay about *Invisible Man*. Willie shot back that he needed a couple more days because he'd been reading a lot of books about Nazis and just hadn't gotten around to reading *Invisible Man*, though it sure sounded like a book he'd like because he loved science fiction. She tapped back that it's not sci-fi, but a serious book about being black in America. And Willie replied that he was an expert on being black in America, so he shouldn't even have to read the book. She signed off by giving him until the end of the week to send her the essay, and she wanted it to be in the form of a comparison/contrast with some other novel Willie had read. More specifically, she wrote, Willie should proceed from a thesis that defines some common features of plot, theme, or characterization, and then compares and contrasts specific details from the two novels. Because he was late with the assignment, it should be six hundred words long rather than four hundred. Willie tapped back that he thought the Emancipation Proclamation meant that black people didn't have to be slaves anymore, but she didn't answer.

Willie hit the turn onto Broadway and spotted the two goons from Alpha Phi, and they saw him, but pretty much looked through him. They didn't even remember him. As he pedaled casually past, they laughed about some story the big one was telling the really big one. They were wearing exactly what they both had worn when they'd chased him. Willie was pissed that they didn't recognize him. He was pissed that he was just another little black dude to them, that one black face pretty much looked like another to their eyes. Willie wanted to pick up a rock and smash in the backs of their heads for not recognizing him and not chasing him, for not trying to half kill him for what he'd done to their car, but they couldn't see him, see the little black dude who'd shot them fuck yous in stereo, and whom they'd chased and popped with a rock and who'd broken one of their windows and spattered dog shit all over their car. All they saw was a black kid.

He stopped the bike and pulled over onto the sidewalk. They were turning onto Willow. Willie wanted to go back and tell them who he was. He'd be much happier if they were chasing him and calling him nigger, because then he wouldn't really be one in their eyes. His eyes teared up a little and he got pissed at himself for wanting to cry. He was really down, now, but he figured listening to Bart's poem would make him feel better, if only because he got such a kick out of telling Bart what a piece of shit it was.

This time the poem talked about music being prayer and how words always screw things up. It said that between words and the world there's a big gap and that's where Hell is, in the gap between words and stuff. Willie wondered why Bart was writing this weird poem, then, because as far as Willie could tell the poem was just words, but then the poem talked about itself as a longing on the other side of the words it's made of, which Willie figured was a load of crap, a chunk of the kind of pretty crap only white people seem interested in.

The poem quit by saying something like you'd better love something so hard it makes you want to die not to have it, because if you don't love like that you're going to fall into the gap and burn forever in your own pettiness. And then Bart said it was done. And Willie said good, but then realized that Bart meant really done, like finished.

Willie got a weird feeling like when his cousin Louie told him Grandma was dead. He'd known he was supposed to feel real bad because he loved her a lot. Later he'd gotten low and cried, but right that moment he'd not felt anything he could hang a name on; he'd felt nothing but weird for feeling nothing. And right now he'd gotten that same weird feeling, and when Bart asked him what he thought, Willie told him it's a piece of shit and he should just burn the whole thing, but he felt bad because he didn't really mean it this time. He didn't think it was worth anything, and Bart didn't have enough money to pay him to sit through it a second time, but somehow he hadn't wanted it to end, and not just because Bart paid him good money to listen to it. In fact, he told Bart that for a piece of weird, worthless shit his poem had not been that bad to listen to.

Bart got tears in his eyes and told Willie that those words meant more to him than the rave he'd gotten last year in the *New York Times*, and Willie just chuckled and tried to imagine what Bart'd do if Willie'd lied and said he really liked the damned thing. Willie figured he'd probably die, which he was going to do soon enough anyway.

Bart pulled out a stack of pages from under the coffee table. He put the pages he'd just read to Willie at the bottom of the stack and asked Willie to carry *The Mystic Pig* to the bedroom and stash it in the bottom drawer of the dresser. Willie said he'd do it for twenty bucks. Bart nodded and said fine, and Willie plucked a twenty from the cookie jar then hauled *The Mystic Pig* into the bedroom.

———————

Since his father died eight months ago, Nat had found it difficult being in the ancestral home. Though his father had not been around much when Nat was growing up – out of the house early, home late, and out of town many week-ends on business – Frederick Michael Moore's calm and tender essence was a strong and abiding feature of Nat's and his mother's lives in that house.

Nat's mother's given name was Eva, and her maiden name was Kohoutova; Nat considered how he'd gotten well into his teens before he'd even asked what her maiden name had been, and how she'd seemed to give even that information grudgingly.

She imparted all information about her life in Czechoslovakia grudgingly, and one day in his late teens, several years after learning he'd been adopted at birth, he'd asked his father why. Freddy–Mike, as his friends had always called him, had responded by assuming a serious and confidential tone to tell Nat how the death of Eva Kohoutova's own mother in London, just three weeks after Eva and Army Intelligence Lieutenant Frederick Michael Moore had met and begun dating, had devastated her.

Eva Kohoutova's mother's brother, a rich contractor who'd gotten even richer collaborating with the Nazis, also had ties to Benes' exiled government, and had funnelled large amounts of money to it. Certain members of Benes' coterie had been more than willing to take in and protect Antonin Vaculik's only surviving family. Eva and her mother had arrived with no money and less English, but Eva had learned quickly, becoming functional within four months, though her mother had learned not a word of a language which sounded too much to her ears like German.

So when the jolly neighbor from across the hall, a fat red-cheeked woman who sang popular songs while she endlessly baked for no one Freddy-Mike had ever seen when he'd come to fetch Eva for dates, shouted at Eva's mother to watch out for that crate, the lanky Czech woman had smiled and waved and tripped over the crate and tumbled down two flights of stairs. At first, Nat's father had reminisced, it had not seemed even a particularly serious accident, much less a fatal one. The robust, middle-aged Czech had risen immediately and walked back up the steps. She had been alarmingly bruised all over and sore, but had seemed otherwise fine. She hadn't even bled, externally, anyway. But then she'd complained of a sharp pain in her chest and all through her woman parts, and Eva had taken her to the hospital where she'd died four days later.

Frederick Michael Moore had confided to his teenage son how the ravishing young woman — his wife, Nat's mother — had seemed more alone in the world than he or Nat could ever imagine. She'd never be able to return to Czechoslovakia after the "Bloodless Coup" of '48. And then Nat could imagine how Freddie-Mike, a Southerner to his core, a young man from old New Orleans money, an old-fashioned gentleman who'd fully expected to return home and marry one of eight or nine aging debutantes still available and acceptable to his family, reacted chivalrously to Eva Kohoutova's dire circumstances. Indeed, Freddy-Mike, Nat later assumed when he himself had received sufficient lessons in such matters, fell in love with his Slavic beauty's grief.

Life had been difficult in Czechoslovakia, and she simply didn't wish to discuss that time in her life. People had been scared, and when tens of thousands of Czechs had stood in Wenceslas Square, soon after Rinholt Heinrik's assassination, to give the Nazi salute even as they sang their own national anthem, they'd done so out of terror. No one wants to recall such terror. Better to recall fairy tales, untranslatable aphorisms one tries to translate anyway and always to hilarious effect... folk songs, recipes.

And there was Jarka. The name floated in his mind since he'd awakened from the dream recalling it, recalling how, when he was three or four, his mother sometimes called him Jarka ("Jarko," in the vocative form), a girl's name. Before his father had explained, Nat had assumed there had been a child named Jarka, in Czechoslovakia, a sister, perhaps, a cousin; Eva Kohoutova had suffered a fever in puberty that had left her barren. Nat had heard the Czech relatives refer to how she'd almost died when she was thirteen. Freddy-Mike of course had known of her condition when he married her, and had accepted with a true gentleman's grit the prospect of no blood heirs. When Nat had discovered that Jarka was a doll, the doll of Eva's best friend, a girl who'd been murdered in a death camp, he'd felt angry at his mother, angry at what seemed juvenile and frivolous. His mother's sorrow, so powerful she'd transferred it from a murdered child to a doll, puzzled Nat. But he'd never pressed the subject. He'd never hear

90

of Jarka from his mother's mouth. He wanted to hear that story; he wanted his mother to tell him about her friend, how they'd parted, and how his mother had come to possess the doomed girl's doll only to lose it.

He recalled how every afternoon of endless childhood his mother would take him to her bed to nap, how she would lie with him, always holding him close, and tell him stories in Czech as he drifted off to sleep, and as he drifted off to sleep he'd breathe in the smell of her skin, with its slight hint of whatever she'd last been cooking, and a hint fainter still of soap. Her breath had always been warm and fragrant, even when a little pungent with the strong coffee she drank. And when he'd awaken and she'd not be there beside him, holding him close to her, he'd panic and scream for her.

The only person besides Sandra he'd told about Jarka was the best friend of his youth. His mother had been extremely fond of Bart Linsey, and Bart had from the beginning shown a regard for her that was surely rooted in the enmity he'd felt for his own cold mother, a woman who'd tolerated, merely and poorly, a son. No, not a son so much as a more or less exact replica of Bart's dreamy father, a man she'd loathed preternaturally because he'd so willingly given her most of his family fortune for the privilege of leaving her. Bart had shuttled between a bemused father and a hateful mother all his life, and had found, it seemed, in Nat's mother a maternal figure worthy of his strong affections.

In his late teens, Nat had at times been uncertain whether his friendship with Bart was really a convenience, a way for Bart to have access to Eva. But Nat had never felt jealous or used, perhaps because he had never experienced sibling rivalry. In any case, he'd won, forever, the unmediated affections of his mother, and her embracing Bart — stuffing him with kolaci, discussing the prose of Capek and Neruda and the verse of Macha and Seifert with him for hours at the dining room table — had allowed Nat to see both his mother and his best friend from different, quite interesting angles.

The Ash Wednesday of their eighteenth year, in their last months at Morgan Heights, Nat had told Bart about Jarka, about how his mother as a girl had had a friend who'd been killed in Auschwitz, and that somehow Eva Kohoutova had acquired the doll but lost it, and that when Nat was very young she'd sometimes call him Jarka, the name of the doll.

Bart had been very troubled by this information, had risen and paced Nat's room. They'd taken numerous hits off of Nat's gourd bong, rich blond hash Nat had won in a poker game. Bart had paced himself into a stoned agitation within minutes of the revelations, and had begun to mumble something in

91

Latin, something from the Mass, from when the wine turns to blood, Nat had been fairly certain, but thinking back, no longer was.

Edie liked to play in Nat's room, the room that had been his until he was twenty and moved into the Quarter. When Nat entered it now, he didn't see the private space of the young man he'd been when he'd last occupied it; that is, he didn't see just that space, but the spaces it had been for each phase of his early life. Of course, he'd never slept with the closet door open as a child because that closet scared him in the dark, and his father had cut a limb off the oak because it cast a shadow through the curtains onto his floor, and when the wind was strong that shadow poked the closet door, and Nat had not been able to sleep. In his early teens, Nat had kept his personal stash on a hidden ledge below the window-sill, one he'd found by accident when very young and had never bothered to mention to his parents. It was just enough space for a lid – a baggied ounce – papers or pipe. He'd kept the stuff he sold, never more than a kilo at a time, on the top shelf of the closet behind a porcelain sink, a white chunk that had been stored there and never used and that was itself behind an inflatable pool he'd used twice when he was nine. Of course the pool and the sink were still there, and Nat was certain that if he ever got up there with a flashlight he'd find seeds. Under his bed, in addition to the witches and monsters who compelled him to sleep with the covers over his seven-year-old face, was the boxing trophy he'd won when he was twelve; Nat had not put it with the eight others, on the shelf his father had built onto the wall over his desk, because his name had been misspelled on it: Nathan Moor. On the five-tiered bookcase, Curious George rubbed against Siddhartha who rubbed against Zhivago who rubbed against Jane Eyre.

Edie liked to sit on the brown throw rug Nat, too, had sat upon "Indian-style" – half-lotus – before the big windows onto the big backyard, and play with Mr Monkey, whom Nat had loved but who became Mr Bad Monkey a few years later while Nat and his buddy Bart were fucked up on hash and laughing fitfully at nothing at all but a sock monkey whose frayed red tongue flapped out of the stitches that were its mouth. Edie liked to hear Nat talk about how he'd slept with Mr Monkey all his childhood, and that even when he'd gotten too old to sleep with Mr Monkey, he'd kept him sitting prominently on his dresser. Of course, what he didn't tell her was that friends in adolescence learned not to fuck with Mr Monkey. Nat had coldcocked a customer, a school acquaintance who'd come over with Bart to purchase a lid, and who'd casually picked Mr Monkey up by the feet and swung him around in a blurred circle as Nat, standing turned away on his chair, reached behind the sink. When Nat turned back holding the plastic garbage bag, and saw Mr Monkey being so mishandled, he'd dropped the pound of "good shit," taken two swift steps and cuffed the startled perpetrator, knocking him to the floor.

Edie propped Mr Monkey against the old blue navy foot-locker where Nat had kept the dross of a good education: report cards, spiral notebooks filled with his sloppy lecture notes, certificates of accomplishment he'd gotten by luck or default. She prepared a meal for Mr Monkey of imaginary stuff she assumed monkeys just naturally liked: bananas, grapes, grass, leaves, and eggs. Nat watched her from the doorway until Marti shouted for them to come to the table.

When Marti and Edie had been ten and three, eleven and four, there had been frequent conflict; the little one learned quickly, or simply knew instinctively, where the big one's buttons were and pushed them extravagantly. Marti's home life had been one long howl of protest against Edie pawing this or that. But over the past year Marti had settled into the oldest child's role of third parent, and had acquired, miraculously it sometimes seemed, a patience beyond her years in her daily dealings with her sister seven years younger. As she helped Edie cut her meat, brow wrinkled at the solemn effort, Edie petted Marti's forearm distractedly.

Nestor was kind to both of his half-sisters, had always been, but having never lived with them, except for brief visits when Bridget and Katie went out of town for a few days or when Nat used to bring him along on weekend family trips to Florida beaches, there was a slight formality, even stiffness, to how he related to them. But Nat was certain that this had nothing to do with resentment. At seven, Nestor had loved the infant Marti, had seemed delighted to witness all the phases of her life preceding and now including adolescence. The infant Edie he'd adored. There was simply an emotional distance twinned to the actual distance between Nestor and the girls.

His mother was telling a story to her grandchildren as they ate the cherry torte whose pale canned cherries had thick seeds that accumulated in clutches at the corners of their plates; she told of how her own grandmother's third husband had done regular business with Franz Kafka's father on Stare Mesto, the Old Town Square where the large, stern man had had his store.

"Who's he?" Marti asked.

"Wasn't he a writer?" Nestor said more as a tentative statement than question.

"Yeah," Nat said.

"He wrote in German," the old woman smiled.

"He wasn't Czech?" Nestor asked.

"Well, it was a complicated time. Prague was a city of two cultures, two languages, Czech and German. Kafka's mother tongue was German, but he also spoke Czech. As a Jew he wasn't liked much by non-Jews, no matter which language they spoke."

Nat was always amazed at how effortlessly his mother spoke about the city of her birth as it had been before she was born, and yet turned silent or coy when asked to speak of what she could recall. "Mama, how'd you lose Jarka?"

After a long silence that even Edie had found puzzling, Nat could tell by the wrinkle of her nose, Eva Kohoutova replied, "I just don't remember, dear," and rose to clear the dessert dishes. Nat motioned for the kids to help her, and they responded quickly, even Edie.

"You mean you don't remember right this second?" Nat followed Edie through the swinging door into the kitchen holding his own plate and utensils.

Eva Kohoutova shuffled between the sink and the stove, where a glass pan and an iron skillet soaked, filled with sudsy water. She directed her grandchildren in small tasks.

"Mama, let me get you a dishwasher," he half-mumbled, and she turned and smiled, shook her head no.

As his mother hugged each of the kids in turn, and as Nestor led the girls to his car, made sure they were strapped in – Nat was proud of his son's thoughtfulness – Nat was filled with dread. He'd not wanted the kids to leave; he'd not wanted to face his mother alone. He didn't want to tell her about Grace. As Nat stood on the porch and watched Nestor's taillights recede toward St Charles, his knees got a little shaky; he turned slowly back to the door of the house that was the home of his heart, his good childhood, the beloved old woman from whose body he had not issued unto the world, yet who embodied everything he knew of "mother." He strode slowly into the living room and chatted about the kids, the restaurant, Lou, Bridget, the weather, the stock market, cherry tortes and why she only used unseeded cherries to make them; he and his mother chatted about cancer and who in the neighborhood had it, and about Lake Pontchartrain and how now it was clean enough to swim in again, as it had been in Nat's boyhood when he and Bart and some of the others, but usually just he and Bart, rode the bus to the lake to swim all day.

He wished his mother could know Sandra. Nat had always regretted that his mother had never met Sandra, would never meet her. His mother would love her even more than she loved Bridget, Nat was certain. Sandra would help him explain to his mother why he'd felt so strongly compelled to seek out Grace, the woman who, as a girl, had given him away.

SECTION TEN

As Nat waited for Bridget, he set his glasses on his nose and read the menu, one he knew well but he'd heard had changed a bit since last he'd lunched at Billy D's, which was the last time he and Bridget had called a powwow to talk about Nestor's future. They loved Billy D's; they'd come here often through their courting phase, such as it had been with Bridget pregnant through most of it, and when Nestor was a baby their waiter Sammy always brought a special spoon for the teething infant, on which he'd tied a piece of napkin so the little one could hold it more easily. Sammy brought Nat's coffee and Nat asked him about the Sweet Potato Redfish with Kumquats. Sammy said it was brand new, and he couldn't honestly say much about it, except that the chef had stolen it from somewhere else in town, though he couldn't recall where. Nat realized that that was the main problem with menu changes: it took a while for waiters to get a feel for an item, what kinds of people might like it, and whether anyone really did. Nat knew this dish from Dominique's. You sliced the sweet potatoes lengthwise into roughly quarter-inch wedges and soaked them in cold water for about half an hour to get out some of the sugar. While they soaked, you heated a splash of olive oil, then threw in some shallots and kumquats and got them soft. Then you deglazed the pan with a squirt of vermouth, scratching up the dark scum from the bottom, and reduced the liquid by about half, stirring in butter until it thickened up and shined a little. Then you preheated the frying oil, and dried the potato wedges as well as you could before deep-frying them until they were crispy.

96

Then you blended the potatoes in a food processor. You brushed the Redfish fillets with what was left of the olive oil and salted and peppered them before sprinkling on the potato flakes and searing them in a frying pan, about a minute on each side. You finished off by popping them in an oven, about 350, for four to five minutes. He ordered that for himself, and grilled shrimp for Bridget because, knowing she might be a bit late, she'd told him what she'd wanted over the phone.

Eva had been so shocked by the news that he'd found his biological mother, he, too, had wept. Why had he sought her out? His mother had not let him begin to explain, answering her own question, saying between small sobs that it was only natural to want to know who one's biological parents are. Nat had nodded, mumbled yes, it was just an urge to know the basics, like whether Grace was even alive, what she did for a living, had she suffered any major diseases, did Nat have siblings, things like that. Eva had pressed about the correspondence, what kind of person Grace seemed. For the first time, his mother had described in detail the day Nat had been brought to her, the joy she'd felt to hold him and know that nothing, no one would ever take him away. She'd talked about the details of that room, an office: the final paperwork she and Freddy-Mike signed; the color of the blanket the infant was wrapped in; the smell of cigarette smoke from the waiting room of that office; and the smell of Nat's skin. She herself had known nothing of the girl except that she was bright, sixteen and white, and that there were no patterns of illness in her family. She'd seemed a little perplexed by the fact that Grace was a feminist. She'd visibly bristled at Nat's scheduled reunion with Grace, but when she'd referred to their getting together on Ash Wednesday as a "reunion," Nat had laughed nervously, saying it was hardly a reunion since they'd never even seen one another, though he'd thought to himself that it would be a rather primal reunion, indeed. He'd told his mother he loved her dearly and that no one could ever replace her, no one, and she'd seemed mildly comforted by that assertion.

It wasn't much of a parenting powwow; their getting together ostensibly to discuss Nestor never really seemed necessary in retrospect because they always agreed about everything. Among other things, they agreed he was a great kid who seemed to be changing into a decent and capable adult, but unfortunately one with a gift and a passion for playing a game at which he'd never make any money. Of course he would never starve; Freddy-Mike had made sure all three children would have trust funds which would pay them, not huge monthly stipends, but enough on which to survive through hard times at least.

The real reason they got together was that they enjoyed one another's company in small doses, and could discuss aspects of their relationships with their respective mates they couldn't confide in anyone else, with the exception in Nat's case, of course and in every sense, of Sandra. The real subject of this date was the fact that Bridget was falling in love with a woman she and Katie saw socially; the woman herself had a partner, and the four women were more and more doing things together. They'd all gone gambling in Biloxi together at Katie's insistence, staying in the same motel room. Bridget and the woman, Pam, had stayed up and talked after Katie and Pam's partner, Lynda, had fallen asleep, and walked on the beach until dawn, holding hands and talking.

This sort of thing had happened before, several times. Bridget would have intense, unrequited relationships with women other than Katie, but would never leave her, would always settle back into their domesticity. It was Nat's job simply to listen and quietly assure her that she's a decent person and that such feelings as she's harboring are not in and of themselves betrayal.

Nat had told her he'd found his birth mother, and Bridget seemed shaken. Nat didn't understand why, except that it was a new X factor entering her life through his, and Bridget, despite her proclivity for clandestine, unrequited romances, didn't fancy actual reconfigurings or whole new patterns in the Mystery of Life. She kept all cosmic bafflements compartmentalized.

"She's a what?" She said, screwing up her pretty face.

"She's a feminist. A writer. You know, she's a professor who writes books nobody can really read but a few people, but they're about how fucked up the world is for women."

Trained as a nurse and mildly sophisticated, Bridget was a feminist who didn't like calling herself one because she thought the term had too much pop culture baggage. But after her initial shock and mild incredulity, she chuckled. "A ball buster?" she asked.

"Actually, I don't think so. She's one of those academic commies, but otherwise she seems okay, kind of a regular person. We've exchanged a few e-mails. They're a little funny because a sort of awkward intimacy seemed possible from the very beginning, so she started right in ragging me about this or that, and I've called her bluff a couple times, but she hasn't put my bad boys in a vice; not yet, anyway," Nat said.

"And she's only, what, about sixty?"

"Yeah, and she's coming into town on Ash Wednesday."

"Jesus, that's less than two weeks," she reminded him, but he didn't need to be reminded. Everything in New Orleans revolved around Carnival; everyone knew, at least from the beginning of the New Year, how long it would be before Mardi Gras. Restaurant owners, especially, gauged their lives, at least a little, by the rhythms of the liturgical calendar.

"Twelve days to Fat Tuesday," he breathed, at once bored with and excited by the prospect.

He got a call on his cell phone, which was always a little startling because he really did try to use it only for emergencies; just eight people had the number. Roberto Mancini was one of them.

"Mr Mancini," Nat rolled his eyes to Bridget, who rolled her own. Their orders arrived, and Nat's appetite evaporated.

"Nat, we've got a problem," Mancini said in an even voice edged not with malice, but something tipping toward it. These were not words one would wish to hear uttered by Roberto Mancini, especially as Nat did not doubt that he, Nathan Moore, was included in the plural pronoun.

"I guess it has to do with Nick," Nat said, his eyes shut tight.

"That's not Nick," the sweet old gangster replied.

"Well, my fix on the situation, Mr Mancini, is..."

"His mother," Mancini interrupted, his voice assuming an oddly endearing edge of desperation, "my daughter Marie is devastated. He told her he's moving out. You have to understand, Nat, he's all she's got."

"I wish there was something..."

"I don't blame you, Nat," he half-whispered, and Nat was extremely happy to receive this information. "But I need you to do me another favor," he continued, and Nat was ready to wrestle an alligator, run naked up Bourbon Street with a fat pink ribbon tied around his pecker.

"Of course, Mr Mancini."

"I want you to convince him not to move away from my sister. He's very fond of you, Nat. He credits you with changing his life," Mancini said, but not in a tone that suggested that he, Roberto Mancini, thought the change was for the best.

"Well, I wouldn't exactly say..."

"My daughter wants her boy back, Nat," and there was no doubting that this was an ultimatum. "Please, talk to him. You're our only hope, Nat. You have to make this happen. Have a good day."

As he stared beyond Bridget, out the window onto St Philip, he saw a clutch of tourists who'd attended, probably the night before, one of the dinky early parades of the season; they wore the cheapest beads but seemed happy to have gleaned even that sad horde; they wore the strings around their necks with the stupid charm of the uninitiated: they'd actually taken them off, slept, bathed, redressed, and donned again the funkiest, cheapest beads in which to bounce about the Quarter, waiting for the next opportunity to scream at floats for more, more, more. The parades would get bigger, the baubles bigger and tackier. Everyone would get happier, more excited, less inhibited. One second Mancini was calling her his sister, and the next he was calling her his daughter.

"You look concerned."

"I am," he admitted.

"Want to talk about it?" She devoured her shrimp as he told her in broad outline the situation with Nick; she, Katie, and Nestor dined sometimes, on Nat's nickel, at Newcastle's, and knew the staff. And of course they'd heard stories about most of them from Nat when he visited the house, though this was the first time Bridget was hearing about Nick's special physical feature, and about his talent for throwing his voice. Nat picked at his redfish. It was slightly overdone.

"Isn't that practicing psychiatry without a license?" she joked.

"I didn't know it could happen that way. I didn't know they could actually switch."

"What can Mancini do to you?" she asked, seeming only a little concerned. Nat knew she loved him, but considered him Lou's problem now, at least for the big stuff.

"It would save time to answer the negative of that question," he replied.

After watching Oprah, Willie watched a little CNN. There was a story about banks in Switzerland owing Jews some money. Willie knew Jews came before Christians, kind of, that Jesus had been a Jew but that other Jews flipped on him to the Romans. Willie was okay with Jesus, but he didn't feel right with all the goings-on in church. Since his grandma died, he hadn't been made to go to church, though his Aunt Bertha was all on his mama about that. She yelled that just because Willie's mama, her younger sister, was high stepping right through the gates of Hell didn't mean that an innocent child had to be dragged there, too.

Uncle Teddy had always said his sister Bertha was full of shit, and that was good enough for Willie. His uncle said Jesus was a good heart, not fear of damnation, and that'd made a lot of sense to Willie even when he was real little. Willie'd already figured out that he couldn't trust anything to be exactly what it seemed like. Church was a good place, but not everything that got said there was good, much less true. There may be a lot of evil in the world; he'd seen some of it in his own life and a lot of it on TV, and now he was reading about evil so big he couldn't begin to get his thinking around it, just like when his grandma had told him how all black people's ancestors used to be slaves that white people brought over in boats, and how some people died in the boats and then when they got to America children were taken from their mamas and everybody got sold like animals and worked to death. After his grandma had told him about it, Willie'd read about slavery a little, but it got him so down he'd had to stop. He'd been too young then. Reading about what the Nazis did to the Jews made him think about his mama's mama's mama's mama's mama getting chased down and chained up and thrown in the dark part of a boat and almost starving there and then getting yanked up into the light and sold to some old white dude who could make her do whatever he wanted her to.

The Nazis were evil, and the white people who owned black people were evil, but all that evil didn't come from some place outside of people; Willie was sure of that. That whole Devil and Hell thing never lay right in his thinking. He certainly knew that just because somebody smiles and acts nice doesn't mean he's not out to steal your wallet, or he's not like that slick Danny Dork peckerwood who made hating both the Jews and black people look about the same as selling cars on TV, but Willie was also pretty sure that Acting Nice and Doing Bad weren't getting sent into people's heads like they're transistor radios, and no devil's sending radio waves into people's heads to be Nazis and murder Jews, or to go to Africa and hunt people down and treat them like animals, and then set them free and keep treating them like animals for over a hundred years. Willie figured that getting treated like an animal was better than getting murdered, though when people on those plantations couldn't take being treated like animals they got murdered, and when people in those concentration camps weren't being murdered they got treated like animals. The difference was just emphasis and degree. Willie shivered thinking about plantations and concentration camps, and got real blue. He knew there was and would always be a lot of evil in the world, and he could see how people would want to blame it on the Devil, because a world without devils and a hell to send really bad people into, even if what they do is because they're like those goddamned remote control toy planes, is even scarier than a world where all the evil comes from inside of people. Willie considered how the idea of the Devil had scared him when he was seven, and now that he was twelve how the idea that there probably wasn't a devil scared him just as much. That Danny Dork dude was on Willie's mind a lot. Most of his life Willie'd been hearing about that white dude who kept running for different stuff and getting lots of votes but not quite enough to win, and Dork had once been in the Klan and still celebrated Hitler's birthday, and how Danny Dork was so slick he seemed kind of reasonable talking about how bad white people've got it, and Willie wanted most of all to understand how the dude's hate could stretch from black people to Jews, because he didn't get the connection, Jews being white. But Willie wanted to understand what it was he felt coming off of most white people like steam, and wanted to know if that's what the Jews felt from other white people who weren't Jews. Willie wanted to know if people like Danny Dork had two hates, one for blacks and one for Jews, or if one gigantic hate covered both. Willie read about how Jews got tricked into taking their clothes off and walking right into places that looked like showers where the Nazis poisoned them, every one of them, even babies. Millions. Because they were Jews. They just kept killing and killing in every way possible, those Nazis, and Willie realized that if there'd been black people around the Nazis would've gotten them, too, like they did the Gypsies, but their main job was killing Jews, and Willie wanted to understand why.

Willie had to get his thinking somewhere else, so he pictured TLC naked, all three of them, and went to the bathroom.

When he was finished, he rode his bike over to Bart's for his last visit; Bart had said there was one more thing Willie could do for him, and that Bart'd pay him real well for doing it.

There were three cases of vodka bottles stacked up in the corner of the living room. Bart was really stinky now, and he seemed to be working real hard to keep his eyes open. Willie asked Bart what it was he wanted Willie to do, and how much he was ready to pay for Willie to do it.

Bart said he'd give Willie ten thousand dollars, and Willie said he wasn't going to kill anybody, even for ten thousand dollars, and Bart said he didn't want Willie to kill anyone; he just wanted Willie to burn *The Mystic Pig*.

Willie asked him was that all he wanted him to do for ten thousand dollars, and Bart said yeah, but that Willie had to take it home and do it after Bart died. Willie asked him why, and Bart said it was because he couldn't bear for it to cease to exist before he did, and Willie asked why it didn't bother him that it'd burn up after he was dead, and Bart smiled funny, coughed up a little blood, and rasped that then it wouldn't matter, but then he wrinkled his brow and got a little mean sounding and said that if Willie didn't want to do it, he wouldn't have any problem finding someone else to do it for ten thousand dollars, and Willie told him to hold his horses he'd do it, he'd do it.

Willie asked Bart how long, roughly, he thought he had left, and Bart shrugged like he was answering a question about something so tiny he didn't really care about it, but Willie knew Bart didn't want to die, and that was probably why he didn't want Willie to burn it up until after he was dead. It kind of made sense.

But then Willie looked hard at Bart and wondered if because he was so close to dead Bart might not know some things. So first Willie asked if Bart believed in a life after death, and Bart took no time at all to say he was pretty sure he was going back to where everybody came from, and Willie said, You mean your mama's pussy? And Bart laughed and called Willie a wiseass, but Willie said he wasn't kidding. After a few seconds Bart said his mama's dead so in a way, yeah, that's where he was going, but Willie couldn't leave it alone; he wondered aloud if people got born all over again like those Hindus think. He'd read about the Hindus, and said that that reincarnation thing didn't sound so bad, except for the part about your coming back as a bug if you were an asshole when you died. Willie figured that that might account for there being so many bugs, especially in Louisiana.

Bart said he talked about all that in the poem, and that if Willie had listened he'd know what Bart thought about death. And Willie shot back that he listened to the creepy piece of crap as best he could, and all he could say for sure is that it's about Bart not wanting to die. Bart smiled and said what else is there, and Willie said there's got to be more than just not wanting to, since nobody'd got any choice.

After a long silence, during which Bart seemed to be thinking so Willie shut up and let him, Bart said he needed to hear some organ music. Willie asked him why, and Bart took a long pull on the vodka bottle he always seemed to be choking with his left hand, and said organ music's serious and dying's a serious activity. He told Willie to get *The Mystic Pig* out of the drawer in the bedroom and put it in a plastic bag from behind the fridge. Willie asked him how he was going to pay Willie after he's dead, and Bart said he'd arranged it with his lawyer, and that Willie would just have to trust him. Willie wasn't big on trusting people about money, but figured he had nothing to lose but the time it would take to burn *The Mystic Pig*, so he said cool, and got the stack of pages and stuffed them in a bag.

Bart rose, shaking like a sick dog. He put the bottle down, and dropped the shawl from around his shoulders. Each step he took toward the door was packed with effort, and Willie asked where he was going since Willie was pretty certain Bart hadn't moved from that couch since he started the poem, and now that Willie had ten grand invested in Bart staying alive long enough to work things out with his lawyer about Willie burning the poem, Willie was none too happy about Bart's sudden burst of activity. Willie asked where he was going, and Bart said there was a service today at Roger's Chapel on the Tulane campus, on the Broadway side, about five blocks away, and if he started now he might make it. He really needed to hear some organ music. Willie said that's pretty close to where he lived, that he passed that little church every day, but he hadn't known it was a real church. Bart just said he wanted Willie to come with him as far as the gate, and Willie said shouldn't Bart call his lawyer first, and Bart said Willie shouldn't worry, it's already been taken care of, he just needed Willie to walk beside him, to let Bart put his hand on his shoulder sometimes for balance, and as they got out the door, and Willie put the bag of pages in his basket and pushed his bike onto the porch as Bart held his shoulder and they went down each of the four steps real slowly, Willie asked why Bart didn't just listen in the apartment to some organ music on that big nasty sound system Bart never listened to, and Bart mumbled something about how he needed to hear it live, in a church, and as they got across the westbound two lanes of St Charles, Willie asked what's the difference, and just as they were making it to the streetcar tracks Bart dropped onto his back and Willie thought oh, shit, there he goes.

From the streetcar, past Lowerline, then Cherokee toward Broadway, Nat glimpsed his best friend, Bart Linsey, who was on his back in the grass of the neutral ground by the tracks. They'd been best friends through elementary, junior high and high school, stayed in close touch through college when Bart went off to UVA but came home every holiday, and about a third of the way into Nat's first marriage. After that, he'd get in touch every couple of years, and reuniting was always a highlight. He'd not heard from Bart in six years, since Nat, Lou and Marti (and Edie, though no one knew it yet) had had him over for Thanksgiving six years ago. Nat sometimes forgot that he had a best male friend, but the shock of seeing Bart passed out, filthy – even from a moving vehicle he could see the filth – and emaciated awoke a powerful feeling of fealty.

Even as he ran he realized he'd left his workout bag on the streetcar. He patted his ass to feel his wallet, which he sometimes threw in the bag before leaving the house, and was relieved it was there. As he stood above Bart, with whom he'd had so little contact over the past decade, he caught an ugly whiff of physical degradation, alcohol and piss. His hair and skin were filthy. The stench of his long-lost best friend reached into Nat and coiled around what little of the redfish he'd been able to get down in his agitation at lunch. Bart had likely not bathed in weeks, and there were sores on his lips and forehead. He wore a nice Italian suit, Gucci shoes, and a Rolex.

Bart had always dreamed of being a famous writer, had written hundreds of stories and poems in his teens, and indeed had begun to publish in some fairly respected venues through his twenties. He'd thrived on the local literary scene and through his thirties had been a local literary lion, publishing poems in *The New Yorker* and in a thin, handsome collection of verse every couple of years. From a wealthy shipping family, Bart had been Nat's only friend growing up who'd come from a family more financially secure than Nat's own, and even as they'd drifted apart, Nat had delighted a little in Bart's literary successes as they were trumpeted from time to time in the *Times-Picayune* Sunday Book section. He'd always wished Bart well with his ambitions, even as other guys, like that idiot Frank Mancini, Roberto Mancini's third son and Nat's and Bart's class-mate at Morgan Heights, howled with laughter every time Bart "the poet" was mentioned. Frank was always quick to point out that only girls and faggots read poetry. Bart, a large athletic kid, would simply good-naturedly knock the shit out of Frank and continue chatting about Whitman. A big hit with the girls, Bart had transcended adolescent prejudices so effortlessly he'd been universally admired, even by Frank and his gang. The only one of Nat's friends from the neighborhood who'd also attended Morgan Heights, Bart had often held forth so eloquently the teachers themselves seemed enthralled. He'd taken that same class from the remarkable little Boston gnome the year before Nat, and had been asked to choose and read aloud a poem at the school's memorial service. He'd read "Ode On a Grecian Urn" in a peculiarly ironic tone, hamming it up as one might have at the beginning of the course. Then he'd recited section six of *Song of Myself* with a joyful and optimistic passion appropriate to the poem, and to the life of a man in love with beauty. Every shocked kid had been healed a little by that performance.

Nat'd tried to read one of Bart's earlier, more successful books, *Checking In at the Entropy Hotel*, while browsing through the Maple Street Bookstore, and had stood for twenty minutes puzzling through it. He'd wanted to buy it, but he simply couldn't justify laying down $18.95 for something which, clearly, he found mildly torturous to read. It had seemed to be smart stuff, even a little witty when comprehensible. But like so much modern and contemporary literature, the poems seemed in a code for which Nat had not been supplied the key.

This sick man, so obviously close to death, was his best buddy with whom Nat had played chess and talked abstractly about life the whole summer of his fourteenth year. Then they'd discovered drugs together. How many joints had they smoked together? How many tabs of acid had they dropped? How many girls had they both, on different occasions of course, "hosed," "popped," "porked"? Nat touched Bart's neck as he'd seen done in movies and felt immediately silly; Bart was heaving breaths, even snoring a little, and Nat didn't really know what he was feeling for. He certainly didn't like touching his old friend, and reflexively wiped his hand on his pant leg.

"Bart," he said and then again, louder, "Bart."

A young, black voice from behind him said that the dude was really fucked up, and then asked how Nat knew him.

Nat asked the boy — a beautiful, small kid holding a bicycle that had a basket on the handlebars spilling the ends of a plastic bag — if he knew this man, and the boy said yes, Bart was a poet, and he was Bart's muse. Nat asked the boy his name, and he said Willie. Nat said Willie what, and the kid said Willie None-your-goddamned-business, then corrected himself, saying it was Mr Willie None-your-goddamned-business.

Okay, Mr Willie, Nat said, and told the boy that he and Bart used to be best friends, that they'd hung out together a lot. Nat then said, with a desperation that was surprising to himself, that he couldn't just leave Bart like that, to which Mr Willie None-your-goddamned-business said it looked to him like Bart'd left himself like that.

Nat pressed again to know how the boy knew Bart; Willie knew Bart was a poet, but Nat didn't get the second part, that the boy was Bart's muse. From his crouch over Bart, he stared hard into the child's eyes to see the truth. Nat was particularly worried about Bart's Rolex.

Willie said again that Bart was a poet, and that he, Willie, was his muse. Then Willie pointed at a large, white house and said that was where Bart lived. Nat recognized it as an old mansion that had recently been converted into expensive apartments.

Then the boy said that Bart gave him good money to buy him booze from

106

over there, but now Bart had four big boxes of booze so he wouldn't be needing Willie for that anymore, or at least for awhile.

Nat did not pursue the assertion that a child was being allowed to purchase liquor from a convenience store, but asked Willie where he lived. Willie answered by asking where he lived, to which Nat answered that he lived only a few blocks away, on Pine. Nat rose and formally introduced himself, extending his hand. Willie let his hand disappear, limp, in Nat's large white hand.

Then Nat asked if Bart lived with anyone, and Willie just stared down and asked Nat if Bart looked like he lived with anyone, and Nat felt ridiculous for having asked the question.

Nat stared down at the dying man; Bart had been one of his most important teachers, the way certain soul-quickened peers help focus the world in adolescence as numb adults may not. He simply couldn't leave Bart there. He asked Willie to help him, said he'd pay Willie for his help. Willie asked how much, and Nat said five bucks, and Willie pointed out that the dude was pretty stinky, and Nat said ten, and Willie said okay.

Nat managed to sit Bart up; Bart's eyes rolled back in his head at first, and Nat figured the best thing would simply be to call an ambulance, but realized he'd left his cell phone in his workout bag. He said shit under his breath, then got a couple quarters out of his pocket and, holding them out to Willie, told him to go over to the payphone and call an ambulance.

"Am I tenured?" Bart blurted.

"What?" Nat said, and Willie said Bart meant dead, that he always said that when he meant dead.

"No, you're not tenured," Nat said earnestly, recalling that Bart had taught for several years at Loyola. Nat recalled, too, the title of Bart's most recent volume, *Teach Me How To Die*, favorably reviewed in the *Times-Picayune*.

"My mother died," Bart said.

"I'm sorry to hear that," Nat said, a bit startled by the non sequitur. Bart's mother, though stiffly patrician, had always been kind to Nat, seeing him as a positive influence on Bart, whom she had seemed to dislike as one might dislike an expensive heirloom.

"Why?" Bart asked, and it seemed he was expecting an answer, until he said, "Excuse me," then turned his head and spewed a reddish torrent onto the grass as Willie moaned and turned away. "Died in her sleep," he finished. The crimson bile dripped down his cheek. "I'd like to stare upon a large body of water as I die. Preferably the ocean, but the lake will do. Will you take me to

107

Lake Pontchartrain? I fancied organ music a moment ago, but now I want to look at the lake."

"Why don't we get you home, clean you up, and call a cab? You need to be in a hospital," Nat said.

"Never!" Bart yelled, suddenly enlivened. "I'll never return to one of those foul places. People die there, you know," he said, but his gallows' humor was lost on Nat, who sought the least filthy part of him to grasp and lift. Bart was startlingly light.

Cowboy-style, Nat had one of Bart's once-muscular, now—frail arms over his own neck, and Willie served as a kind of walking stick, Bart's quivering hand lightly grasping Willie's skull for balance as Willie walked his bike. They got him across the tracks, the double left lane of St Charles, but nearly dropped him as they squeezed awkwardly through the low gate to the house. Hobbling up the porch steps Bart crashed to his knees but recovered, under the circumstances, almost gracefully.

Once they'd wedged through the main entrance of Bart's building, which to Nat's surprise was unlocked, Willie led them down a sour hall to a door that was opened a crack.

As Nat gently dumped his rank cargo onto the sofa, he marveled at how relatively well kept the apartment was, in dramatic contrast to its occupant. The furniture was an odd though tasteful mixture of modern and Art Deco, with much fine wood that had been recently polished. Two broad bookshelves that reached almost to the twelve-foot ceiling were packed and orderly, and as Nat glanced at them, obviously alphabetized. "You need a bath, pal," Nat said.

"I need a drink," Bart corrected. "Willie, fetch me a bottle from the top case over there," Bart ordered, and Willie said he didn't fetch for anyone.

"Take a twenty out of the cookie jar, then, and bring me a bottle, my little friend."

"Who in God's name sells liquor to a child?" Nat blurted, and Willie said that his mama owned the store across the street, and she knew who the booze was for. Willie added that she often came over and helped Bart out.

"Help out how?" Nat inquired, and Willie said he should look around and ask himself if he thought Bart was keeping the place looking so nice.

"The cookie jar," Bart reminded Willie.

Willie reminded Nat that he owed Willie ten bucks. Nat peeled a ten from his clip. Then Willie headed for the kitchen.

"Cool it," Nat said. "This guy doesn't need any more booze. I'll make him some coffee and try to get some food in him." Nat wheeled into the kitchen and yanked open the fridge: a withered grapefruit, a small jar containing a few green olives suspended in a filmy liquid, two plastic bottles of Canada Dry tonic water, and an all-but-empty Hellmann's jar.

There was indeed a cookie jar. Nat lifted the round belly of the jolly brown bear: packed with twenties. Nat plucked one out. "Mr Willie, run across the street and get a quart of milk and some saltines. Keep the change."

Nat called Lou at the shop, told her he wouldn't be able to pick up Edie and wasn't sure if he'd be able to make the game with Marti tonight. He told her he'd run into Bart, and needed to help him with something. She was mildly upset he'd not be able to pick up Edie because some customers were lingering and she wasn't sure she'd be able to get them out in time to close the shop twenty minutes early, but she heard the edge in his voice, and didn't press; then he called Birdsong to remind her that several thousand Shriners were in town so she should probably order three or four extra butts from Benny, because those old boys suck down a few raw oysters as a concession to local color then go straight for the red meat.

"You're a busy fellow," Bart observed, his torso slumped forward and to the right, held up by the couch arm. His eyes were closed. Nat strode back into the kitchen and looked into the cupboard over the sink, and then the one over the immaculate electric stove – Nat guessed that it had never been turned on – and found an unopened jar of Community instant. It stood between a battered paperback of *Atlas Shrugged* and a huge jar of pickled pigs' feet that at first glance Nat thought, startled, contained a fetus. The cupboards were otherwise empty, except for numerous roach motels. There was a pot in the sink; Nat put on some water to boil, and looked around for a cup. Next to the happy bear was a mug with PERFECTION SUCKS stenciled in black on its glossy vanilla surface, and numerous pencils and pens sticking out of it which Nat dumped on the counter. He rinsed the mug in the sink.

He put the strong brew on the coffee table in front of Bart, at first looking around for a coaster then feeling stupid for doing so.

"Lord," Bart breathed, his eyes still closed, his face propped by his left elbow so that the heel of his hand held his cheek, pushing it into his eye socket. "What is that foul aroma?"

"Drink it," Nat ordered, "then take your clothes off."

"But darling, we haven't even kissed," Bart quipped, not opening his eyes or moving. Nat began to assist Bart with his jacket and then his pants. Bart turned into a stinking rag doll. When Nat'd gotten him down to his sock (he'd only been wearing the left one) and unspeakably disgusting briefs, he trotted into the bathroom and started the hot water.

He let Bart stew languidly for awhile, checking often to be sure he'd not slipped under.

Three empty aspirin bottles lay on their sides in the medicine cabinet; one half-full stood upright. Nat sprinkled five or six into his palm. When Willie returned, Nat forced Bart to swallow the aspirins and wash them down with big swallows of the cold milk. Then, while Bart still sprawled in the tub, he forced him to eat some crackers and swallow some more milk. To Nat's mild astonishment, Bart kept it all down. Then Nat made him swallow the now-cool coffee, and even with this it all stayed down.

Nat reached in and drained almost all the filthy water, then ran some more up to Bart's chest. On his own initiative, Bart actually dug out with his long filthy nails a petrified sliver of soap that had eons ago molecularly bonded with the crusty chrome. He began to wash himself. Nat drained the tub twice more, and reminded his old friend to get his hair, which, awkwardly with the soap sliver, Bart did until Nat found an all-but-empty Head & Shoulders bottle, filled it with hot water and anointed Bart's greasy head with the suds of the shampoo residue. Then he gingerly rubbed the suds in then poured clean hot water over Bart's head with a bucket from under the sink. Bart's body resembled the photographs of ancient carcasses scooped from bogs, and Nat did not doubt that the man was dying.

As Bart, revived, began to dress himself in quite nice clothes that no longer fit him, Nat glanced out the front window. One of the smaller parades, a new one on a route that had never been tried before – skimming down St Charles from Carrollton before turning onto Nashville – would roll in a few hours; people already milling about, staking out prime spots for families: coolers, ladders with jerry-built seats for the wee ones, lawn chairs and blankets. Willie turned and pumped down Broadway.

"When did you come to this, Boo?" Nat asked gently, using his private name for his old friend. Nat had told him, after a long discussion about *Catcher In the Rye* one summer evening on Nat's porch, that Bart scared the living shit out of him sometimes. Bart had laughed, then ceased suddenly, made his eyes big and wild, and said in a voice so soft as to be barely audible, "Boo."

"Difficult to say," he replied. "I got on the ol' slippery slope about twenty years ago. Things went really bullshit just over a year ago." He fell back upon the sofa, closed his eyes.

"What happened?"

"What usually happens to destroy one's self-esteem and crush one's life?"

"A woman kicked your ass. You fell in love and got your heart stomped," Nat guessed.

"I was in love, old friend, and my heart got crushed. But it had nothing to do with a woman, except in some psychosexual sense. I mean, if one wishes to factor my warped affections for Mother into the nasty little equation, one may. I certainly don't."

Nat stared at him. Bart's head was pressed back against the wall over the sofa cushion. His eyes remained shut. He was so thin his once barrel chest was sunken. Not all the sores on this body, Nat suddenly realized, were the wounds of an unsteady drunk. His color was ghastly. Glancing at Bart when he was folded into the tub, Nat had assumed, with shivers, that he was witnessing the result of life wholly in the bottle.

"You taking medication? He finally asked. "AZT? Any of that stuff?"

No answer. Half a minute passed. Nat sat down. "You've got lots of money. You could've lived a long time."

"Money money money..." Bart breathed, eyes closed, tapping his finger on the arm of the couch as he chanted. "Money money everywhere and ne'er a drop to drink," he mumbled. "I need a drink, Natty."

SECTION ELEVEN

THE NIGHT BEFORE, Nat had roughly chopped red, yellow, and green peppers, an onion, and an ample bunch of spring onions, and dropped the pieces into the processor with some thyme, chili paste, whole cloves, the juice of four jalapenos, nutmeg and allspice and cinnamon and cardamom and coriander with three limes and a little more than a cup of brown sugar and a dash of salt. He'd let it all get chewed together in the machine as he added olive oil, little by little, until a thickish marinade emerged. Then he'd peeled and veined the jumbos, washed them, buried them in the marinade in a three-inch glass cooking dish he'd then covered with wrap and left in the fridge overnight.

Nat fired up the grill just as Lou came in with the girls, shedding stuff just purchased.

Lou was stunned by Bart's appearance, Edie clearly frightened. Marti vaguely recalled him, but this person before her did not much resemble the robust and chatty man who'd swung her around in the backyard and blown farts on her neck.

"Bart's sick," Nat gently explained to Edie, who was doing her shy number, hiding behind Nat's leg, staring from behind it at Bart in obvious distress. Bart occupied the first of the three lawn chairs beside the redwood picnic table on the patio, shadowed raggedly by a fat frond of the banana tree. He smiled at Edie, giving a coy little wave as he did so.

"Bart's going to stay with us for awhile," Nat announced.

"Oh, good," Lou said, wrinkling her brow as she always did when she lied.

"How long?" Marti asked.

"Until he dies, honey," Nat answered then blew on the coals.

Marti looked at Bart, who smiled weakly, then at Nat. Lou's mouth was open.

"We gotta talk, Nathan," Lou said. She wore short white shorts and a white blouse buttoned to her cleavage, and her skin was flushing pink against the bright white.

"Sweetie, I've got to get these puppies on the fire. I forgot the basting brush. Marti, could you run in and get me the basting brush? It's in the third drawer to the right of the stove."

"Nat please," Lou said. Nat had noticed the paperback she was currently reading splayed open towards the middle, spine up, on the coffee table. On the emerald cover a perfect woman was held from behind by a perfect man in a garden or jungle, and something about them was forbidden, according to the title. "Louie, baby, I tried to talk him out of this," Bart said. "He brought me here against my will. He could get ten to twenty for kidnapping a corpse. You still like gin and tonics?"

Lou nodded yes.

"I'll have one, too," Nat smiled.

Lou went into the kitchen. Edie ran after her.

"You've gotten big, dear," Bart said to Marti, who seemed not to have heard Nat's request she fetch the basting brush. "And that's one of those stupid-ass things adults always say, isn't it?"

Marti gave a little affirmative smile.

"Still got Marlene?" Bart asked.

"You know about Marlene?" she squeaked, not recalling that Bart had given her the stuffed mouse. Nat reminded her and she narrowed her eyes to concentrate her memory.

"I got her for Christmas," she seemed vaguely to recall.

"Yeah, and Bart got her for you," Nat said.

Thanks," she smiled at Bart. "I still sleep with her," she added

"Does your father still sleep with Mr Monkey?" Bart asked.

Marti cracked up.

"He would, but Babicka won't let him take it out of his old room," she giggled.

"Bad monkey," Nat said almost in a whisper.

"Very bad monkey," Bart echoed.

Marti laughed with them, but then asked what was so funny. Nat told her it was a long story, and that when she was older he'd tell it to her, maybe.

Lou returned with a tray of G&T's. She handed them out, then heaved a breath and said, "Okay, boys, let's start over. I wish I could say it's good to see you, Bart, but you're obviously real sick and need to be in a hospital."

"He won't go to a hospital," Nat said evenly. Bart smiled, and nodded.

"He's right. I won't," he said.

"You got the flu?" Edie chirped; she'd returned with Lou, and no longer hid behind Nat's leg, but kept one hand on it as she stared at Bart.

"How old is this pumpkin seed?" Bart asked.

"I'm five, and I'm not a pumpkin anything. You got the flu?"

"Sweetie, I've got the mother of all flus."

"All the others are the babies?" she said and smiled.

"Okay, let's shoot some answers here. I think you already know the questions," Lou said. She was being butch. Nat knew she couldn't sustain the disposition for long. It was too contrary to her nature.

"Louie, I'm dying. It'll be very soon. Nat happened along when I was... well, in a compromised position. But I've got everything taken care of."

"He was my best friend," Nat said as he angled the marinated shrimp on the grill. "Marti, didn't I ask you to get me the basting brush?"

"I'll get it if you guys promise not to say anything while I'm gone," she said.

"Scoot!" Nat shouted, and Marti ran.

"Flu Mama!" Edie blurted, then giggled.

"Natty must have had you knocked up with the wee one that last time I was here," Bart calculated.

Marti came back breathless, "What'd you say?" she blurted, throwing the brush to Nat who caught it between two fingers the way he used to catch a joint.

"Still got the touch!" Bart said.

"Why aren't you in a hospital?" Lou pressed. Nat knew she'd always liked Bart, the way all females, with the exception of Bart's own mother, had always liked him.

He looked up into her eyes. "I just can't, Lou. I can't go."

So you're just going to die?"

"I could say the same to you," he replied, smiling slyly, but Lou didn't get it.

"He's going to die here?" Lou said to Nat, who was leaning away from a plume of smoke rising from the grill.

"Maybe not," Bart answered before Nat could. "I'm going to take a cab to the lake. I'd like to pass while gazing upon a body of water," he said evenly. "I thought about the river, but it's not the same thing if you can see the other side. The lake is better for dying."

"You know, it's funny, Boo, but I was kind of thinking the same thing when we were at the beach, that when I check out I want to be near a body of water."

"Out of the cradle endlessly rocking…" Bart whispered.

"You really going to die?" Marti asked.

"Yes, dear," he answered.

Nat flipped the shrimp with tongs, though he had to use the spatula to unstick them a little.

"I don't know about this," Lou said. Bart knocked back his drink and eyed Lou's. She gave it to him. She was slow to process harsh realities if they weren't packed in the prose of romance. Poon shuffled onto the patio, and she scooped him up, stroked him slowly as she stared beyond the banana fronds.

"We're putting him in Edie's room. Edie ends up in bed with us every night, anyway," Nat said, fiddling with the sizzling shrimp, poking and nudging with the tongs.

Lou fell back into a lawn chair; Poon curled himself, with great quivering effort, in her lap. She positioned her fingertips on her forehead as though she were trying to keep a mask on. Nat knew hysteria was gathering within her, that she was controlling it just barely and with considerable effort. "Bart, darling, you know you're always welcome in this house. I've really missed you. I've often asked Nat about you, haven't I Nat? Haven't I wondered about him, Nat?"

"She's definitely wondered," Nat offered, moving the shrimp to the cooler edges of the grill and lining up veg kabobs over the strongest heat.

"I just don't know," Lou continued, staring beyond the banana tree into the ivy-covered wall of their backyard. "This doesn't seem right. I've never heard of something like this," her voice trailed.

"What's that, Mom?" Marti asked.

"This is difficult for her, sweetie," Bart sympathized. "That's why I'm leaving after you people eat. You can call me a cab."

"You're not going anywhere," Nat announced, and smiled at everyone. He felt that he must seem happier than he'd seemed in a long while. Surely Lou could see how happy he was to have Bart in the house, how important it was to him that Bart should stay, that this best friend of his youth should die in his, in their, house and home.

"You can't dictate to people like that," Lou said.

"I know, honey, and I'm sorry for how that sounded. But let me put it to you this way. I couldn't live with myself if I let him die alone. No one should have to. I mean, that's one of the main things families are for. And now we can be Bart's family." Nat looked at Marti looking at Bart.

"Well, like, what do we have to do, Dad?" Marti asked.

"Nothing! Just go about your life. We'll even go to the game on Monday."

"I may be a moot point by then," Bart said, and though he was serene his breathing was labored.

"Are you in pain?" Lou asked almost in a whisper.

"Yes, dear, but another one of those delightful Beefeaters on the rocks will help. Hold the tonic."

"We're going to have something for that," Nat said. "I already called Bridget and Katie, and they're sending something over with Nestor. When we've taken care of the pain, my old friend and I are going out on the town! We're going down to the Quarter to cause trouble, like we used to."

"Hardly like we used to, Natty. You never had to carry me."

"I'm not carrying you, you ol' bugger! We're going in style!"

"What are you talking about, Nat?" Lou asked. She was utterly overwhelmed now. She'd go along with anything when she was utterly overwhelmed.

"When he comes over with the goodies, Nestor's bringing a wheelchair Katie pinched from Touro."

Nat suddenly noticed that Edie had inched away from his leg and was now standing beside Bart, gripping the arm of the half-reclined lawn chair. Bart noticed her there the same moment, and turned and stared into her eyes, then made his eyes big and whispered, "Boo," and she giggled.

———————————

No matter where he put *The Mystic Pig*, under the bed, in the closet, behind the curtain on the floor, between Reverend Jackson's litter box and the washing machine, Willie couldn't help thinking about it being there. He couldn't wait to burn it, even though he knew that to feel that way was to want Bart to die. But it wasn't so much that he wanted Bart dead as he just wanted him to finish dying. He was glad that the funny white dude popped up, saying he was Bart's friend and acting so polite he was ridiculous, shaking Willie's hand like Willie didn't know the dude was playing him, trying to get on his good side the way white people sometimes do, acting more polite with black people than even they do with themselves, and thinking that the black people don't know they're being played. White people were funny as hell. Some of them, anyway.

Willie picked up the plastic bag *The Mystic Pig* was in and carried it from the kitchen to the bathroom, opened the towel cabinet and tucked it up under the bottom towels that never got used. But then when he tried to think of TLC, all three of them, naked, and stood in front of the toilet and imagined what he'd do with them, he couldn't stop thinking that *The Mystic Pig* was in the cabinet under those towels, and he was able to do what he'd set out to do, but with considerably more effort and concentration than he usually had to put out. And just as he was finishing, just as Left Eye was doing something so nasty he could only think about it when he was standing right there with his eyes closed, Reverend Jackson rubbed against his leg messing up the picture he had in his head, so just as he was finishing all he had in his head was that goddamned plastic bag with *The Mystic Pig* in it under the towels that never got used because the top ones keep getting used and washed and put back again before Willie and his mama could get down to them, and as he washed his hands he gave Reverend Jackson a good kick.

Willie had told his cousin Benedict, who was almost as old as Willie's mama, that he'd come over and hang out with him and his wife and the kids, all younger than Willie; Benedict had said they could all go down to Prytania which was just a couple blocks from Benedict's house and watch a parade that was rolling tonight, but Willie knew the main reason Benedict and his wife Louella wanted him to come was because he always got stuck watching the two youngest of their four kids, and Willie really liked the little one Tina, but he was in no mood for a parade.

The last parade he'd attended had been last year's Bacchus. There'd been a dude standing on a red cooler saying come here little fella and have a beer, but Willie'd said he didn't drink beer because it makes people stupid, and the fat old white dude had cracked up laughing and put his elbow into another old white dude who was also standing on a red cooler and who was even uglier, and he'd said did you hear that little monkey, he says beer makes you stupid. His buddy hadn't been listening, because another float had been groaning behind a really shitty band of white kids from Wisconsin, and Willie remembered wondering why the hell they brought some white band all the way from somewhere where there probably weren't any black people just to march like robots and play shitty when there were so many good black bands right in New Orleans, but then he'd

figured they were so shitty because they were tired. In Wisconsin they'd probably never marched and played for half the day without stopping.

Willie remembered that he'd been over halfway up St Charles, a bad place
for beads because they usually throw a lot at the beginning, then realize they've
got to make it all the way down Canal, so near the middle they got stingy. One
old fat white woman had flashed her tits so she'd gotten a lot, but it'd looked
like some of the guys on the float had just been trying to hit her with the beads
because she was so ugly. What teeth she'd had were pretty messed up and crooked,
and she'd had real ugly little eyes. Her tits'd been pretty big, but sloppy.

Willie recalled the moment he'd realized that everyone around him was
fat, ugly and white, a really bad combination, and he hadn't known how he'd
gotten himself in among so many of them. He'd been begging for beads one
minute with his cousins Louisa and Benedict, and then they'd slipped away to
somewhere else and while he'd been looking up and begging, all those fat, ugly
white people had just popped up. And then one of them had called him a goddamned monkey, and then the Kong family had come along, and Willie had
always liked them the best. Everybody always threw beads back at the giant ape
and ape mama and baby ape. But some fat son of a bitch had just called him a
monkey, so Willie hadn't been able to enjoy the Kongs the way he had the year
before and the one before that and the one before that, and before that Willie
couldn't remember much about the Kongs. Willie remembered turning his back
on the Kongs and going up to the fat white dude saying I'm not a monkey, you
fat fuck, but the dude hadn't heard him because of the noise and because he'd
been yelling so loudly himself, so Willie'd screamed I'm not a monkey, shithead,
and the dude still hadn't heard because he'd been yelling at the Kong family, so
Willie'd punched him square in the nuts.

Then he'd walked just a few steps away into the thick crowd. Through arms
and legs moving back and forth, Willie'd seen the dude folded over, still standing
on the red cooler, puking beer and what looked like nachos, and Willie'd been
sure the dude hadn't even known what'd zapped him, and that was okay. Pig,
Willie said aloud, but no one could have heard him because they'd been shouting
at the Kongs. Pig, he'd screamed, laughing. If I'm a monkey, you're a pig.

After that, Willie'd lost interest in parades. And he figured he'd blow this
one off, though he'd have to get out of the house, because that damned plastic
bag under the towels that never get used was driving him crazy. And now whenever he thought about *The Mystic Pig* he didn't just think about Bart Linsey being
dead. He thought about people getting poisoned in fake showers by the Nazis,

and about people from Africa starving and shitting all over themselves in the bellies of big boats, and about that goddamned Danny Dork smiling on TV like he was somebody you'd want to hang out with, and about an orchard of rotting fruit. And he thought about Uncle Teddy driving his beautiful car into an oak tree in City Park.

———————————

As they rolled onto Rampart it was just past dusk, and the lights of the Quarter seemed as vivid against the rapidly blackening western tinge as after a rain. They'd laughed from uptown to downtown, Bart sloshing a sixteen-ounce Proteus go-cup filled with Beefeaters. Lou'd given him the cup as Nat gingerly wedged the folded-up wheelchair into the back seat. Cruising down St Charles, they'd joked about all the shit they'd pulled as kids. Every block Nat or Bart had pointed at something and recalled some shenanigans someone, living or dead, had pulled, and they'd talked of the dead, the conscripts killed in Vietnam, the suicides, the ODs, the ones eaten by cancer and the ones ripped open or smashed in all forms of accidents, and they'd marveled at the tally, how many peers before or by mid-life had been ended.

Nat wrestled with the cheap aluminum and canvas contraption, and Bart reminded him of a similar event almost twenty years ago, when Bart and Nat had been charged with taking the infant Nestor to City Park while Bridget worked the tail end of a double shift; Nat had spent twenty minutes trying to open the baby's stroller. Nat was the least handy male anyone he knew had ever known, and though he often tried to fix things, the results were usually hilarious or vexing, or hilarious and vexing.

After several minutes of thick-fingered fiddling with the wheelchair, Nat lifted Bart as though he were a child, placed him in the chair, and rolled him from the Riverwalk parking lot.

Bart drained his go-cup and Nat got it filled again with Absolut, and Nat bought a Cajun Bloody Mary for himself and pushed Bart with one hand through the light crowd on St Louis between Royal and Decatur. As they turned onto Royal, passing the Napoleon House, Bart mentioned that it was there he and Teddy would meet for dates; they'd sit in the courtyard and drink Ramos Gin Fizzes. Nat pressed about Teddy, what he did for a living.

"Mad Dog? You were fucking Teddy 'Mad Dog' Singer?"

"We didn't actually fuck..."

"Please!" Nat shouted, "Spare me the details! I'm just getting used to the fact that my old buddy's a cocksucker."

"I wasn't back then, Natty, when I first met you. I mean, I didn't know what I was until we were about sixteen. Or I didn't know what to do about it. By the time we were adults we didn't see each other so often that I felt like I needed to tell you. It didn't seem to matter."

"But all those girls! Boo, you got laid more than any of us!" Nat exclaimed. Three Shriners toting go-cups turned to stare at Bart, who smiled and shrugged.

"I had sex with very few of them. Usually we just stayed up all night talking and reading poetry. If young heteros only understood the power of patience," he said, and chuckled.

"You scared of pussy?" Nat blurted.

"No, Natty, I've just never fancied it."

They got fresh drinks at Lafitte's Blacksmith Shop and rolled back up toward the heart of the Quarter on Bourbon. Bart could not lift the cup to his mouth now. Nat wedged it between Bart's spindly legs, and every few yards paused to lift it to his mouth. Nat became adept at pushing and steering with one hand, using his foot to brace the chair getting down and up curbs.

The Mardi Gras spirit was on a low burn, which was where Nat liked it. He'd always preferred the week and weekend before Carnival week; that concentrated and accelerating rush of nerve and slosh and color and blithe fellowship which were the eight days preceding Fat Tuesday. And as this sentiment coursed through him, the pleasant, manageable crowds parted for the chair, and everyone smiled at Bart who smiled back up at them, but he was growing more abstracted, and Nat wondered if he was beginning the final fade. The Percodan were working, Bart had assured him in the car, and he'd downed quite a few. Perhaps the drug patina was being further shaded by the alcohol toward the darkness behind sleep, but Nat didn't want Bart to slip away yet.

Nat wanted to see everything again, the past, he wanted to see the past again, not through the gauze of booze-dulled and lonely recollection, but with a friend; he wanted to talk the past back for awhile with Bart, not because it'd been so wonderful, not because it was superior to the present. Nothing could make him happier than his children, at precisely the ages they were, made him feel, and nothing could be more engaging to him than the work he was doing at this moment of his life, and he loved his wife and he loved his ex-wife and he adored Sandra, yes, adored her, for she was the woman he first loved and continued to love and would love unto death. Loving Sandra deepened his love for his children, and mellowed his affection for his wife, and sweetened the compassion he felt for his ex-wife, and now that love was compelling his desire to massage the past from these moments with someone he'd loved, yes loved as a boy and a young man, someone he'd always felt was his brother of the heart, a boy who had dared to talk serenely of beauty, who'd declared to other children – for they had only been children- that poetry was the purest form of the only enduring beauty, and that that purity was the only valid religion, all others being false for their subterfuge, their denial of the finality of death.

"How you holding up, partner?" Nat asked, steering the chair around a clump of kids begging for change. One grungy, angel-faced boy, sixteen maybe, who reeked of hash and body odor squatted down to beg money from Bart: "Hey, man, you got some change?" he said gently. Bart's expensive clothes – wrinkled and already reeking a little on his sour body – his pants and shirt tailored for the man he'd been, not the dissipated creature upon whom they now hung, all the same signaled "money" to a street urchin.

Bart was willing each breath now. "Sweetheart, I would give you enough change to change your life, except that I would trade mine for yours," Bart wheezed, and touched the boy's cheek. Nat pulled a couple of bills from his pants and tossed them at the boy with no malice, and the kid plucked them up and backed away.

In their junior year, Bart had had a job as busboy at the Court of Two Sisters; he'd gotten it to piss off his mother, and had succeeded. She'd been terrified that someone might "see" him there bussing tables, though she'd surely realized it was unlikely that anyone she'd known would dine at such a place where so many tourists got siphoned off of Bourbon and Royal. Both working in the Quarter, Nat and Bart had arranged their schedules to coincide, and on workdays during the week would leave straight from Morgan Heights for the Quarter, usually riding the streetcar to Canal and hoofing in on Bourbon.

One night, scrubbing pots in the Newcastle's scullery, Nat had slipped on the gunk that always collected over the course of the night around the old dishwasher, and caught his chin on the chrome rim of the machine's feeder tray, biting a chunk out of his lower lip. Teddy had pressed crushed ice wrapped in washcloths to his bleeding chin and his bleeding lip, and the blood had slowed but wouldn't stop. Sixteen, embarrassed, scared, all Nat could think to do was find Bart. The Old Queens had insisted that he let one of them take him to the hospital to get stitches, but he had just wanted to find his friend because he'd promised Bart he'd swing by the Court of Two Sisters and walk with him back to Canal to jump on the streetcar. Now Nat stared at the top of Bart's wobbly head, the thousands of flakes of dead skin littering his thinned hair, and looked up at the sky, which was now grinding with clouds and coming night as he steered the chair onto Royal, and that manager at the Court of Two sisters, a Mafia wannabe who terrorized the waiters as he robbed them, had screamed at Bart because Nat had strolled wild-eyed through the foyer holding a bloody towel to his chin; it had been toward the end of the evening and Nat had still worn his blood-and–grease-splotched blue scullery apron. The front wheels of the silver chair got snagged on a crack, and Bart slunk forward and almost fell on his face except that Nat scotched the wheels out of the deep groove, rocking side to side a little, and a very drunk pudgy woman dressed cowgirlish-expensive tossed a paper flower in Bart's lap, the kind of green paper bloom on a wire stem passed out at the St Patrick's Day parade through the Quarter. Bart raised his hand a few inches from the chair arm to wave, but Annie Oakley was far past and the manager had shoved Nat into the bussing pantry, yelled at him not to go back on the floor looking like that, and when Bart had entered toting a tray covered with dirty platters and silver covers and utensils the manager, skinny with slicked-back black hair and acne scars and ratty eyes, had followed him through the swinging door screaming about the stupid little faggot bleeding all over the fucking restaurant and Bart had been startled to see Nat and asked what had happened even as the wannabe gangster had kept yelling and as they reached the entrance of the Court of Two Sisters Nat stopped pushing and said, "What was that guy's name? Your boss he... Drano, Fago..."

"Plato."

"Jesus, that's right. How could I have forgott..."

"He was my first."

"First what?"

"Lover."

"Oh, shit, don't tell me that," Nat moaned, and as Plato had continued to yell at Bart, screaming obscenities, Bart had calmly checked Nat's chin and lip and told him he should get some stitches, and Plato had screamed that Bart should just drop to his knees and suck the little fairy's dick, and Bart had grabbed a silver pot of coffee tucked under the tap of the ten gallon electric machine and wheeled around splattering the hot liquid all over Plato's tuxedo and Nat pushed Bart into the foyer and glanced around.

"Whatever happened to Plato?"

"He owns a golf course in the northern part of Alabama. Pillar of the community."

Nat parked the chair past the service bar and the kitchen onto the patio, whispering to the manager that they were just passing through to the Bourbon Street exit. The fellow looked annoyed but waved them by. Two old waiters, portly light-skinned black men with poofed 70s hair, glanced at Bart as Nat pushed him through the twilit fern-pretty patio that was half filled with tourists at the various stages of dining. The right footrest of the chair brushed against the stem of a silver ice bucket, and Nat lurched to catch it. He apologized to the couple whose Mouton Cade he'd just saved, and they smiled indifference.

"Has it changed?" he asked Bart. He himself had not been there since his early thirties. The waiters wore white shirts and black bow ties, black pants, and green jackets not unlike those worn at Pat O'Brien's. On the left, running the length of a brick wall crumbling with charm, two rows of deuces and four-tops were elevated on a long dais covered by a green canopy. The other tables were exposed to the sky. A fountain splashed through the chatter, the gentle scraping and tinkle of something that at least approximated fine dining. Candles flickered. The wheels of the chair stuck every couple of feet on the stone floor.

As they wheeled back onto the clogged sidewalk of Bourbon, Nat recalled the night he'd told Bart on the phone that he'd fallen in love; snorting laughter had been the reply. Bart had begun graduate work at Virginia, and they had been at the point in their friendship when they'd talked on the phone every couple of weeks. Bart had called him a slut, a slobbering pussy hound, insisting between yucks that Nat should, since Bart wasn't there to do it for him, smack himself hard up 'side the head. Nat had chuckled along with the ribbing, but had insisted that he'd met the woman, Sandra, with whom he wanted to spend the rest of his life.

A fuzzy silence had ensued, then Bart had said simply that he was happy for Nat, though he'd added that he'd bet half his inheritance that Nat would be back to dogging poozle within a month.

Bart had always delighted in Nat's joyful, non-predatory carousing, and had always nudged Nat to supply him with narrative details of amorous encounters, which, it had been understood, Nat would offer only to a point. Though he was not a Southern Gentleman, Nat had been raised in proximity to one, and had absorbed from his father at least a measure of gentlemanly discretion. Bart had always himself been the genuine article, albeit a postmodern Southern Gentleman, which meant he could dance nimbly around the condition's codes of discourse without transgression. He'd referred vaguely to innumerable dalliances and erotic peccadilloes, but otherwise had always charmed Nat into talking about his own escapades.

Bart had wanted to know how this one, this Sandra, was different, and Nat had only been able to speak about her effect upon him, how she'd changed him.

A cop exiting held open the door of Felix's so Nat could push Bart through. In the fluorescent light, Bart looked ghastly. Nat figured if Bart could get down some protein he might rally. Nat arced the chair around the oyster bar to the rear section, which was a bit darker, or less starkly bright, than the bar area. Several tables were open, but all had remnants of previous customers. Nat bussed a table by the window, moving two trays of empty plates and glasses to an adjoining table. He ordered beers and two dozen oysters.

"Hungry?" Bart said, the lids of his eyes dropping, his head wobbling.

"You didn't touch the shrimp. I want you to get down some oysters. You need protein."

"Why are you enjoying my death, old chum?"

"What are you saying?"

"I'm saying I'm not sure who's sicker, you or me. You have so much joy in your life and so many days and nights left to embrace it all, and yet you're pitiable."

Nat could not reply. Bart had never insulted him before except in jest.

"Can't get pissed at a dying man, can you?" Bart rasped, chuckling.

"I can get pissed. I just can't say anything. An argument right now would seem a waste of time."

"You're wrong. A good row is the only thing I need from you."

The oysters and beers arrived. A muffled "Penny Lane" was drifting from a cheap sound system. Nat mixed the catsup and horseradish and squeezed lemon into the pink paste. He forked a fat gray glob and swirled it in the pink. Then he held it out to Bart's moth.

"Open up," he said, and Bart did, and swallowed it. Nat got several more down him, and swallowed four or five himself.

"Boo, I don't want to talk about me, however fucked up you may think I am," Nat said finally. "I don't want to use the time for that. I want to use it for you. What can I do for you?"

Bart closed his eyes; his body began to shake. "Tell me your heart," Bart said.

"I don't follow," Nat said.

"I'll show you," Bart said, then heaved a sigh and continued to shiver. "I loved

Teddy. Teddy killed himself. In the midst of my grief, I had a revelation: Beauty is dead. It's a simple enough thing to grasp. It's one of those things you know, but continue living as though it weren't true. But from the pit of my grief I couldn't deny what I knew any longer; I couldn't continue denying. So it wasn't a revelation so much as an awakening. My lover was dead, and my passion, that which had always been the source of my deepest passion, was dead. When I realized I could no longer live denying what I knew to be the truth, I decided I would stop fighting death. And stop delaying it."

"Are you scared?"

"Unutterably. Of both living and dying. Teddy had made me a little less scared of living. But that's finished." The shaking subsided, but he could keep his eyes open only with the greatest effort.

"I think I know what you mean," Nat said.

"Perhaps you do, but I doubt it. Now tell me your heart."

Nat spoke of Sandra, and Bart got tears in his eyes as Nat spoke. Nat described his and Sandra's twenty-year relationship through two marriages and the births of three children, how she'd encouraged his marriages, and how she collected birds, how her home was filled with birds.

"You poor man," Bart whispered, tears coursing down his cheeks. "You poor, sweet, sick thing," he whispered.

"You ask me to tell my heart, and when I do you call it sick," Nat said, not angry but deeply perplexed and hurt.

"Take me home," Bart said. "Let's go back to your place or take me back to mine. I don't care. Just let's get out of here. I'm sorry I asked you. I'm so sorry."

Willie's Uncle Jimmy was not really his uncle, but his dead grandma's best friend after his granddaddy died which was when Willie's mama was a little girl, so Willie's mama grew up calling Jimmy "Crawfish" Krews Uncle Jimmy even though she said he was more like a daddy. Uncle Teddy had even called him Pops, and everybody was real proud of the old man, how much respect he got for how he used to be able to play his horn. His name was always showing up in books about jazz, and when he was young Louis Armstrong himself said Crawfish blew one of the best horns anywhere.

Willie could go over and visit the old man just about any time he wanted to because lately Uncle Jimmy hadn't been getting out much. He had a pretty big upstairs apartment that he kind of owned with big balconies front and back and a big courtyard with lots of banana trees, and he had some money not from his horn but from buying some land cheap and selling it for a lot a long time ago, so he could hire somebody to buy his groceries and help with laundry and cleaning and to read to him some. Uncle Jimmy liked it when Willie read to him, said his eyes were getting so bad it was too hard to read to himself, but Willie knew the old man just never learned to read too well, and that was why he liked it when people read to him. He'd been buying tapes and CDs for blind people and could sit all day listening to a book. At night he put a boom box out on the back patio and played his own old music for about two hours because a writer who lived across the street wrote in a magazine that Jimmy "Crawfish" Krews was a great live performer, but unfortunately hadn't gotten around to making any decent recordings. Uncle Jimmy made Willie read that magazine story about him out loud sometimes even though his lips moved like he'd had it memorized. Every night Uncle Jimmy put some of his old music on the boom box and cranked it up, then closed the storm doors to his balcony so he could watch TV. He sat and chuckled, and talked under his breath about how his music was going to last at least until he's dead, and that greasy son of a bitch across the street was going to have to listen to it whether he wanted to or not. The cops had come a couple times to check with Crawfish about the loud music, but they couldn't really do much to an eighty-six-year-old music legend, and that was what Uncle Jimmy'd been called a lot, a music legend, and besides, Uncle Jimmy only played the music a couple of hours, so everybody in that part of the Quarter had pretty much gotten used to it, including the greasy son of a bitch across the street.

It was a long pull from uptown to the back of the Quarter. Going home would be easier because it would be full-on night and riding a bike in the dark just seemed easier, like you can go faster with less effort. Willie knew that wasn't really possible, but it still felt that way.

He hit the buzzer and knew it'd take awhile for Uncle Jimmy to push out of his big soft chair and make it to the speaker.

His old-man voice was crackly and thin through the intercom, and he said he was really happy it was Willie, and buzzed him in.

Willie pushed his bike through the narrow space between a high wall and a building, but it opened up onto a courtyard and Willie propped his bike against a fountain that had a red light in the water, and lots of goldfish, so many they bumped into each other swooshing around that light.

As soon as he got in Uncle Jimmy was stomping his foot and yelling about his cat Bubbles getting out, but she wasn't out hunting birds and getting into mischief; she was out stuck somewhere because she was so damned old she often forgot that she couldn't do much but lie around. Uncle Jimmy said Bubbles was old when Willie was born and she was probably stuck over on the other side of the wall and Willie had to go get her.

Willie hated looking for Bubbles, and now he wished he hadn't come all the way down to the Quarter just to go all over yelling Bubbles, Bubbles, and shaking a box of dried cat food until she heard and meowed.

Uncle Jimmy said she'd climbed the banana tree and gone over the wall, and Willie said shit, he hated going over that damned wall after that damned cat, but Uncle Jimmy smacked him in the head, and it was like getting smacked with a rag he was so old and skinny and weak, and Uncle Jimmy said Willie was a child and children shouldn't swear, and to get his butt over the wall and fetch Bubbles.

The wall was high. The bricks were so crusty and dark Willie could hardly see it on nights when the red light in the fountain was off. The only way to get over it was to shimmy up one of the round white beams of the balcony running from the floor to the roof of the overhang. On the other side everything was situated real nicely for Willie to climb onto a wide ledge right next to some steps that went down to the courtyard. A dim light was always on inside. Willie shook the box and whispered Bubbles real loud, but then felt silly for whispering and said Bubbles in his normal voice, shaking the box.

Willie looked at the big cage that was all rusted from being in the rain and whatnot for who knew how long. And he tried not to look at the ridiculous pink plastic bird because those things always gave him the creeps. His mama had said his cousin Maurice chased Willie with one when Willie was a baby barely walking, and that was probably why Willie hated them.

The door of the place was open a little, which it had never been, and Willie thought oh, shit what if Bubbles got in there. The porch light was gold and dim, and the light inside was small.

Willie pushed the door, and called to Bubbles. He shook the box so it sounded like those big baby rattles they used for rhythm in Mexican music, and he called for Bubbles a little louder. He felt for a light switch and flipped it, but it turned on a little lamp and not an overhead light. There was already the same kind of little lamp on, one with a green lampshade and not kicking out much light, and so another one being on didn't do much.

127

It looked like a place you keep stuff until you need it. There were boxes stacked everywhere, and jars of stuff. One stack of boxes shot from the floor almost to the ceiling and each box had OLIVE OIL on it. There was an old beat-up looking machine by the window in the back, and Willie saw that god-damned cat curled up in the middle of it, one of those giant silver dishwashers like the one in the cafeteria in the school he used to go to but didn't have to anymore.

As he stepped forward to get that old orange cat something crunched under his shoe. Dried-up roses.

SECTION TWELVE

N AT GOOSED JIMMY "Crawfish" Krews' "Better than Butter" from the *Masters of Jazz: The Lost Years CD*; if Bart was not dead, he was nearly so, and Nat did not wish to bring a corpse back to his house. The point had been for Bart to die as if among family, not be dead among them. So he turned onto Louisiana and headed toward Touro.

"Hey, Boo," he said, and shook Bart's arm. "Bart, you with me, partner?"

His head was tipped back, his mouth open. He'd continued to weep all the way to the car, and then from Decatur to Lee Circle tears had squeezed from his eyes, but he'd remained quiet. "I'm sorry, Natty," had been his only utterance as they'd headed up St Charles.

"Boo," Nat said over the slow, sexy horn solo. "Hang with me, pal," he said as he pulled into the Touro ER drive-up, but then he curled back out, hit Magazine and took it a few blocks before heading right, back to St Charles, then up to Carrollton for the twenty-minute pull to the lake. Nat parked facing the delicate looping lines of the structure that had been built as a stage for the Pope's visit a few years before. It was haloed, comically Nat thought, by the lights of the Lakefront Arena parking lot. Only the stick-domed top of it was visible above the gentle mound of the levy. The silhouette of an elaborate jungle gym and swings attached to a closed and darkened snack bar foregrounded it. There were two other cars parked at a right angle to the street that ran along the lake, past a tiny barbed wire-encircled National Guard and Naval Reserve installation, to the Seabrook Bridge.

Nat lifted Bart from the seat and carried him across the street to the cement steps of Lake Pontchartrain. The nasty water, in which Nat and Bart had soused, legally, when they were boys, lapped up to the third step, so Nat put Bart down on the first, and sat next to him, propping him up. A tiny, protracted hiss issued from Bart's head, but he didn't seem to breathe. Nat hoped there was still enough of him tethered to the world that could feel the chill of the mist that got thrown up by each lapping of the mildly toxic lake water onto the third step below. "They say you can swim in it again, Boo," he whispered.

The Lakefront Airport hummed to their right, across the Seabrook, and beyond the runways the riverboat casino glittered in its more or less permanent mooring. A few stars above the lake didn't get smeared away by the city light behind them, and the moon, what there was of it, lay blocked by the only cloud in Nat's field of vision.

"You shouldn't feel sorry for me, Boo," he said, his arm around the corpse of his boyhood friend. "It's how I live. It's my secret life."

A corporate jet banked out over the water and quietly swooshed toward the east-west runway.

"It's so hard to keep it out. At first I couldn't keep it out." The hiss from Bart's head quieted.

"She was a beautiful kid. I loved her the way you can only love when you're young. And I still love her exactly like that."

An NOPD white Taurus slowed down behind them; Nat glanced back and smiled. It sped away.

"They made me watch, Boo. I never told you about that. First the little one held the shotgun to my temple and told me to keep my eyes open or he'd blow my brains out. Then the young one stuck it in my ear. Then the leader, a bald fat guy with a snake tattooed..."

A couple from one of the other parked cars was arguing. She wanted to go home. He wanted her to have another drink and chill.

"The whole time she looked into my eyes over their shoulders. The snake guy said if I closed my eyes he'd kill both of us. She didn't cry.

"What do we really know, Boo? In my secret life she overcomes everything. And I'm not a coward. I don't weep and beg for my life while she lies smeared with blood and cum, because I'm not there. I don't get laughed at and pissed on and left tied to a tree so I can watch her bleed to death. I don't stare at her for two more days. I don't see what happens to her. How she changes.

"It works for me, Boo. I can live this way."

130

With his free hand he worked a cell phone out of his opposite pocket, the one between him and Bart's body. It was awkward, but he just didn't want to let Bart's body fall back. He called Lou, and told her Bart had passed and where they were. She sounded relieved and sad, and even told Nat she was proud of him, proud of his loyalty. He said nothing to this, not feeling particularly loyal. Nat said he thought he should handle talking to the girls about it, and she agreed. Then he told her it would take quite awhile to deal with all the details, not to wait up for him.

Then he called Bridget. They'd already talked through what he should do, how she would help. She'd already discussed the situation with colleagues at Touro, though she'd thought the plan was that Bart would pass away at Nat's home, not sitting on the steps of Lake Pontchartrain.

The ambulance arrived, no sirens but with lights flashing, in what Nat judged to be forty minutes, the police very soon after. Katie, who was on duty, had come with the ambulance to help Nat out with the police and get his emotional bearings. He was grateful, and he was allowed to leave while the ambulance and two police cars were still silently flashing, and the officers and medics proceeded through the first stages of the bureaucracy of death. Before leaving his apartment Bart had gathered his ID, and dictated to Nat instructions that Nat had written down and sealed in an envelope. Nat had suggested to the police that they check Bart's ID in his left inside jacket pocket, and also that they read what was sealed in the envelope they would find there as well. Bart's lawyer already knew what to do; she would take care of everything.

Nathan Moore walked past his car onto the playground, past the swings to the cropped grass teeming with shadows, and paused, the lake and a dead friend at his back, to consider the halo of light along the levy. Then he climbed the steep hill and stared southeast at the lights of downtown. "Jarka," he said.

Grace:
The best friend of my youth died tonight. His name was Bart Linsey, and he was a poet, a real one I think, though I'm not sure what that means. We were the same age, but I always looked up to him because he was obviously so much smarter and wiser than I. He died of AIDS.

I spent the last hours of his life with him and yet I can't call him my friend. We'd been out of contact for almost six years, and the decade before that we'd come together happily, familiarly, once in awhile, but those occasions were already steeped in nostalgia. Even as I held him, as he was becoming a corpse, I couldn't regard him as a friend.

And even as I mourn him, I'm quite contented to know that he took my youth with him, a fair chunk of it, anyway.

It's late. I'm exhausted. But as I tap these words to you I am filled with the sense of how blessed I am, though I can't fix to the dark beneath these words an image or even the most abstract conception of what may be the agent of that blessing. Bart Linsey was not gathered to the bosom of an infinitely loving and knowing progenitor. The trillions of little lights comprising him simply burned out in a grand cascade. What has blessed me confounds me precisely because I don't doubt that I am comprised likewise of trillions of tiny lights that in due course will flicker out with a rapidity unmatched except on those unimaginable scales at either extreme of nature.

I'll see you soon.

He turned off the computer, put on his jacket. He flipped the switch on the light to the walk-in, stuck his head in and did a quick inventory, then went back into the office to go over the books again because he had a feeling he'd missed something, and indeed he had. He noticed that he needed to write two more checks for Peggy to send on Monday. He wrote them out. Then he had a feeling he'd missed something when he'd looked into the walk-in, so he yanked it open again, flipped on the light. He counted the trays stacked around the perimeter of the space on shelves three deep, then the five-gallon aluminum pots covered with clear wrap and lining the floor beneath the bottom shelves. On a hunch he stepped in and peered into a five-inch deep rectangular pan on the top shelf, and was alarmed that only a third of the white chocolate bread pudding was left. He ticked off two large parties of regulars he'd noticed listed in the reservation book, folks who always made a point of ordering it for dessert. Birdsong was a dream, a consummate pro who got almost everything right, but she was a bit too cocky. She made decisions based more on her own experience at other restaurants than on the history and quirks of Newcastle's, even though the kitchen staff and waiters were more than willing to educate her. Surely someone had told her she needed to make another flat of bread pudding, and she'd nixed the proposal. Nat would find out. Meanwhile, someone had to make the pudding. Birdsong and Paul would have their hands full in the morning with the normal prep. Nat sighed, slipping out of his coat and into an apron.

It took about ten minutes to get everything ready, and to fire up the oven to 350. There was plenty of stale bread in the pantry, which was a pleasant surprise because the twins usually took it home when it wasn't immediately used for the pudding. He set everything up on the cooking ledge: whipping cream, milk, white chocolate someone had already broken into little pieces (perhaps Paul had already started the prep and Birdsong had gotten him onto something else), sugar, lots of eggs — he'd use a half-dozen or so whole ones, and twenty or so yolks; this was not a dessert for the weak of heart — three stale loaves. He heated the cream, milk and sugar — a couple cups of sugar, ten cups of whipping cream and about a quart of milk — over medium heat. When it was steaming but not boiling he took it from the flame and stirred in the chocolate until it melted. Then he quickly separated out about twenty yolks and cracked in eight or ten whole eggs with them, whipping them together. He heated the cream up a bit more, then gingerly poured the hot cream-milk-sugar into the yolky egg goo, whipping vigorously. Then he sliced the bread and placed it in the long pan and poured about half the goo over the slices. He pressed the bread with his fingertips to make sure it got soggy, then poured in the rest of the goo. He covered the pan with foil and popped it in the oven. After fifty minutes or so, during which he watched CNN on the TV in the employee lounge, he poured about a cup and a half of whipping cream into a medium saucepan and brought it to a boil. He took it off the heat and sprinkled in about half a pound of the "best white chocolate west of the Alps," and considering what Nat paid it had better be. He stirred until the sauce was utterly smooth, then took the cooked bread pudding out of the oven. He put it in the walk-in for a few minutes to cool it down, but just a little. Then he poured the sauce over it while it was still warm. Then he covered the pan with clear wrap and put it in the walk-in. Additional hot sauce would be added before serving, he reminded Birdsong in the note he wrote and left on the counter in front of the grill. She'd thought it barbaric that he let a glaze of the sauce harden on the pudding, only to add another layer of it hot before serving, but he explained that that's the way it had been done at Newcastle's since before Noah built the ark, and that her innovations were to be in addition to what the restaurant had always done, not instead of. The natural and quite healthy tension between a fine chef and a committed owner was beginning to bubble, and they both knew they had to ride it out.

Nat cleaned up, threw the apron in the hamper — it could have been reused except that he'd gotten a dot of egg smeared on it — turned off the TV in the employee lounge, put on his jacket, set the alarm and locked behind him. He emerged from the alley onto Dauphine.

Dawn was an hour or so away. He was glad he'd made the pudding. He always felt better after cooking something.

When he got to Zimple, Willie decided to walk his bike the rest of the way because something was blooming and smelled real good, and the air just felt real good, and the small sounds coming from the white people's big houses made a kind of overall music he wanted to listen to while he thought about how glad he was not to be old Bart Linsey. But then he thought about *The Mystic Pig*, and about naked people gagging on gas and screaming and little babies choking and a big dude was staring at his house through the high hedge. He was an ugly black dude wearing floppy dark clothes, and the hood of his sweatshirt was up over his head, though his big ugly face was poking out. He had a bandage on his right hand. He was just standing there looking at the front door.

Willie angled across to the rear patio, slipped in, leaving his bike on its side by the gate. He ran through the house and peeked again between the curtains; Ugly was still there.

Willie dialed 911 and his mama came out of her room and heard him explaining to the police operator, and she looked through the curtain then hustled back into her room. She came back out with a robe over her slip and the gun in her hand by her side. She yelled at Willie not to come out no matter what, then threw the door open and ran past the yellow porch light.

Even Willie was scared of her now; she screamed I seen you motherfucker, I seen you in my store and I seen you following me and I know you the one shot into my house now I'm going to shoot you in the dick. She was telling Ugly over and over how she was going to shoot him in the dick, and when Willie looked through the curtains at how his mama pointed the gun down at Ugly's pleasure unit, as his uncle used to call it, and how big Ugly's eyes were, almost all white with little dots, and how his mouth was open making him look doubly stupid, Willie knew the dude was definitely scared shitless, and when Willie's mama said she was going to shoot him in the dick now and next time blow his fucking brains out, Ugly held both hands over his crotch and started grunting about how he hadn't done anything, that Willie's mama was crazy and that it was a free country so he could hang there and check things out if he wanted to.

134

Willie's mama just told him again he was getting a bullet in his dick, but if he showed her his gun maybe she'd just blow one of his balls off. Ugly said he didn't have a gun, but Willie's mama aimed real carefully, holding the gun with two hands now like she was just now going to let one rip, and Ugly screamed he didn't have a gun and Willie's mama said he better pull one out of his asshole, then, and counted one, two, and Ugly yanked up the front of his sweatshirt and pressed into his jelly belly was a little gun with a white handle, and Willie's mama told Ugly to take it out with two fingers and drop it on the grass or she'd shoot him in the dick right this second. Ugly plucked out the gun and dropped it on the grass, and that was when the cops got there.

They jumped out and Ugly ran, and Willie's mama dropped her gun on the grass just as a big black cop started peeling out his gun. He cuffed her while the white cop sprinted after Ugly, who didn't look in shape to get very far.

Willie came out and yelled at the black cop that his mama hadn't done anything wrong. The cop told him to shut up and get in the house. Willie watched from the window as his mama sat in the back of the white Taurus whose blue light splashed over all the houses across the street, and his mama's white Toyota Corolla was bluish from it, too. The black cop talked to her, trying to calm her down, then listened a long time, it seemed, while she talked. The white cop came back with Ugly cuffed in front of him; Ugly's nose was bleeding pretty badly. More cops came. The whole neighborhood was flashing blue and now some red, too. Six cops stood around talking while Willie's mama sat cuffed in the back of one car, and Ugly was in the back of another. Everything was flashing blue and red, and now some people, mostly kids about Willie's age and a little older, including Maurice from two doors down who got knocked in the head so bad last year all he could do now was watch TV, stood around with their arms folded checking everything out. Willie hated that people in the neighborhood, people he and his mama saw almost everyday, were staring at her sitting in the back of a police car with her hands behind her back. The cops were acting like this was a social occasion; the ones who weren't talking to Willie's mama or to Ugly were leaning against the police cars with their arms crossed, just shooting the breeze like they hadn't seen each other for awhile so now they were just hanging out. They laughed and spit and yawned and glanced at their watches.

One of the white cops came over and talked to Willie's mama a long time, then he helped her out of the car and took the cuffs off. The cops picked up the guns and put them in plastic baggies, then rolled away with Ugly. Willie's mama came back into the house.

She threw herself onto the couch and shook all over with her face pressed into a cushion. Willie stood over her and rubbed her on the back. That's all he could do. She mumbled something about Ugly being wanted for murder. She mumbled about being so tired. And Willie told his mama to go to bed; he'd lock up and clean up and turn out lights. He told her they can even open up the couch and lie on it and watch a movie together, and she said okay that would be best, and dried her face with the sleeve of her robe, and pulled herself off the couch to move the coffee table and open up the couch, and Willie fetched the pillows off her bed.

SECTION THIRTEEN

"Jack, we've got to talk," Nat said, through the doorway of the employee room. "When you're finished here, come see me in the Bienville Room."

"Yeah you right, boss," Jack answered with a smile.

"Help! Help!" Nick screamed.

"Hey, Jack!" greeted Stinkfinger as he and Puddin' Head breezed through. "How you hangin'?"

"Like a chandelier at Versailles, Stink m'man!" Jack answered, and Stinkfinger laughed, though he obviously wasn't sure at what.

"What's cookin', Jack!" said one of the twins as he passed, though because they weren't together Nat couldn't tell which.

"A rack of your mama's spare ribs, Rudy boy, and they're all for you!"

"Help! Help! Please, help!"

"How you doing, Jack!" greeted Danny passing through, already in his tux, his bow tie dangling untied from his open collar.

"Somewhere a pipe is calling for you, Danny boy!"

"Somebody help! Mr Moore! Help!"

Everybody loved Jack, and Jack loved himself, Nat observed, and as he entered the dark Bienville Room, which that night wasn't booked, Nat still hadn't shaped a strategy, a compelling argument as to why Jack should go back in the dark and let Nick drive the bus again.

"Hey, boss," Jack said.

"Sit down, Jack," Nat said from the head of the long banquet table.

"Would you like some coffee? I used to have to tank up on java before a long night's work," Nat said with a strained joviality.

"Nope. I just chew NoDoz all night," he answered, and plucked one from his shirt pocket and popped it in his mouth, smiling. "Saves time."

Nat had told Paul to put a fresh pot of coffee on the table, and two cups and saucers. Nat poured himself some. "Jack, I think everybody in the restaurant's happy with your transformation."

"Help! Mr Moore!"

"Is there anything you can do about that?" Nat asked, interrupting himself, and Jack eased into the chair two down to the left of Nat, and slowly crossed his legs.

"That should shut him up for a while," Jack smiled.

"He keeps quiet while you're working the floor?" Nat had to know.

"Oh, yeah, he's a stupid monkey, but we do share certain professional principles," Jack said.

"Please don't call him a monkey," Nat said.

"Why not?"

"Personal reasons," Nat sighed. "Jack, your grandfather called me and said you're moving out of your mother's house. He's disturbed because she's so upset, and I'll be straight with you, pal, Roberto Mancini's distress is my distress."

"Why's that, boss?"

"Help, Mr Moore!" Nick gurgled, as though he was being strangled.

"Well, you know I grew up with your Uncle Frank," Nat began.

"Who got whacked."

"Nobody really knows that for sure, Jack," Nat said, frowning, though of course everybody knew Frank Mancini'd had the mother of all gambling problems, and drowned in eighteen inches of water off the Gulfport beach, wearing his best suit, owing almost half a million to one of Roberto Mancini's friendly competitors who himself was no longer counted among the living.

"Yeah, and Art Garfunkel was the talented one," Jack smiled.

"My point here, Jack, is that I went to your uncle's wake, and saw your grandfather there, of course, and he remembered me from when I was a kid and used to go over to his place across the lake with Frank and some of our buddies."

"Yeah, I like it over there," Jack said. "Got some nice horseflesh," he added.

"Yeah, we used to ride his horses," Nat remembered wistfully. There was a single candle in the middle of the long table. Jack/Nick seemed almost angelic backlit by its flickering. "Anyway, I was the floor captain back then, making good money, and I'd just inherited a bundle from my father's sister, and already had quite a bit put away. Everybody knew Kent Newcastle was looking to sell the place, and I had the crazy idea I wanted to buy it. Newcastle laughed in my face. I mentioned to your grandfather at Frank's wake that my dream was to own Newcastle's, but old man Newcastle wouldn't sell it to me even though I had cash up front and could get the financing. Two days later Newcastle calls me into this room and he's sitting where I'm sitting right now, and I was about where you are now, and he told me he'd take my offer."

"What was the big deal in the first place? I mean, if you had the money?"

"Oh, it makes perfect sense, especially to me now. It wasn't just about money. When I bought the restaurant, I bought the name, the tradition. Kent Newcastle's grandfather created the place, and the only reason it didn't stay in the family was that he had three daughters who married complete and utter assholes, Yankees with those fucking Yankee attitudes the old man hated like he hated cooks who burn food and call it cuisine. No, it wasn't just about money. It was about legacy. I'd be just as picky about who I sold the place to, and my name's not even on it."

"So you think Grandpa made the deal."

"Of course he did. And he's only asked one favor of me in return," Nat lied; Jack had certainly figured out that the only reason Nick had been hired and then tolerated was whose grandson or nephew he happened to be, but Nat didn't feel that point needed to be pressed. "He wants me to talk you into letting Nick take over again, but I can't do that, partly because I know you won't, and partly because I don't think it would be right. But I do want you to consider staying at your mother's house, Jack. It would mean a lot to me, more than I can tell you."

"I'm twenty-six," Jack said.

"Be that as it may, Roberto Mancini thinks it would be the best thing," Nat said half-heartedly.

"I want to get laid," Jack said.

"That's understandable," Nat said, his own reasonableness clogging his sense of self-preservation.

"I mean, like, boss, I *really* want to get laid," Jack insisted.

"What does your mother have to do with it?" Nat asked lamely.

Jack laughed. "The same things every mother has to do with it, only factor that by the number of times I've whacked off in my life and you've got a numerical value, expressing my mother's particular investment in my not getting laid. She's a religious nut, boss, a certifiable psycho. She wanted to be a nun. The way I heard it from cousin Ferdy, my old man was some kind of monk or something who slipped Mom a mickey at a summer retreat and had his way with her, for which he got whacked, of course, but dum-dum was already in the ol' oven, the leavened loaf of a mortal sin. In the middle of the living room of her house has always stood a three-foot Virgin gazing down from an altar. Nick would sit on the couch and stare into it like it was TV. That's Mom's idea of family entertainment. She weeps every fucking night on her knees in front of the three-foot Virgin in her bedroom. Every room in the house has a three foot Virgin except the bathroom, where a square-foot portrait of the Virgin Mother stares right at you while you're taking a dump, or worse. Mama weeps and prays, prays and weeps, clicking those fucking beads, moaning to Mary that she wants me to be a priest. Me, a fucking priest! Or Nick? Nick a fucking priest? When Nick was little she said I was a Siamese twin who never fully developed, and that my little soul was in Purgatory.

"Well, boss, I ain't in Purgatory. I'm in the world. And I want to get laid, and I don't want to go to bed every night to the clattering of beads and the weepy mumbling of prayers, and get up every morning to the same thing."

"So I guess I can't talk you out of it," Nat sighed, defeated.

"Boss, I owe you a lot. I don't want to put you on the spot with Grandpa. But that woman's nuts," Jack said, reaching into his shirt pocket, then popping a NoDoz into his mouth.

"You're not exactly a poster boy for good mental health, Jack. I mean, you've got some kind of split personality thing going there, don't you think?"

"Hey, I'm not perched on a school roof at recess picking off the wee ones with a semi-automatic," Jack pointed out.

"I'm a father. I don't find that humorous," Nat informed him.

"I didn't mean it to be. Sure, I'm a sick motherfucker, but as far as I can see you've got two basic kinds of men, you got your cocksuckers, and you got your motherfuckers. I don't know much about cocksuckers. But I do know that motherfuckers divide yet again. You got your sick motherfuckers who just got to do damage, and sick motherfuckers trying not to get damaged."

"That's oddly eloquent," Nat said.

"Thanks, boss. Look, I'll talk to Grandpapa. Maybe we can work out something. See, I really think my old lady's off her nut, like, she should be committed or something. Maybe I can talk Grandpapa into getting her into a nice place, like over in Mandeville. They can stick her in a rubber room with one of those freaky statues; let her pray her guts out. Hell, maybe I can put her away by myself!" Jack blurted, radiant with the prospect.

"Jack, I don't know if the judgment of someone who's been taken over by the personality he's invested in his penis is likely to sway the authorities in such a matter."

"You don't think?"

"I think you may have some problems there, pal."

"But I'm exhibit Number One! I'm proof positive she's loony!"

"I don't think it works that way, or two-thirds of all parents would be committed for excessive praying. I think there's some kind of First Amendment thing there. You certainly couldn't make it stick in Orleans Parish."

"But it's crazy!" Jack almost screamed.

"Some people would consider talking to a dick crazy, but I don't think I could be committed for participating in this conversation."

"But boss, she never stops. She weeps and prays, prays and weeps. She clicks her beads from dawn to dusk. She kneels all day in front of that statue. It's crazy. If she's not crazy, nobody is."

"How did Nick deal with it?"

"She made him pray with her a lot. So he thought a lot about fucking the Holy Virgin. You know, because she's pretty cute. Nice skin. Nice features, like, really pretty eyes and that pretty little mouth. And she's nice and slim. Of course, whenever he thought about fucking the Holy Virgin, I popped up, sometimes right out of his jammies, and he'd get beaten up pretty bad when she saw that. One time she broke a mop handle across his back."

"The woman does sound sick. Obviously, Nick was an abused child."

"Like, duh! You think? Of course he was abused! I'm telling you, boss, she's sick. She should be put away."

"Yeah, well, if you move out, the only thing I can think to do is offer to take your place," Nat sighed, defeated. "Why does he care so much?" Nat finally asked.

"About me staying with her?"

"About her generally. He sounded desperate when he asked me to talk to you. And he's referred to your mother as his sister. That's weird."

"Yeah, but it's also true," Jack said. "Here's the deal: back in the Old Country he knocked up a gypsy when he was fifteen. When my mama was born, my great-grandparents adopted her and raised her. Technically, Grandpapa's also my uncle. Fuckin' Greeks got nothin' on us!" Jack chuckled.

For a couple of days, Willie's mama'd had to go back down to the police station it seemed like every ten minutes, and they were constantly calling her to come down or just answer more questions over the phone; at first Uncle Lester was going to be her lawyer because he was almost one, but as it turned out she didn't need a lawyer. Willie's mama had been told she was okay, that nothing was going to happen to her for having that gun and saying she was going to shoot Ugly in his dick. She'd told the police she'd bought the gun from somebody she'd never seen before, somebody who'd come into the store a few times, got to talking with her about how dangerous it is not to have a gun, and that he could sell her a good one. The police had been okay with the story, but they'd wanted to know more about the other times she'd seen Ugly, the times he'd followed her from the store and watched her get into her car, or sometimes when she just walked home because it wasn't that far, he'd seemed like he was following her all the way up Maple to PJ's where she'd sit and drink a cup of coffee until Ugly was gone and she could go home without him following.

They were trying to make it so Ugly'd die by lethal injection, and they needed Willie's mama to go to court when they told her to and say what she had to say so the jury wouldn't have any doubts, so the detectives and their partners who do the court stuff had to make sure Willie's mama said everything right, so they'd talked to her a lot, and to a bunch of other people who'd run into Ugly while he was killing four people uptown the last couple months, not all at once, his mama had explained, but here and there at different times. Ugly'd killed three women and a girl, the seven-year-old daughter of one of the women he'd killed, the police told Willie's mama, who told Willie she'd help all she could to get Ugly shot up with poison and put down like a dog, because he was no better than a mangy old dog, no, he wasn't nearly as good as one, and if anyone deserved to get poisoned to death it was a man who killed women and little girls. Besides, he'd almost gotten Willie, too.

Now it was his mama's birthday, so Willie was going to make her an extra special dinner, then give her the present he bought. It looked like she finally had that police stuff behind her, except when she would go to court, which probably wouldn't be for awhile. She'd been pretty blue about what'd happened, so Willie wanted to make an extra special birthday dinner for her, and he'd invited Uncle Jimmy who'd come over in a cab Willie'd already fixed up for him, and Aunt Bertha because he had to but wished he didn't.

Instead of regular old cake he was going to make yam and praline cheesecake because it was his mama's favorite when Aunt Bertha made it, and Willie thought he could do it better and Uncle Jimmy'd tell the truth if he did, and that'd really piss off old Bertha, and Willie'd really like to see that.

He took the Graham cracker crumbs he'd just made by smashing the crackers with the flat end of a Pepsi bottle and measured not quite two cups, then mixed in about a third of a cup of sugar. Then he dripped about six little spoons of butter to get it like mud as he mixed it all together. He washed his hands again, then pressed the mud over the bottom of the kind of pan you can snap the sides off of. When he'd gotten the crust the way he wanted it, he squeezed a lemon all over it and put it in the fridge. Then he turned on the oven to 350, lighting it with the last match in the box so he had to be real careful.

He got down the biggest bowl and wiped it out with a paper towel just in case there was some dust in it, then dropped in three slabs of cream cheese he'd gotten soft in a little pan first, not quite a cup of sour cream, half a cup of heavy whipping cream, a cup and a half of sugar, half a little spoon of nutmeg; then he used his mama's old hand mixer – because the processor'd gotten jammed – to smooth it all up so there weren't any lumps from the cream cheese. Then he broke in five eggs, one at a time beating each one in before adding the next. Then he put in a little praline liqueur his mama kept for some of her own cooking – about three splashes – and about a cup of yams he'd turned into orange paste with the mixer and put in the fridge an hour ago, and a couple of handfuls of chopped up pecans. Then he got the crust from the fridge and poured the good stuff into it, dropping in the rest of the yams so they'd stick out a little. Then he put it in the oven.

Willie cleaned up the mess from the cheesecake, and set everything up for the Chicken Etouffee. He measured out a cup of flour, two cups of chicken stock he got from cans but toughened up with some chicken-flavored cubes, a half cup of olive oil, five onions he chopped up pretty small, a cup each of chopped up green peppers and celery, about ten cloves of garlic smashed up, a bunch of chopped up green onions, four or five bay leaves, some salt and pepper and some Chef Paul Prudhomme seasoning which his mama had bought so he had to use up. Then he cut up about ten thighs into little pieces.

He got the olive oil hot in the iron skillet, and stirred in some flour for the roux; he'd had his share of disasters burning roux, so he kept stirring until it turned nice and muddy looking. In his mama's biggest pot he dripped in a few drops of oil and washed it around with a paper towel. Then he dropped in a little more than half of his onions and peppers, and stirred them around for a little over five minutes with the fire about half way. Then he plopped in the roux and the rest of the onions and peppers, and the green onions. Then he crumbled a chicken-flavored cube over it and poured in the chicken stock from the cans a little at a time while he stirred with the big wooden spoon that used to be his grandma's and which Bertha wanted but Willie was going to hide before she came over. When he had a gravy that was exactly how he liked it he dropped in the rest of the stuff, lastly the chicken pieces. Then he started the rice. He had to stand there for twenty minutes stirring so it wouldn't stick. Reverend Jackson threaded through his legs and Willie kicked him in the head just hard enough to piss him off, and laughed at how the Reverend hauled ass towards Willie's mama's bedroom, but then he remembered *The Mystic Pig* in that plastic bag under the towels that never got used, and he wished he could go back about two minutes when he actually wasn't thinking about the thing, because now he won't be able to get it out of his head again. All through his mama's birthday dinner which was supposed to be a time of laughing and eating and the grown-ups drinking a little whiskey and beer, he'd be thinking about that damned thing, and about those Nazis dropping poison into those fake showers and babies gagging and blood coming out of the sun and blue soldiers and people with tickets in their heads and what really worked his nerves now was that he couldn't be sure the situation was going to change after he'd burned it up. Ten thousand dollars is a lot of money, especially for just burning a bunch of pages, except that now all he could think about was that goddamned soda-cracker-silly-ass-butt-ugly-dog-shit poem and all the sad things about the world it talked about in that weird-ass poem way.

So when Bart's lawyer called as Willie was taking the rice off the stove and told him Bart was dead and that Willie may now perform the task he and Bart had negotiated and get his ten grand right after, Willie asked how the lawyer was going to know that Willie actually did what he and Bart made a deal for him to do, and the lawyer said she was instructed to take it on faith. Willie said that if people could really be trusted like that there wouldn't be any need for lawyers. The lawyer laughed, though Willie didn't know why.

He had about half an hour before Uncle Jimmy got there in a cab, and his mama would come in about forty minutes and Aunt Bertha would get there

144

when she felt like it, which Willie hoped was in time to hear Uncle Jimmy say Willie's cheesecake was the best.

He went to the bathroom and got *The Mystic Pig*. Reverend Jackson rubbed on his leg as Willie stood at the sink and stared at the plastic bag, and Willie didn't even kick him. Willie was hearing Bart's voice, and seeing Bart's face as Bart talked the words he'd written on those pages Willie was holding in a plastic bag that had a speedboat on it and a white man and a white woman in the boat really loving the cigarettes they were smoking. Willie thought about the giant ovens he'd seen in books and so many people getting killed and their bodies thrown in those ovens and burned up so that the ashes filled the air all around and got into everything, what people drank and ate even. And he thought about people dying in the big dark bellies of ships and those that live having to be with the dead for so many days without much light that the smell of the dead starts to be normal and all there is to life.

Willie'd seen lots of dead bodies on CNN, and he'd smelled dead animals under houses and such, and figured that dead people probably aren't that different. Death is so sweet smelling it's beyond sweet. There's no rot like animal rot, and humans are animals. He was certain of that. Bart's dead, he said out loud, and it sounded peculiar. A weird dude had sat dying for weeks and scribbled what was in his head onto the pages Willie was cradling. He'd said Willie was his muse, and all Willie'd ever done was sit and listen then tell him it was a piece of shit, which it was. Bart was dead, Willie said out loud, and got tears in his eyes but he wasn't crying, not really. It was more like he was so pissed he could rip the asshole out of an elephant, except that he was so little. He was pissed at the world for being like it is, and for making a poor dying dude spend so much of what little life he had left on such a sorry piece of shit as Willie was holding in his arms.

SECTION FOURTEEN

ILLIE LAID HIS bike down by the library steps. Sad Eyes was still behind the desk. Willie told the tall skinny white dude he had a problem and he needed to talk to somebody who knew something about books. Sad Eyes asked what his problem was. Willie said he had an epic poem in the bag, and if he burned it up he'd get ten thousand dollars, but really all he had to do was say he torched it because the lawyer of the dude who wrote it said that was all he had to do. The problem was that he couldn't burn it, and Sad Eyes shouldn't ask him why that was, either.

Sad Eyes told Willie his name was Larry Lux, and that Willie could call him Larry. Larry Lux stuck out his hand to shake and while Willie shook it he wondered why he would call Larry anything but Larry if that was his name, unless Larry meant Willie didn't have to call him Mr Lux, which Willie wouldn't have done anyway.

Larry asked Willie who wrote the poem, and Willie told him Bart Linsey, and Larry looked surprised. He said didn't he just die, that he'd read in the paper that Bart Linsey died. Willie said yeah, he just died, but before he did he stuck Willie with this ridiculous epic poem he'd paid Willie to listen to because Willie was his muse, the way his uncle used to be Bart's muse.

Larry had confusion in his face, and Willie knew this must all be hard to get straight when it's told flat out like this, but he'd figured coming in he'd dump everything out first and then do the sorting and piecing together, like with a puzzle.

After shaking his head a little and looking like he had a cat turd in his mouth, Larry asked to see the manuscript. Willie slid the bag across the counter. Larry pulled out the stack of pages. Looking at the top one, his mouth opened and he looked like something just popped him on the back so hard his breath got knocked out. He said the thing was dedicated to Theodore Singer, and the name sounded familiar, and Willie chimed that it should, because Teddy "Mad Dog" Singer was the greatest middle linebacker ever played the game, and he was Willie's uncle and he and Bart had been best friends, but nobody could figure out why because they were so different.

Larry shook off his surprise and said Bart Linsey was a pretty famous poet and that some of his books were in the library. He told Willie to wait.

He came back in about ten minutes with four thin books. They had weird, kind of pretty covers, like on one two birds of fire were hugging in the air above some kind of strange city with castles and spaceships all over and the moon was melting. Larry said they were all published by a big company called Morton in New York, and Willie should call them and see if they wanted the book. Willie asked Larry if he wanted to read *The Mystic Pig*, and Larry smiled and held up his hands as if to stop something and said he didn't read poetry, but he'd heard that Bart Linsey is, then he said was, a pretty famous poet.

Willie thanked Larry for the advice about Morton, and as he took back the stack, half at a time because he had to hold the bag open with one hand and he couldn't get his other hand around all of *The Mystic Pig*, he read for the first time the dedication:

> *In memory of Theodore Singer, my Teddy,*
> *the most beautiful man I have ever known,*
> *and the love of my life.*

Nat:

I'm sorry about your friend. Loss is the one thing we can't accommodate, not really. All that "coming to terms" crap is just rhetorical sugar. We either learn to unlove the dead just enough to keep living, or join them.

You seem a person of deep, if rather sloppy, feeling. Depth of feeling is usually an indication of character. Such sloppiness is

147

probably just an indication of poor potty training. Who knows...

Anyway, you've felt it necessary to zap me intense, if cryptic, missives, and I'll simply take them, and any that may follow, at face value. As I've already indicated, you seem a very troubled fellow, and I'm not sure if I'm ready to sign on as your heart's sounding board, though I guess in some sense I've already become that. Even so, you're working very hard not to tell me something. Whatever it is, you should probably keep working hard.

Well, you've expressed interest in my life; I'll nutshell it for you so we don't have to hash it over when we meet in a few days. I'll skip the parts you already know: I graduated from high school toward the top of my class without really trying. Most of my brighter peers ended up in the armed services or married to men who ended up there, or they took over their fathers' businesses or simply got as far away as they could manage and still get by speaking some form of English. I went to college because my dear father thought atypically that it was okay for a girl to do that and besides, no one had asked me to marry. In college I got married, and though I was on scholarship worked six nights a week for most of the five years of my undergraduate studies because hubby was in med school. I actually served cocktails in joints where some guys rode horses to get there, and those who didn't rode in on choppers big as horses. I got knocked up twice, and lost both, thank Nothing. It was the old story: I put him through then he dumped me before he started to make the big bucks, and of course acquired as soon as he did begin to rake in the greenbacks what's called (though the term is probably already passé) a trophy wife, a set of knockers with the IQ of a hamster. Bitter? You betchem! To this day. I'll not deny it. He still lives here, and I can't tell you how many times I've happened upon his mauve Mercedes in a parking lot and come oh so close to jabbing the blade of my Swiss army knife into one or more of his whitewalls. Hell hath no fury like a woman who worked to put a man through med school and then got dumped.

Well, then I went to grad school, first Brown then Yale, then managed to get hired back at UT mainly because of a dear woman who'd mentored me when I was slogging through classes and slinging cocktails and trying to keep intact a hopeless marriage to

148

a hopelessly narcissistic boy. She was a closet feminist at a time in academe, especially academe in Texas, when one didn't wag a finger at vicious and antiquated rape laws, much less question the whole structure of authority in which they were nestled. She'd contrived to get tenured, and once having achieved that blessed state, by sleeping with the chairman and the dean and the provost, not to mention the vice-chairman of the Promotion and Tenure Committee, she acted as though none of them existed except as pesky functionaries from whom she received memos from time to time and to whose memos she deigned to reply from time to time. She gathered about her as many bright young women as she could find, and didn't mother them, never that, but instructed them brilliantly. My best friends to this day, a couple being the ones for whom you are an unknown Intimate Detail, are women I met at that time of my life under the influence of that remarkable woman.

Anyway, I got hired ABD (All But Dissertation), and finished my thesis the autumn of my second year, getting four good articles out of it and eventually sprucing it up to be my first book, a pretty lame monograph by my present standards regarding theory, but solid in its research; in fact it still gets cited. Well, that was around '67, and the rest is history. Our mentor died of ovarian cancer, but I and my bosom buddies, all at different institutions but in constant contact, networked madly among ourselves and with other women, and there are days now when I despair that nothing's really changed, but in my better moments I know the world has changed, if but a little, and that I've had a hand in that change. Forgive the boastful tone of this… actually don't forgive it, but do note it. Isn't it odd to hear a woman exult in her accomplishments? Boasting, that particular rhetorical field, is but another example of male hegemony (by the way, I was impressed by how well you slung the ol' lingo!), and indeed my first impulse above was to beg forgiveness (from a male!) for simply noting that I was among those who created within academe the present conditions in which a woman's more likely to get a fair shake than was the case for us and those who preceded us.

I met a hell of a guy soon after I got back to Austin, Martha's father. He was a landscape gardener who'd never read a book, and I never tried to make him. He wasn't exactly a Lawrencian lover, and I was certainly no Lady, but we fit. You know what I mean? We fit great. He loved me and knew I was only truly happy working, so he created the space for me to work, and our world was beautiful, filled with fecundity and quiet honesty and passion, and he loved his kid when she came into our lives. When he found out he was dying he asked me to marry him; he'd understood before that I couldn't, that I didn't believe in it, but when he asked me, after we'd lived together for seven years, I felt like a girlie girl and said yes yes yes, and we did and he died.

Oh, I've had many lovers since. I used to love traipsing off to conferences to give papers, because there were three or four guys on the circuit I could always count on for a good tumble. I learned early it was better to get it on the road because when you got it close to home they'd howl for weeks like dogs at your window. The men, anyway.

Okay, here's a summary of 1970 to the present! ... a good and successful daughter; nearly a hundred articles published mostly in leading venues; seven books; appearances on national news talk shows when the subject is women's rights in marriage; listings in most of the Who's Whos; too many conference panel appearances to count; an endowed chair; four very good friends; a great condo; presently a love interest that's not solid but not gaga (I'm twenty years too old for gaga; the guy massages my feet, and it doesn't get any better than that); relatively good health (occasional IBS, oy vay!... at least menopause finally finished); and yes, now you, Nat Moore, a son of my girlhood, a middle-aged man who has my genetic code wound up with that of someone I never knew. Nathan Moore, the owner of a fancy restaurant (which of course I've heard of! I almost went there when I was in New Orleans three years ago. We ended up going to Commander's Palace), a deep-feeling bright fellow who flouts to a mother he's never seen and cannot know a "secret life" which sounds to her mother ears like an emotional quagmire too gummed up and mucky to imagine without getting very sad.

I'll look forward to seeing you, Nathan, and to be perfectly honest I also fear it, not because I in any sense fear you; I simply fear the complexity I'll find in you, all the tiny and stubborn knots to be picked at and bitten into.

The children are angry; they shout at Nat to let them out, to break the wall and set them free. They threaten to kill Jarka if he doesn't break the wall. The silhouette of a large child grabs her by the hair and drags her to the wall and shoves her face into it and the face is Sandra's, he sees as through ice, so he lifts the hammer and swings it hard, giving over his dream shoulders to the dream swing of the huge hammer, and the wall shatters and he is eight, and he and his mother are standing on the curb near the Montellion on Royal in the Quarter, and a parade is passing and Nat says parades no longer roll through the Quarter, but his mother, who is young and beautiful says to him *Ovšem delou!* Of course they do! And catches a glimmering string of beads and puts them around his neck and says with pride they were made in Jablonec nad Nisou; all the beads for Mardi Gras, she says are made at a factory in that little city on a little river in Bohemia, and he fingers the beads around his neck and they are fine glass, and recalls the sound of glass beads crunching under his shoes and his mother is holding him in her bed and she is young and beautiful and weeping Jarko, Jarko, Jarko, and it is Sandra whose arms and legs are wrapping him and she is covered in blood and cum and her eyes are wide open and he can't get loose and he screams —

— and Lou shook him screaming his name, and he was awake sobbing, still screaming. The girls cried, and finally he got control of his breathing and shivered in a fetal position under the covers for half a minute. Then he rose.

"Nat, my God," Lou whispered as she stroked his shoulder, weeping gently, her hands shaking.

"Daddy, what happened?" Marti asked, her voice a rasping quiver. Edie was whining with her head under the pillow.

"Had a bad dream," he said almost in a whisper.

They knew about scary nights with Nat, with Daddy; a couple years earlier, when he was drinking the heaviest, he would on occasion sleepwalk, and three or four times had pissed on the floor in the hall, thinking he was in the bathroom. Once, he'd pissed on Poon, which, when he awoke and was informed of the deed, he'd considered the one redeeming feature of an otherwise embarrassing episode.

He stood with his hands against the wall, his head down.

"I'm sorry, girls."

"You okay, Daddy?" Marti asked.

"I'm okay, Chump Change," he assured her. "What time is it?" he asked Lou.

"Four-forty," she answered.

"Baby, I'm sorry," he said, his palms flat against the wall, his head down.

"You've got nothing to be sorry for. You've been through a lot," she patted his back.

"Daddy?" came Edie's voice as small as she could make it and still be heard.

"Hey, sweet stuff, had a bad dream. That's all."

"Dream about Bart?" Marti asked.

"Yeah," he lied, even as he realized it probably wasn't a lie.

"Look, you guys try to get back to sleep. I've got to get up now, okay? Will you be able to get back to sleep?"

"I'm sleepy," Edie said, yawning.

"You know me," Lou said, referring to her uncanny ability to fall asleep at will any place, any time.

"I don't know about me," Marti said, "but I'll just lay here and rest."

"Lie," Nat corrected, turned from the wall, bent down and kissed each female on the forehead, then left the bedroom closing the door behind him.

It wasn't working anymore. He couldn't do the trick. He couldn't say Sandra is there in the Quarter and she's dead, I saw her die and watched her body change for two days and she's forty-four years old and beautiful and keeps birds all over the courtyard and in her apartment and we make love feelingly when we have the time and we talk about everything but she's dead and I saw the tattoo jam the barrel and the blood and they left and I watched her die and she's independently wealthy and is a painter and her work shows in other cities and she loves Nat and knows everything about his wives and children and even loves his children through him and bugs crawled on her and into her and the trick doesn't work it doesn't work his secret life is dissolving and of course it had dissolved before and often did but he always got it back and he hoped he would get it back because she was sleeping now, in her room in the Quarter and her birds were sleeping, their cages covered by black silk, and Rachmaninoff is swelling gently through the large many-windowed high-ceilinged space and windows are cracked to the soft muffled roar of the Quarter like the ocean and she's sipping an earthy red and thinking about the picture she is working on that stands more than half-finished in the studio downstairs where she lets Nat store things for the restaurant, like that funky old dishwasher he thinks he can sell and stuff he's bought in bulk and doesn't have space for in the storeroom of the restaurant and considers how much she loves him but must put her foot down about that damned machine because she needs the space for canvasses and when the men from the road crew found him he'd been sleeping they'd said, though he'd not been able to recall sleeping, not at all those two days, and when the police and the ambulance had arrived he'd calmly explained what had happened, and they'd seemed to pity him but had also seemed a little disgusted with him for being alive, and one had even asked him why he thought they'd let him live, and Nat had said he didn't know, but it was the cruelest thing they could have done to him, leaving him tied to the tree to watch her die and then smell her body for two days and all Nat had been able to tell them was that two of the killers were white and one was black, and the two white ones were a little fat and middle aged and the black one was young and they seemed like old friends, and the leader was the bald white one with a snake tattoo and they had a shotgun and he'd told the police how they'd held the shotgun to his head and made him watch and the more he told them the more disgusted with him for being alive they seemed and of course he didn't tell them how he'd begged and cried and pleaded with the monsters not to kill him and they'd laughed and cackled and pissed on him and he'd pissed and shat on himself two days bound to the tree a limb arced out over the water and it was a sweet and gentle arc the limb assumed and squirrels shuttled it and the sun rose up to it and the half-moon seemed to hang at the end of it once a plane crossed it at dusk and the odor of the decaying body of his lover overcame the odor of his own living body and what it emitted into his clothes and Sandra sometimes gets up and paints because the spirit moves her and because she is independently wealthy she does not need, has never needed to keep regular hours she is free free free and if she wishes to rise at five-fourteen in the dark morning and drink wine and paint until eight she simply does so then sleeps as long as she wishes and Nat will come and make love to her and then she will sleep some more and rise and tend to her birds and paint some more and drink good wine and watch a movie and cook something light and good and paint some more and the police hated him for stinking of shit and piss and shaking all over and crying but stopping suddenly and seeming wholly composed but then blubbering sobbing and they hated him for not being dead though they didn't know he'd begged for his life and he'd not closed his eyes still they hated him because they could feel how much he hated himself for being too much the coward not to witness what was done to his lover but when she'd worked as a volunteer at the Bird Rehab Center of Audubon Zoo she'd bring home eggs from nests fallen from drainpipes and branches and other hidden crotches and raise them to set them free and once the keepers asked her to rehabilitate a Snowy Owl that was blind and had but one wing and that meant simply getting it to eat and she indeed coaxed it to tear at the dead rodents she left in the cage with the moist cat food she fed all the birds and Nat hated those smug sons of bitches who had never been bound to a tree and pissed on and threatened death if they didn't watch the loves of their lives brutalized unspeakably and Nat had to cook something.

He poured a tumbler full of Jameson, knocked half of it back, then clapped his hands and rubbed them together. The girls loved his chocolate cookies. They'd have warm chocolate cookies for breakfast. He thought that maybe warm chocolate cookies would make up for the pre-dawn horror show.

He fetched from the fridge unsalted butter, three eggs and some sour cream that had languished behind the mayonnaise through at least two shopping cycles so was probably getting used just in time. He checked for chocolate; he'd need unsweetened and semisweet, and he had plenty of the latter and not as much as he wanted of the former, but that would be no problem. He pulled down the sea salt, baking powder, sugar, flour. He got down his favorite mixing bowl; Marti had dubbed it the Green Monster. He plopped five tablespoons of the butter, about two ounces of unsweetened and three ounces of semisweet chocolate into the Green Monster, which he then placed on a double boiler at just a shade over medium heat. After about ten minutes, during which Nat knocked back the whiskey and poured another, the chocolate was smooth. Then he got the electric mixer and attached the paddle; he dropped in about a cup of sugar and cracked the three eggs over it and beat them on low for about four minutes. Then he dumped in the buttered chocolate and beat it all for about a minute and a half, then dropped in about a half-cup of flour, two pinches of salt, roughly a teaspoon of baking soda, and beat on low for about three minutes. Finally, he folded in about a third of a cup of the sour cream, and dumped the rest down the garbage disposal.

He pulled two cookie sheets from under the shelf to the right of the sink; the pots and pans were tossed in any old way, as his father would have characterized the clutter; he made a small racket extricating the flat racks from the junkyard mangle, and as he tossed back his whiskey he scraped cement-hard yellow-cheese char from one of the sheets with his thumbnail. He cranked up the oven to 350 because it had seemed to be heating a few degrees cooler lately, and buttered the sheets before plopping two spoons of batter for each cookie, keeping about three inches between each double plop of batter. He baked each rack for twenty minutes, rotating the racks every ten.

He sat down at the table with three fingers more of the good Irish whiskey, two warm cookies, and a tumbler of cold skimmed milk. He ate the cookies slowly, sipping the cold milk with each bite. They were perfect. When he finished the cookies and the milk, he poured another glass of milk and chugged it. Then he knocked back the whiskey, sat back and felt it course down into him.

The cops didn't care that he was fouled by his own waste, that he'd been forced to witness the death of beauty and the death of human decency and the death of hope. They wanted him to recount details, because he was an eyewitness and must recall everything, every detail because he should have been dead and they were disgusted, he could tell, how deeply disgusted they were with him for not being dead, for having had his manhood completely humiliated. They couldn't look him in the eye when they spoke to him, when they pumped him for details, and even when the medics insisted they had to take Nat to the hospital, that he would need medical attention and should be checked thoroughly by a doctor the police kept pumping him and hating him for not being dead and now Sandra was sleeping, and would sleep through the morning and early afternoon.

SECTION FIFTEEN

WILLIE COULDN'T SLEEP. He rode his bike up to Carrollton and crossed over to the levy, walked his bike over the steep angle, and now he was staring into the river because sometimes that's all a person can do.

Before he'd left the house he'd stood at the toilet thinking about Left Eye but that hadn't worked so he'd brought in the other two and that hadn't worked so he'd brought in Whitney Houston but that never worked because she looked too much like his mama so he'd brought in Janet Jackson and that'd almost worked but then he'd brought in Brandy and that'd really worked. He figured he'd be seeing a lot more of her.

The reason it'd taken getting all the way to Brandy was that he couldn't get Uncle Teddy being a queer out of his head, and every time he thought about it he got sick in his stomach. He'd heard a lot of people say that something or other made them sick in their stomachs, but this was the first time it was happening to him. The river was chugging by and barges on the other side seemed to quiver in their moorings. He knew all about it, like when dudes went to jail a long time it made them a little crazy and they treated each other like one was a girl, and he knew about men liking boys because men had acted weird and friendly with him but he'd always gotten away before they could mess with him. But Mad Dog, Uncle Teddy, had been a big man other men had looked up to. When he'd taken Willie out to do stuff people had treated him like he was a king or a president and nothing had been more fun than going in a restaurant and seeing how people would run into each other to do stuff for Uncle Teddy, and people would come out of kitchens to peek around corners because they'd heard Mad Dog was in the house.

He'd gotten famous by being one of the greatest middle linebackers ever to play, and also for the commercials where he was naked except for shorts so all his huge muscles showed, and he wore a collar and chain around his neck and growled and barked while a fat ugly little white dude who was old and talked funny even for a white dude walked around a Sport Utility Vehicle and said it was a great car that was loaded with everything a family needed except the dog. They'd have to get their own, and Uncle Teddy had made a noise then like a sad little dog, and Willie'd heard an old white woman tell Uncle Teddy in a restaurant that he was adorable in that commercial, and that had pissed Willie off, though Uncle Teddy had laughed and said it was good that old white women thought he was adorable because that just meant he'd make more money for doing commercials, and considering he was getting too old to play football it was a damned good thing old white women thought he was adorable.

Uncle Teddy had introduced Willie to Bart when Willie was nine. Bart had met Willie's mama, Uncle Teddy, Uncle Jimmy and Willie on the balcony of the Chart House, but Willie hadn't seen much of him after that until Uncle Teddy'd killed himself and Willie'd become Bart's muse.

A tug huffed against the hustling current, and somewhere close, though he couldn't tell exactly where, cats started going at it, screeching like they were killing each other. He could hear the morning traffic on Carrollton getting thick.

Willie's daddy had gone on a trip when Willie was four and never came back. Willie'd missed him a lot, though it wasn't like he'd been around much before the trip. He'd played tenor sax and gigged all night and slept most the day. Willie's best memories were of how he'd crawled all over his daddy while the big man had still been half asleep in the afternoon, because it had been Willie's job to get him up to go back to work. Sometimes his daddy had grabbed him suddenly, when Willie'd thought he was asleep, and pulled him under the covers and tickled him until Willie had been about to pee he'd laughed so hard.

But his daddy had gotten a great gig touring with a famous band called Jetstream and had sent good money back to Willie's mama for a long time but he'd never come back and he'd never called and Willie didn't care much because if his daddy was the kind of man who could leave a woman like Willie's mama and a little boy who loved him he wasn't somebody Willie cared to know.

Uncle Teddy had always been around. Even though he'd been so busy, he still always had time for Willie, and he used to take Willie places, even to meet the other Saints, which hadn't been that big a deal because they'd lost so much, but once he'd gotten to meet some of the Buffalo Bills, guys Uncle Teddy'd gone to college with, when they were in town to whip the Saints, and that'd been cool, and he'd bought Willie his first Mac and he'd put some money in the Whitney, in something called CDs, so Willie'd be able to go to any college he'd want to, and some of it went to pay his tutor now. And when Willie's twenty-five he'll get a pretty good chunk of money that Uncle Teddy gave to a guy named Dean Witter, who does weird commercials, to take care of for Willie, and that chunk was getting a little bigger every year. Uncle Teddy'd loved him, there was no getting around that, and Willie was so proud that everybody liked Teddy "Mad Dog" Singer, liked him for hurting other dudes on the football field, hitting them so hard sometimes they just laid there twitching like bugs, and liked him for being adorable in the commercials and being such a gentleman when he wasn't wearing his uniform and making dudes twitch on the ground.

The day his mama had come into his room with tears spilling from her eyes and said Uncle Teddy died in a car wreck was the worst in Willie's life. His grandma had been old and was supposed to die pretty soon, anyway, but Uncle Teddy had still been pretty young. The dudes who'd written about him in the newspapers and magazines and talked about him on ESPN, at the beginning of each season, since Willie was about seven, had said Mad Dog maybe had one more good year left in him, and at the end of each year they'd had to say he probably had one more. Uncle Teddy used to laugh and say he was a dinosaur and they'd have to hit him with a big-ass asteroid to make him quit football.

But then after he died someone had written in the paper that maybe Uncle Teddy had committed suicide, that the police had said the accident seemed like Uncle Teddy'd just aimed for that tree.

Willie at first told himself Bart calling Uncle Teddy the love of his life didn't have to mean they were queer, but Willie wasn't going to lie to himself. Bart calling Teddy the love of his life could only mean they were both queer for each other, and it made Willie shiver to think about, and he got tears in his eyes but he wasn't crying, not officially.

Willie hated it when something he thought was one way ended up another. It meant he had to start all over looking at whatever it was that switched. When he was real little he'd thought his daddy loved him. Also when he was little he'd thought that being black was bad, but then he'd found out it wasn't bad, just hard. A little while ago he'd thought Bart's epic poem was a piece of shit that should be burned. Now he just thought it was a piece of shit, because he couldn't make himself burn it.

But nothing came close to the switch Uncle Teddy'd made since Willie'd read he was the love of Bart's life.

In the deepest sense, Newcastle's belonged more to Robby, Kenny and Danny than to Nat. He'd been a boy scrubbing pots in the scullery, concentrating earnestly on his first remunerated tasks, when they, grown men, first spotted him: his had been the only white face in the scullery or the kitchen besides that of old Chef Holditchovitch himself, the brilliant, dyspeptic, mean-spirited little czar of the Newcastle kitchen for thirty-seven years. Nat had been skinny and pretty and obviously had tried to be so butch when any of the gay waiters were around.

Robby, Kenny, Danny and the others issued from remarkably similar backgrounds: they'd grown up in small Southern towns; experienced the horrors of shaping homosexual identities through adolescence in such a context, which included breaking through thick and thorny hedges of Christian guilt and surviving the physical threats from boys who preyed on peers with sensitive natures, anyone unwilling or unable to participate in the communal brutalities of adolescent male bonding. They'd all, or nearly all, formed strong attachments to the black women who'd been their surrogate mothers and indeed those women had been their earliest and strongest gender models, such that Danny's camp, the same in kind as that of the others though more elegant in its timing and grander in its scale, always had about it the edginess of a black femininity expressing itself through a Southern white man's body and, by extension, history, and early on Nat had found the layered ironies of such a persona fascinating, though he'd not in the beginning been entirely certain what he was observing in Danny and the others. On the floor they'd seemed – when he'd finally been allowed out of the scullery to bus a couple nights a week – prim and proper, by turns stiff and pissy and blithely graceful. They haunted their stations gloriously. Once they'd engaged a group, done what talking was required (and they never said a word more than was necessary, unlike those chummy Yats at so many French Quarter tourist traps who played customers like they were rubes), they silently, inauspiciously tended to the needs and desires of patrons, anticipating everything. No one ever lit her own cigarette at the Old Queens' tables; no one had to ask where the restrooms were located; no one had to ask to see the dessert cart; rarely did anyone even have to ask for the check.

It was in the kitchen the Old Queens became their mammies, and in their own ways were just as tough as those women. Once, in the late seventies, a new broiler man hassled Robby, who in response blew the large, dumpy fellow a kiss. The cook had then made the mistake of curling around the serving counter and getting in Robby's eyes, threatening to bust up his pussy face, to which Robby had responded by swiftly and efficiently kicking the guy's ass right in front of the service counter, pounding him bloody and semi-conscious before Kenny — pausing first to admire his colleague's work — dragged Robby off the poor fellow. Kent Newcastle blew in through the swinging door and fired the new guy on the spot, which is to say as he lay dripping blood, shocked and utterly humbled on the red cement floor of the kitchen. The lesson to Nat had been that one does not, even figuratively, fuck with nelly fags, given the crucible of violence the world is for them; some become quite proficient at giving as well as they take.

And if the Old Queens had ever fancied him sexually, they never expressed such attraction overtly. They were good looking men who got plenty of action anytime they wanted it from the legions of other attractive gay men in the Quarter; they hadn't been inclined to moon over pretty straight boys.

But they had seemed to be attracted to something in Nat, something in his character, though he'd never quite understood what. And once he'd moved beyond the shyness, that is, his fear, his predictable boyish homophobia, he'd gotten on with them extremely well, Danny especially. They'd taught him to be a very good waiter.

Nat usually consulted the Old Queens about everything, though he had not consulted them about hiring Birdsong. He wanted to get them together before opening, away from the others, and, in effect, apologize for not having first consulted them regarding such a hugely important hire. He also wanted to get their opinions as to how she was doing.

They made good money at Newcastle's, but not as much as legend suggested venerable old waiters earned in the French Quarter's more famous establishments. Each took home, on nights of at least two turns, after tipping out the busboy, service bartender, kitchen and scullery, only about a hundred and forty, but of course they paid almost no taxes on any of it. Each also made twelve-hundred a month for, in effect, group-managing the restaurant for and with Nat. But all of them earned almost twice again what they made at Newcastle's at sidelines: Robby owned an antique restoration business with his life-partner — his partner Billy was the craftsman, Robby handled the business; Kenny'd been sub-contracting for two decades to the major hotels as a French Quarter

160

walking tour guide; and Danny had simply invested brilliantly over the years in rental properties on Magazine and Prytania, and had lived since the mid-80's with one of New Orleans' more successful corporate lawyers. None needed his job at Newcastle's, except perhaps emotionally. All three seemed to relish with almost a religious purity the formalities of waiting tables in a fine restaurant. Nat became depressed considering that someday, probably quite soon, they would all three, however reluctantly, retire.

Nat would talk with the Old Queens in the Bienville Room, then hustle to pick up Marti for the game. He looked out onto the main dining room, the "floor," and motioned to one of the part-time busboys, Dickey or Ricky or Mickey, he couldn't remember, a quiet black kid about twenty from the Dominican Republic. Nat had hired him as a favor to the maître d' at Broussard's who was repaying a favor to the owner of Brennan's who was repaying a favor to one of his captains who owed money to his bookie whose recently arrived cousin the kid most likely was. Dickey/Ricky/Mickey seemed to understand a little English, but couldn't speak a lick. Robby spoke Spanish to him, and surprisingly Stinkfinger, whose wick otherwise seemed to burn pretty low, chatted airily in Spanish with the kid, who was indeed a very good worker. He at least understood "Old Queens" and "employee room" and "come... here," because in a minute and a half they joined Nat in the Bienville Room.

Nat had poured four shot glasses half full of Grand Salute. For years, they'd performed the ritual of toasting when they met all together in the Bienville Room. They toasted the memories of their fallen colleagues, the dead Old Queens, and then to a good night's work. Then Nat poured coffee all around. The room was lit by three candles all at the opposite end of the room.

"Well, ladies, the main thing I need to know is how our little Xena Warrior Stove Jockey's doing back there."

They all three nodded thoughtfully in silence for a couple of seconds, then Robby said, "She's good, Nat. You knew that when you hired her. She runs a tight kitchen, so everything's been coming out pretty much on time."

"Except maybe the pompano," Kenny added, "because she changed the line, got Paul working the fish station and moved Stinkfinger to the grill and sauces. You know how they have to put the pompano on the top rack, and Paul's so short he's got to really work to angle that spatula under the fish boats on the top rack."

"But it's not that bad. It's working out," Robby assured Nat, as the other two nodded their heads in agreement.

"So we keep her?" Nat asked, half joking.

Danny chuckled. "Yeah, right, about six months I'll give her. Then she'll take over her daddy's place on Rampart."

"That place is a dive," Nat said, puzzled.

"You ever went to K-Paul's back when people lined up to get in?" Danny said. "Nat, come on. It'd make perfect sense. I heard from Christi Mastree who does Lisa at the Peach Pit that she and Suzi Dreamcheese were in the Birdsong at four PM last Friday and the old man bragged to any drag queen who'd listen about how his girl's run the kitchens of three major New Orleans restaurants, and how she's running things at Newcastle's now. And Christi said he kept saying she's building up her resume before taking over the Birdsong. And think about it. The place could seat eighteen to twenty-five if you configured it right, and you wouldn't have to do much to the kitchen."

"Except clean it," Robby added, and everyone smiled or chuckled. The Birdsong was notoriously funky.

"And you've noticed how much time she spends working the floor. Whenever there's a lull she's out front schmoozing with the clientele," Kenny said. Nat believed it was a good thing for chefs to make nightly appearances, but Birdsong did seem to spend more time fraternizing than was usual. She always lingered with VIPs, and always wanted to know when she was cooking for one.

"Well, shit," Nat sighed. But then brightened. "I didn't think I was going to keep her more than a year. I bet she stays through Christmas. That'd be, what, about ten months? She's not going to open a new place over the summer. That'd be suicide," he calculated.

"She wouldn't be opening a new place, would she?" Kenny said. "But I get your point. But look, the way she does it, I figure, is she works on the joint over the summer, renovating, ripping out the counter, modifying the kitchen, and stays on here because during the summer the work'll be pretty light, anyway, and she'll have time to schlep around on Rampart fixing up the greasy spoon. I'll put money on her leaving in late August," he finished.

"Ouch, that would definitely suck," Nat said. "By the way, none of you old girls is going away any time soon, are you?"

"They'll carry me out feet first," Kenny assured Nat.

"I'm like an old piece of soap that's stuck to the soap dish," Robby said.

"Well, we're all going away someday," Danny sighed.

"Oh, sweet Jesus, she's soooo deep!" Robby said.

"Old Queens never die. They just fade, fade away," Kenny crooned.

"No, honey, fade? Away? Fade away?" Robby said. "I'm checking out on a Saturday night right here in this room. Ricky Martin's coming in with his entourage and Nat's going to seat him in here and I'm going to plush him out!" Do you hear me? Plush him out all night and right after I lay the check I'm going into cardiac arrest and Ricky's getting down on his hands and knees on this carpet to give me mouth-to-mouth..."

"Oh, shut up, Princess Fish Breath!" shouted Kenny.

"And I'm going to die with that adorable boy's lips pressed to mine," Robby finished.

"JesusJosephandMary! That's the best you can do?" Danny whined. "You're a fucking fifty-eight-year-old Catholic schoolgirl!"

"Thank you," Robby whispered.

SECTION SIXTEEN

A S THEY PULLED into the Lakeside Arena parking lot, hard-looking young men wearing orange-glow vests directed them with flashlights. They'd stopped at the Smoothy King next to what Nat wished was still Shwegmann's, across from the arena, and gotten a Protein Blast and a Muscle Punch, respectively a milky banana-flavored concoction loaded with protein powder and a red nondescriptly fruity drink likewise loaded. They took turns on each. Marti liked them equally, and powered back about a third of both before she and Nat had gotten out of the car.

"Buuurrp... excuse me," she said nonchalantly.

"Feel any stronger?" he asked, sucking the Protein Blast rather daintily through a straw.

"You betchum. I could rip Godzilla's balls off!"

Nat glanced around nervously. "Chump Change, please don't talk like that in public."

She giggled. "You running for mayor?"

He swatted her on the rear. She swatted him back.

Nat had good, lower-level half court seats. He'd gotten first shot at his regular-season seats, and scooped them up, as had, it seemed as he surveyed the stands, most of the regulars. Unfortunately, it was late in the season and this was only the third game he and Marti had been able to attend, and because of their schedules they could never make any of the women's games.

The arena, a typical modern ten thousand capacity structure, was less than

164

half-filled – in the dozens or so years since the arena opened, attendance averaged under three thousand a game. The problem was obvious: demographics and a state university system grounded in a Bizarro World apartheid in which African-American politicians and their buddies, the all-black university administrators, conspired to keep a separate all-black university network. The University of New Orleans was really the University of Anywhere But, or White Flight U. Black kids, quite simply, went to Dillard or Southern, a few to a very good Xavier.

The university built a damned fine arena, recruited damned fine athletes, and for several years won twenty games or more a season and/or played into the post-season. All this success was witnessed by a corps of middle-aged white business men who loved the game and adopted the team, a smattering of actual UNO students trying pathetically to wring a typical college experience out of a quite good though demographically gerrymandered and atypical institution, and scads of faculty, alums, and of course, administrators, the latter gathering each time as though their collective bureaucratic will held the magical potential to fill the stands. UNO was playing Auburn, and already, twenty minutes before tip-off, the place was half-filled with Alabamians dressed in orange and blue. The opponent's fans, once again, would outnumber the local faithful.

As the teams warmed up (as always dreamily, Nat thought; the big graceful kids of the sport always seemed so loose, so slowed-down, even somnolent during warm-ups), Marti asked the question Nat had been waiting for since she was five, but had not formulated a pat response to yet: "Why are almost all of 'em black, Poops, I mean Pops?" Unfortunately for Nat, a black UNO administrator, a gray and eminent fellow the institution trotted out as often as it could for visual effect, sat directly in front of Marti, and conspicuously cocked his left ear, the one nearest Nat. This was an oral exam, and Nat stiffened.

"Whywhywhywhywhy...?" Marti pressed.

"Because for very complex historical and social reasons many black people in the first years of this century moved from the country into the cities. Basketball is a game which accommodates an urban context."

"Talk English and stop trying to sound smart," she scolded.

The Gray Eminence gave a little nod of approval to Marti's critique.

"It's easier to nail up a basket and throw a ball into it in a city than it is to play, say, football and baseball."

"Yeah, well, black guys mostly play those things, too, so it ain't that city stuff," she said. "How come so many black people are good at playing sports?"

She broadened the inquiry, and turned the screw another notch, putting the squeeze on Nat's social conscience.

"Because for so long sport has been the only way many poor people could advance in a racist society. A large percentage of black people have been poor, so more of them have tried hard in sports."

"But why are they so good?"

"Because they try hard," he said lamely.

"Baloneeeeey," she said.

"Why do you think?" he asked.

"I don't know," Marti admitted, "but Lucia Herringbone's dad says it's because when Africans were brought over in ships, all the weak ones died and the slaves then were the strong ones. And then they treated them like farm animals and made the strong ones have babies with other strong ones, and so now their kid's kid's kid's kid's, I don't know how many times, they're just, you know, bigger and faster and stronger. Just plain better."

Nat wanted a soft, dark pit to open up below him. He wanted a quick exit. "Baby, Lucia Herringbone's dad's a right-wing creep. If there's any truth in all that, it's small and barely significant. People are what they are by a very complex interplay of biology, culture and history. You could spend your whole life trying to figure out why this or that group of people is like it is, and I hope you do. And I don't know much, except there aren't any easy answers, and people who tell you there are are usually schmucks, like Herr Herringbone. Just watch these guys. See how beautiful they are. That's what's important."

Auburn had a little guy, maybe five-seven, skimming the three-point line, popping a shot, side-stepping a few feet to the left and popping another. He shot off his ear, and everything went in. Marti's wild, dark eyes followed him. "That kid's no poster child for eugenics," Nat breathed, and Marti, mesmerized by the kid's fluid, flawless shot, let the big word slide. "He's here because he spent four hours every day of his adolescence on a playground, and then in a gym, popping shots. He's in love," Nat concluded, and remembering the Gray Eminence flicked a glance up to him; G.E. chortled softly to a colleague, oblivious to Nat's homily, as was Marti, who wide-eyed studied the kid's moves along the three-point arc.

Nat glanced around. Lesley Parks, half-owner of the meat distributor most of the French Quarter restaurants used, sat on the other side of the arena, the south side, and gave Nat a little salute. Nat raised his chin and smiled. In the floor area, on the opposite length of the court, a flock of wheelchaired kids

166

lined up to watch the game. One, strapped into his chair, was hideously frail and bent, like something warped by weathering. He could not be long for life, that one, and his head, held up by a strap, cocked at an odd William Buckley angle, seemed too delicate for life. He was a bird, just hatched and wet, who'd fallen from a drainpipe nest. His eyes, too, Nat was certain even from the distance, were fixed on that little Auburn shooter.

"Mr Nat!" Nat felt a tap on his shoulder.

"Hey, Tank, what's cookin'?" It was Leonard's eight year old; after holding season tickets for a few years, always getting the same seats among other season ticket holders who themselves kept their same seats, everyone within a couple of rows knew everyone else's first name. Nat had adopted the UNO team and ignored the one representing his alma mater, the latter playing its games within walking distance of Nat's house on Pine, because so many of the kids who worked for him over the years but weren't permanent employees, busboys who came and went like weather systems, and some of the prep and custodial workers, seemed permanently enrolled as part-time students at the LSU-system's urban university. He felt, oddly, more strongly connected, through his transient employees, to the commuter campus than to his own "Harvard of the South." In fact, Tank's dad Leonard had prepped for Newcastle's for a few months back when Nat was still a waiter; he'd attended UNO for nine years, gotten a degree in history, and now ran his father's very successful plumbing business. Leonard smiled when Nat winked at him over Tank's shoulder. He was a ruddy, wiry little man about Nat's age. Tank was about five-one and at least a hundred and ten, solid. Nat recalled when Leonard wore Tank to the games strapped sleeping to his chest.

"Nothin' much, Mr Nat," the giant child said, and smiled. Many teeth were gone.

"How you doing, Tank?" Marti asked.

"I'm okay, but Mama's got the crud."

"Well, I hope she gets better," Marti said, and Tank sidestepped across the aisle to the steps, probably headed for the concession.

"What's the crud?" Marti half-whispered.

"Bad cold, or flu," Nat answered.

"I think I'm getting some," she said matter-of-factly. Nat put the backs of his fingers to her cheek, then her forehead. She was warm.

"Something going around school?"

"Yeah, even Johnston's got it. Good thing."

167

"Why's that good?"

"She wasn't around today when I kicked Michael Rollin's ass," she said coolly.

"Oh, shit."

"Don't worry. Mr Dill said he isn't going to tell her. He saw me sock Mikey. He was right behind me and I didn't even see him. And we were on the dirt next to the sidewalk in front, so technically..."

"Technically you were still on the school grounds, you little twit."

"I tried to get him across the street, but he wouldn't go."

"So what was it about?"

She cupped his ear in her hands and whispered. "He called me a nigger lover."

"Jesus Christ. Where did that come from?" Nat asked, truly stunned.

"Because I hang out with Louella and Beatrice," she said. "And we were listening to Puff Daddy on B's CD player at lunch."

Nat digested this, stared off for a few seconds. He flicked a glance at the dying baby bird strapped into a battery-powered chair the child controlled by two fingers of his right hand; someone had had to position his fingers at the control stick. "Next time, just make sure you get him across the street," he said finally.

"Poops, I mean Pops, Mama said Bart's funeral is Thursday. You going?"

"Yeah, sure." He said, scanning the opposite stands. "In fact, Bart's lawyer called and said Bart'd requested that I be one of the speakers at the service." Sandra was home painting, she would paint until around midnight and then she would bathe. He loved arriving just as she was getting out of the tub.

"Can I go?"

Nat was taken aback. "Why do you want to go?"

"Because he was funny. And he gave me Bartina."

"Bartina?"

"I changed her name."

"That's pretty radical."

"I just felt like it. I mean, I remember seeing her under the tree and how funny she looked and I've slept with her every night and didn't even know Bart gave her to me. And besides, I never knew anybody who died before except Granddad, and it's not like I saw him the same day he died."

Nat's father had loved the kids, but had never really been available enough to bond with them. Many months had separated Marti's last visit and the old

Southern Gentleman's death.

"It doesn't scare you?"

"What?"

"The idea? The idea that Bart's dead?"

She thought about it. "Yeah, I guess it scares me."

"And you still want to go?"

"That's why I want to go," she concluded, as though she were realizing the truth of what she was saying as she said it.

Marti fell asleep in the car. She, like her sister, was a drooler. Nat felt a wet spot spreading warmly on his right pant leg where Marti's head now lay in profile. He'd let her undo her seatbelt and put her head on his thigh the third time her chin hit her chest and her head bounced back up. Her mother, he knew, would be, and properly so, horrified. If Lou had had her way airbags would remain inflated when children rode in cars, and all humans under fourteen years of age would be required to wear multiple tethers.

He stroked his daughter's brow. It was still warm. Perhaps she was coming down with the crud. It felt as though Lake Drool had grown about an inch, so as he stopped at the light where Esplanade withers onto the entrance of City Park, crossing Bayou St John and encircling the statue of Beauregard, he reached across her body and got the all-purpose orange rag out of the glove compartment and wedged it between her parted lips and his pant leg.

When Nat had met Lou, she'd been involved with Gary, a dumb, pretty, artsy young guy who'd troubled the bars on Decatur, mostly Molly's Irish Pub. Gary had been lead singer in Yellow Stains, a Doors clone in the early 80s, and, like Morrison, had been a soulfully bad poet. Nat had run into him a couple of times at Snug Harbor on Frenchman, where Nat and Lou had snuck off to drink past midnight and swim in jazz.

The first weeks of his friendship with her had consisted of his complaining abstractly about Bridget, and Lou lamenting her attachment to a dour pretty-boy poet with a double digit IQ. Nat would saunter into The Bookworm two or three late afternoons a week, cruise the aisles a bit, purchase a paperback, then chat an hour or so with the gorgeous redhead minding the register. When she'd get off work, they'd stroll Decatur then cross Esplanade to Frenchman, wafting in and out of bars and cafes, chatting, commiserating. Gary had introduced himself to Nat (the second time) on a night one of the lesser Nevilles crooned the boxy black room off Snug Harbor's bar. Six-two, a hundred and sixty, maybe, the tubular, girlishly handsome wannabe rocker had imposed himself upon Lou and Nat who'd occupied a little table near the stage. Lou had spent the past three weeks working hard at being apart from him; Nat had been a good friend, a man sensitive to a woman's need to talk talk talk talk her swelling disaffection.

That he'd lusted after her, though he'd worn his lust lightly, had also been charmingly obvious. It was obvious, for example, that the flicking glances at her breasts wanted to be lingering stares. It was obvious that the more-or-less permanent bulge in his pants had not been a small flashlight he'd happened to keep in his pocket.

As Gary had stood there between sets, tucking his beautiful brown hair behind his beautiful ears, smiling beautifully, chatting about his next gig, winking and shooting little salutes of recognition to the droop-eyed, resting drummer — who'd patted his brow with a hanky and sipped a beer, having obviously no idea why the pretty white boy was making such a silly show of false familiarity — Nat had wanted suddenly to kick the living shit out of Gary, fuck him up but good.

"Get the fuck out of here, you phony fuck," Nat had blurted, only a few moments after shaking the fellow's bony hand, and had wished immediately he'd waited a couple seconds more to speak, and in that time had come up with something a bit wittier.

Gary had been thrown off a bit, but had recovered with shocking suddenness. The beautiful smile had returned to his beautiful face; he'd tucked again his beautiful hair behind his beautiful ears, and said, "No need to get hostile, dude. Me and Lou's just old friends. I'm not trying to squeeze in on your play here, dude, I'm just…"

Nat had popped him across the face, a good hard flat-handed slap across the guy's beautiful chops. It'd felt so good he'd done it again, but with the other hand. For weeks, he'd been hearing what a bona fide narcissistic dickhead Gary was from a bright and gorgeous sexy woman he'd wanted ferociously to fuck and impregnate, and now he was, in the parlance, bitch slapping the fellow in a public forum. Heady with testosterone delight, he'd popped Gary twice more, swiftly and hard. Gary's face had darkened in the gloomy jazz light; his nose had gushed blood. "Dude, dude, dude," was all Gary had gotten out after each slap.

The first two hours in the holding tank of Central Lockup had not been so bad, except for the smell, the claustrophobic discomfort, and the general sense that at any moment any one or all of his compatriots — all black and all ignoring him with such a fury as to suggest they were collectively and painfully self-conscious of his being the only white guy there — would turn on him and fuck him up unspeakably.

The second two hours had been a little less comfortable. A large fellow who'd worn a Jazz Fest '83 sweatshirt had stared at Nat without blinking — Nat somehow intuited with peripheral vision, for he'd dared not look into the frowning man's eyes — sitting on his ass in the corner of the tank opposite Nat. Finally, the solid three-hundred pounder had said, "Gotta smoke?" There had been eleven other guys in the tank. Everyone, without even looking, had known who'd been addressed, including Nat, even as he'd stared into his knees.

"Don't smoke," Nat had grunted.

"You too good?" the fellow'd inquired, raising himself to full height, ducking so as not to hit his head on the rounded ceiling of the tank.

"No, man, I ain't too good for nothin'," Nat had said, sounding ridiculous to himself. "I just don't smoke. Both my parents died of lung cancer," he'd added, praying for the sympathy vote as the guy loomed.

"Watchu in fo'," the fellow had asked.

"Assault and battery," Nat had stated almost cheerily, with pride, reckoning that being accused of such an offense credentialed him for acceptance into this transient community. "What're you in for?" Nat had asked, figuring it the polite thing to do.

"They say I beat my daddy to deaf," Goliath had answered, and at that Nat had looked into his eyes for the first time since becoming the huge man's interlocutor and had known immediately what it means for a human to have absolutely nothing to lose.

The door of the holding tank, reminding Nat of submarine doors he'd seen in movies, had creaked open, and he and three others, by what method of selection he'd no idea but for which he was grateful, had exited the gray tube and been escorted to the dark stack of cages comprising the heart of Central Lockup.

Nat had been led to a cell already occupied by a young black man. Within, he'd sat on the edge of a cot and waited. He'd slipped his mother's number to Lou as the cops entered the small dim performance space from the bar. Nat had suddenly stopped slapping Gary after the thirtieth time or so not because Lou had screamed "Stop! Stop!" She hadn't. Not because Gary's face had been a bloody mess, though it had been. Not because Nat had felt sorry for Gary, because he'd not – he'd done Gary the great favor of doing exactly to him what might break him out of his lurid self-regard, compel him to be a more compassionate, engaging human being. He'd stopped slapping Gary because his hand had gotten too sore to continue without considerable discomfort, and since the whole point had been to cause Gary, not himself, pain, Nat had ceased, and just in time to slip his mother's number to Lou.

In the cell, a wiry little guy in a black nylon running suit and red, black and white running shoes worth more than Nat's best suit, had sat on the floor, his back against the bars on the left-front corner of the cell, his skinny left arm dangling out between the bars of the lower-left front of the cell, flicking ashes of his cigarette. His distraction, his utter boredom, had seemed to Nat mildly heroic.

When Nat had been released in the morning, he'd found Lou and his mother chatting gloriously in the waiting area. He'd spied them before they him, and at the sight of his mother smiling and Lou gesticulating about something cheerier than the present circumstance, he'd known his procreative fate was sealed.

He stroked his daughter's hair as he steered with the middle finger of his left hand, just touching the wheel. Lou had had the big sex talk with Marti more than a year earlier. He still hadn't had the serious talk with her about violence, mainly because he dreaded lying to his children, telling them what any responsible parent must, planting Ideas, knowing that lovely abstractions, such shimmering values, turned to dried cat turds under the pressure of experience. Violence Is Wrong. But if any puke-for-brains skinhead neo-Nazi starts spouting off in a bar, you kick the shit out of him, if indeed you are physically able. Violence Is Wrong. But if any living thing harms your children, you kill it with your bare hands, or by any means available. Violence Is Wrong. But Evil Is Real, and cannot otherwise be addressed. Nat knew this at the very core of his being, not just abstractly. He'd stared into the face of Evil, been profoundly humiliated by it. His life issued from it because it had spared him and crushed the love of his life, lifted him into the purgatory of his secret life. And it had, wretched irony of ironies, given him the particular children he loved so dearly.

When Nat thought about his children, singularly or as a collective, he got choked up. It had always been the case. When Nestor was tiny, Nat would tear up just thinking about him while driving or walking.

When Lou had learned Gary and his band had been killed on their way back from a gig in Jackson, she'd been inconsolable for days. Their van had run into the back of an eighteen-wheeler, a freak accident on a perfectly dry and windless Friday night, and Lou was certain that if she'd been more understanding

172

of Gary, listened to him more soulfully, been like a sister to him even about the breakup, somehow the accident would not have occurred. That Sunday, Nat'd had Nestor for the day and brought the pretty little boy to the bookstore. The child had stationed himself in the children's section, and with quiet cheer sampled the picture books. Nat had then spent the next twenty minutes all but yelling at Lou that her guilt was wholly inappropriate, that she'd had nothing to do with the accident. When the little bell on the door had tinkled as a customer entered, Nat had lowered his voice, and when the same customer had left his voice lifted again. He'd explained how silly it was to feel guilt over an event for which one could not possibly have exerted any influence, and the passion of his argument had far exceeded its occasion; he'd even scared Lou a little talking about guilt and powerlessness. Lou had burst into tears.

"What's wrong with Lou?" Nestor, suddenly at Nat's side, had asked, pulling on his father's pant leg.

"Something very bad happened to a friend," Nat had said almost in a whisper, transfixed suddenly by Lou's sobs.

"Did her friend get hurt?"

"Yes, sweetheart."

"Is her friend dead?" Nestor pressed.

"Yes," Nat answered.

"You don't understand!" Lou had exploded between sobs. A white haired oldster, a tiny woman in a ridiculous but comely red beret, then tinkled the bell on the door while peering in; she was frightened away immediately by Lou's weeping.

"What don't he understand?"

Lou answered as though Nat had spoken, "He called the night before and asked to see me. He'd said he'd blow off the gig in Jackson if I'd have a drink with him. That's all he wanted," Lou had concluded. "All he wanted was to talk to me."

Nat had been immediately delighted that Lou had had the strength to resist the creep's emotional blackmail, mindful of course that that resistance, as bleak fate would have it, ultimately allowed the snuffing out of the creep's unenviable life.

A wisp of a smile had blown across Nat's face, and he saw the shock begin to collect in Lou's contorted, wet expression, and so he'd willed the nasty little smile into a look of brow-stitched generic concern.

"Don't worry, Lou," Nestor had said. "Your friend's probably in Heaven."

Nat had been shocked. When and where had the child gleaned the concept? Certainly not from family. "If there is one," he'd added after a moment. "And if there isn't, it doesn't matter."

At this, Lou had ceased mid-sob and stared over the counter and down at the angelic boy, puzzled. Nat, too, had been puzzled, but by then was used to such puzzlement regarding the child.

"Wake up, Chump Change," Nat said gently, shaking Marti, then swatted her lightly on the rear. She roused a little, and Nat knew that she knew if she just lay there a little longer he'd simply scoop her up and carry her in, and he did.

SECTION SEVENTEEN

WILLIE WANTED TO like him because his mama seemed to like him a lot, but he was sloppy big, not hard big like his Uncle Teddy had been, and he just took up too much damned space on the couch. He tried to make Willie like him; Willie gave him that much, and even though he was ugly he dressed nice. He was a detective on the NOPD, and Willie's mama'd already had one date with him that Willie hadn't even known about. Now only on the second date she was hooking Sloppy Big up with Willie to see if Willie will like him okay. Willie's mama had only brought two men around to meet Willie, and they'd been two she really liked. But she'd found out one was already married with three kids and the other was the kind who could act real normal but was really crazy. She got asked out a lot because she looked like Whitney Houston, especially when she got all fixed up with her hair combed out the way Whitney used to wear it, and she'd go out with the ones who seemed okay but she'd never brought somebody home to meet Willie after only one date, and besides, all the other dudes Willie ever saw her with, like when they brought her home and she kissed them on the step or just said good night and kind of ran in the house, had been good looking men, and Willie's mama always said she needs a slender man, no fat men for her, and this dude wasn't exactly fat but he was sloppy looking, like he had some muscles but they were floating around in a lot of soft stuff. And now he was smiling at Willie and asking him what his favorite subject was and Willie said history, and he was hearing himself say it

175

for the first time and actually he'd never really thought about it before but yeah, history was his favorite subject. He was good at everything but most stuff made him bored. They said he was super at math, but it really got him bored. And his tutor Ms Millie said he had to work more on his writing because he wrote too much like he talked, and Willie'd asked her wasn't writing just talking on paper, and she'd said not exactly, but she'd explain next time and that would be the Thursday after Mardi Gras.

His name was Boris, Lieutenant Boris Black, and Willie flat out told him he'd never heard of a black man named Boris, and Boris laughed and said he got that name because he was found just after he was a baby and put in an orphanage, and they'd had to name him something, and somebody was watching Rocky and Bullwinkle and just named him after the little Russian spy. This cracked Willie up a little, and he said okay Lieutenant Black, I guess you don't have to tell me how they come up with your last name! And they both laughed but Lieutenant Boris Black said he got his last name later when his aunt found him, so it was his real name. He'd been almost four when she'd found him, already used to being called Boris, so even though she'd said he used to be called Rodney, she'd just kept calling him Boris because it was easier.

There were lots of questions floating around to be asked about what Lieutenant Boris Black just told him, but Willie figured now wasn't the time to get into it. Boris asked what history Willie now was reading about, and Willie told him the Holocaust.

Boris' nice smile turned into a question face, and he asked why Willie was reading about that, and Willie said that Danny Dork guy used to throw a birthday party for Adolph Hitler even though Hitler was dead, and Willie'd wondered about that so he'd read about Hitler, and in those books was where he'd learned about the Holocaust and then got some books just about that.

Boris seemed a little dizzy. He seemed to want to say something but he couldn't seem to find the words. Willie's mama came out of her room looking real fine in her green shiny dress and all made up and her hair combed out just right. Willie was proud of how pretty she looked. She said that before she and Boris went out she'd get drinks for everybody and they'd make a toast.

She brought three glasses on a tray, which was kind of funny because she'd never have done that if Boris hadn't been there, and she gave Willie a glass of Pepsi with a little bit of red Big Shot mixed in, and something kind of yellow in little glasses to her and Boris, and Boris put his glass in the air and said to new friendships, and Willie's mama clinked her glass against his and Willie did too and they all took sips. Then Boris asked shouldn't the sitter be here by now, and Willie's mama looked a little embarrassed to say she hadn't had to have anybody watch Willie since he was eight, so Willie said the old lady next door checked in on him, and it's only kind of a lie because even though she was as old as rocks and never stopped watching TV, Willie knew he could go there if he needed to. Boris wasn't exactly okay with the situation, Willie could tell, which was ridiculous, but instead of making him mad, it made him kind of like old sloppy, big and ugly Lieutenant Boris Black a little.

Willie's mama kissed him goodbye, and Boris put out his hand; Willie shook it. Boris promised to have Willie's mama home by midnight, and that almost cracked Willie up but he made himself not laugh, and just said cool, Lieutenant Black.

Bart's lawyer had called back and said Bart had written a letter saying that he'd wanted Willie to be one of the people who would talk at the funeral. She'd said three other people would talk also; one was a famous writer who'd talk about what a good poet Bart had been. One was the mayor because Bart's family was so rich and the mayor knew Bart's mama and daddy both. And that dude who'd taken Bart out to die, Nathan Moore, because he'd known Bart a long time.

Willie'd never stood up in front of a lot of people to talk before, and the lawyer had said a lot of people were going to be at the Bolten Funeral Home when they turned Bart's body into ashes. Willie wondered where the hell everybody'd been when Bart had actually been doing the dying, and got a little pissed thinking about people showing up for the funeral of somebody they hadn't bothered with while he was dying, but Willie knew Bart had kind of fixed it that way, kind of fixed it so he'd be alone to write *The Mystic Pig* while he was dying.

Did Willie have to do this? The way he figured, he didn't have to do a damned thing for old dead Bart Linsey who'd been queer with his Uncle Teddy and who'd made Willie a damned muse without even asking him.

Why did Bart do this to him? Why had Bart made Willie a muse, and then stuck him with *The Mystic Pig*, which was back under those damned towels that never got used, and now why'd Willie have to stand up in front of a bunch of people, probably mostly white people except for the mayor and all his flunkies – Uncle Teddy'd known the mayor and said he had lots of flunkies – and talk about somebody he didn't even really much like, especially now that he knew Bart'd been queer with Uncle Teddy?

Willie'd gone to his grandma's funeral, but'd been too upset to go to his Uncle Teddy's. Willie felt bad that he hadn't gone to his Uncle Teddy's, and felt that going to Bart's would kind of make up for it. He hated that he felt going to Bart's funeral would make up for his not going to Uncle Teddy's but that's how he felt and he couldn't turn the feeling into anything else.

Willie clicked on C-SPAN to see if anybody was giving a speech he could watch to think about how to do it. There was one of those things on where people were sitting in chairs in front of a long table where other people were lined up behind it in chairs and took turns going up to the middle part to talk. Now an old white woman in a red dress with a big blue handkerchief around her neck was talking about Social Security, which Uncle Teddy had said is going to dry up like a Dixie ditch so Willie'd better not count on it. He'd told Willie he shouldn't count on anybody or anything but Willie, and that Willie should never do any kind of work for nothing. He'd shown Willie his contract with the Saints one time, and it had cracked Willie up, because of course no normal person was supposed to be able to understand it, but Willie had been able to see how Uncle Teddy had had it broken down to get paid for every little thing he did. Willie'd joked with Uncle Teddy that he was getting paid for everything but taking a crap, and Uncle Teddy'd laughed real deep like Willie loved to hear, then said that was in there, under incentives.

Willie clicked to C-SPAN 2, and there was a black dude in a black suit giving a speech, and he sounded just like a white dude. And that was no big deal, because Willie heard white people who sounded like black people, and a lot of black people who sounded like white people in their voice, how they said words, but this dude was all the way, how he sounded and what he was saying, which had something to do with Affirmative Action, which Uncle Teddy used to say was a hornet's nest he'd just as soon not put his hand into. Willie knew it was about the government making people play fair. Uncle Teddy used to say the best government was like the best zebras in a game; the less you noticed it the better it was doing its job, but the main thing it had to do was keep the game fair, but of course people were going to see what's fair differently from one another. Willie didn't mind that the black dude on C-SPAN 2 sounded white, but it did bother him that the dude seemed like the only black thing about him was his skin, like he'd been raised by white people. Willie got a whistle up his spine when he thought of that.

Grace:

It's two AM. My oldest is coughing in her sleep. It's nothing
serious, but impossible to ignore. Soon, I will carry her into
this room and put her on the couch and tuck her in, as though
coughing in the same room where I'm tapping on a computer will
be healthier for her.

There… I've done it, and managed to pour some Robitussin into
her. Your biological granddaughter hacks away now within my field
of vision, and I, even if she is not, am better for it.

I know I'll see you in a few days, but how much can we say to one
another in three or four hours? Let me just say now, partly in response
to your last e-mail, that I'm sorry if it's seemed that I've used my
communication with you as some kind of therapy. If I've done that,
I haven't meant to, and certainly don't think it would be fair to you.
What I said in my first letter was the truth. I'm mainly curious. I don't
expect or want anything like mother love from you. I've gotten plenty
of that, maybe too much. And yet over the last few years curiosity
about my origins has become a small obsession to look into your
face. Does that sound strange or creepy? I hope not. I don't know
how you and I will get along; I'm intimidated by your learning but feel
as well that you're at least partially full of shit. Your self-assuredness,
which is probably real enough to you, your life, is what I think is false
in relation to the world. You think there are aspects of life that can be
known, understood, which I simply think are unknowable. I don't think
evil can be known, understood. I think it is something like an ultimate
mystery. It has no single agent or origin, and it's everywhere. All you
can do is fight it, hit back, on some level become it for the purpose of
fighting it. All of life's formalities, from organized sport to fine dining
to High Mass, are temporary stays against evil, which at its core is
all that's random. People emphasize how highly formalized was the
treachery and brutality of the Nazis. Yet what's truly horrifying is how
the massive machinery of the Nazi's hatred was brought to bear so
arbitrarily. Jews didn't evoke hatred, didn't somehow create it within
Christian Germans; it was already there simply needing an object,
any object. And I think it's always that way. You say it's got a structure.
I say what's truly horrifying is that it doesn't. There is no God and She
is merciful; the mercy of a godless universe is that we may imagine

it otherwise. And what we know, to the very lowest rack of our DNA, that horror we may suspend in our hearts next to what we imagine, and the mild current thus created, is our glory and our madness.

I want to look into your face, see the life in your eyes. I don't want to love you. I don't even really want to like you. I just want to see the flesh from which I issued, look into the eyes of the woman who gave me this life, the only one I'll ever have.

As you can probably tell, I'm a little drunk. I get philosophical when I drink. I become a spewer of cosmic bullshit. This only happens late at night, and only occasionally. I'm actually a good social drinker, and hope we can get tipsy together in my restaurant.

Nat

The children were playing like children, the wall was outside, the sky pink going to mauve. He stood in a garden and felt a breeze crawl over his skin. A withered boy strapped into a wheelchair wept. Nat approached him and asked if he was uncomfortable, if the belts binding him to the chair, keeping him from collapsing forward into a pathetic heap onto the ground, were too tight, they appeared too tight, but the boy ignored or did not hear him, and Nat spoke louder, asking if there was anything he could do for the boy. At this the boy looked up, that is his eyes rolled up in his head and he stared at Nat. I can't even jerk off, the kid sobbed, and Nat cringed, ran away, but then felt guilt for deserting the poor quadriplegic, and turned back, but Nat was now in a grove, a green place ringed by towering tailored shrubs in which many delicate trees, no taller than Nat, yet seeming to be fully developed, stood in rows. Nat can hear the children playing like children but he can't see the wall for the shrubs, the ground among the trees is busy with gaudy blooms whose names Nat cannot recall, and there is a fountain, at the center of the lush enclosure, of dazzling white marble. Nat circles to face the figure from whose mouth the green water is spouting. It is the kid from the wheelchair, naked and with little wings sprouting from his delicate shoulders, frozen in a ridiculous parody of a balletic pose, holding a tiny bow and arrow, and sporting a timeless hard-on; Bart crawls out of the fountain, dripping, wearing a tux and red sneakers, the pair from Maison Blanche he bought as a kid and wore proudly for years, even after they'd become worn and stained into something resembling muddy blood-soaked bandages. Now they're as new, and even shine a little; Nat asks if he's dead, and he says in a manner of speaking, and then Nat turns and his waiters are conducting a funeral. Danny is the priest, and chants slowly in a loud and formal voice the chorus of 'Life Is a Cabaret' as the others lower the white coffin into the ground on silk ropes. Marking the grave is a six-foot tall slot machine, golden and studded with sapphires and rubies, balanced on an inverted cross. When he's finished the recitation, Danny closes the black book from which he's read, turns, and pulls the lever on the slot, and Nat hears sobbing and turns. His mother, Bridget, Lou, Edie and Marti, all dressed in long black dresses, walk with dirge-like solemnity, holding their faces in their hands as though their hands were masks, and another woman, wearing a black veil, comes last and Nat fears and hates her and doesn't know why. He picks up a large stone and heaves it at her, knocking her head from her body, and the veiled head rolls toward Nat and stops at his feet; a breeze blows the veil up –

Poon was whining as Nat awoke, startled, in a sitting position where he'd wedged between the couch arm and Marti's feet; Marti had left the comforter on the couch and gone to bed with Lou and Edie. Nat was alone with Poon. He switched on the lamp. The tiny dog's distress had awakened him. Poon was hunched in the middle of the linoleum convulsing, regurgitating bloody bits of whatever he'd eaten. He could barely breathe.

Pumped suddenly full of adrenaline so soon from sleep, the sticky dew of strange dreams clinging still to his vision, he dropped on hands and knees and crawled to the animal. Poon shook and gagged. Nat wanted to stop the torment. He felt a strong urge to rise and flee the room, shut the door on the creature's suffering until it was finished. But he knew he'd hate himself for running away, so remained riveted.

He reached to touch it, but it was oblivious to his touch. He realized he could pinch its tiny throat and make it die more quickly. He reached for the creature's convulsing throat, but when he touched it drew back in horror.

Then he leaped up and ran to the kitchen. He grabbed the iron skillet and ran back to Poon. He whacked it hard on the skull. It fell on its side but continued to convulse. He came down with his full weight on the side of the dog's head and something gave. It twitched once and became still. Blood trickled from its ears. Its eyes were open.

Nat wept. He sat on the floor, clutched his knees and heaved a dozen huge wet sobs. Then he calmed, grew quiet.

It was six-eighteen. He'd only slept an hour and a half.

He took the skillet and the empty bottle by the computer back to the kitchen, and washed off the skillet and hung it back on the hook on the side of the oven.

He took a pillowcase from the bathroom closet off the den. He couldn't bring himself to perform the simple task of grabbing the carcass by the rear legs and dropping it in the pillowcase. He touched a leg, then tried to grip it, but involuntarily pulled back as from a hot surface. The previous day's *Times Picayune* lay folded on the TV. He dropped it in layers over the dead animal until the bloody thing and its pool of bile was covered by newsprint and car ads. Then he shoved the pile with one hand toward the pillowcase, which he held open with the other.

Awkwardly, slowly, he worked the pile into the pillowcase and knotted the end. A little blood soaked through.

The garbage truck was grinding its teeth a block away. He shoved the pillowcase into the black plastic, nearly-full waist high container and pushed down hard on the lid, compacting the contents so the lid would close all the way.

Back in the den, he cleaned the bloody mess in the middle of the linoleum with paper towels, then with Lysol and a sponge. Then he threw away Poon's food and water dish, his blanket, and the straw mat he slept on. He threw away Poon's rubber ball and leash.

He woke Marti, checked her temperature, got her moving through her morning regimen. Then he went into his wife's bedroom. He shook her awake, and sat on the edge of the bed. He was wearing the jogging shorts and tank top he always wore around the house. He felt he should have dressed before waking her. He told her Poon had died last night. He'd died in his sleep.

SECTION EIGHTEEN

WILLIE'D BEEN WORKING on his speech all morning. He'd flipped back and forth between C-SPAN and C-SPAN 2 some more but hadn't seen anything that helped him figure out how to do what he had to do. He hated preachers. He could never have stood up in front of al lot of people and acted like that, yelling and screaming and waving his arms around like loving Jesus just makes you crazy. And he could never have made his voice all deep and important like Dr King's in that I Have a Dream speech. Willie would be embarrassed for people to think he thought he had anything that important to say that he would sing it with his talking voice the way Dr King did, though Willie wondered what it must feel like to know you've got something that important to say the way Dr King had. It must have felt wonderful, Willie thought. That moment he'd stood outside in front of a zillion people and started talking what he'd already figured out he was going to say, then he must have felt how those zillion people liked what he was saying, and that must have felt real good, because he'd sounded like he felt good about what he was saying, serious but good.

Willie wasn't going to stand up in front of a lot of people and try to act so serious and important they'd laugh at him, even though they'd be at a funeral. And Willie thought that to get laughed at for what you say in front of people at a funeral you'd have to look and sound pretty ridiculous, like his Uncle Buster had at his grandma's funeral, when old Buster had stood up all skinny and serious and bald in a suit too small for him and talked about how full of the

183

Holy Spirit Grandma had been, how she'd prayed all the time and had Bibles all over her house, and had even kept one by the toilet, and some of the kids had cracked up and the grown-ups he could tell had been fighting to keep from laughing, and dumb old Uncle Buster had just looked down real puzzled at everybody. Willie definitely wanted to avoid pulling an Uncle Buster.

The only reason he was doing it was to make up for missing Uncle Teddy's funeral, and he hated that he felt that way, that saying this speech would be a make-up. But he couldn't talk at Bart's funeral about what he felt for his Uncle Teddy, and how weird he felt about the big switch Uncle Teddy made in Willie's head now that Willie had to think about him being queer with Bart. He had to talk in front of all those rich white people and the mayor and all his flunkies about what he'd felt about Bart, and about *The Mystic Pig*.

Willie's mama slept late. She'd come in right at midnight with Boris. Willie'd been reading in bed, but he'd flipped the light off when he'd heard the jingling at the door. He hadn't been waiting for her, exactly, but since Boris had made such a fuss about getting her home he'd wanted to see if Boris could pull it off; Willie knew how his mama was once she got started, how she could party like a hurricane right into daylight, dancing men right into the floor she always said and laughed about it, because she did love to dance, and sometimes when she cleaned up around the house, like on weekends, she'd put the music so loud Willie'd have to get out so she could dance and clean and sing along with Ella Fitzgerald and Bob Marley and the Supremes and the Four Tops and Lauren Hill and dance around kind of crazy and sing and clean. She didn't sing too well, which was good reason in itself for Willie to get out of the house and go over and lie down in the grass on Tulane campus and read, but she danced pretty, and when she got going you'd think a broom was alive and dancing with her.

Boris had come in with her and they'd had drinks and she'd put on Lena Horne, so Willie hadn't been able to make out everything they were saying, but then Willie'd peeked out and they were dancing real slow in front of the darkened TV, and Willie'd seen his mama's face pressed against Boris' big sloppy chest, and her eyes had been closed and she'd been smiling and looked real happy, and they'd danced like that until the record finished on one side, and then they'd finished the other, then Willie's mama had put on a CD of something slow with no singing and they'd danced that all up, and then Boris'd kissed her goodnight a long time and left.

Willie wanted to make his mama something good for breakfast. He checked the fridge, and saw he had what he needed. So he pulled out the butter, some smoked ham he'd been saving for beans but figured he'd just get some hot sausage from the store for that later, and the whole carton of eggs that hadn't been put already in their little slots on the door. Then he pulled down the red wine vinegar and cayenne pepper, and checked the box for English muffins and he was relieved that there were three left, though he was pissed that they were so hard. Toasting would fix that some, but it would be better if they were fresh.

Willie dropped a glob of butter into a saucepan over a halfway flame then quickly separated out four yolks. He tried to break one with one hand like his Uncle Teddy used to and like the chefs on TV did it, but it just slopped onto the counter so he quickly scooped the mess into the sink and broke the next ones with both hands. Then he skimmed the gunk off the top of the butter and put what was left over a real low fire. Then he dropped the yolks into another pan and splashed in a little vinegar and two big pinches of cayenne and a little salt and then poured all that into a silver metal bowl and got the whisk and whipped it up a little. Then he got another pan, just big enough to rest the bowl in, and put in water about a knuckle deep and got it just about to boiling and set the bowl into it, making sure the water didn't actually touch the bowl. Then he whipped some more and put the clear liquid butter over the smooth yolks, whipping fast. Then he poured in just a tiny bit of water. He poured the sauce into a gravy boat that his grandma gave to Willie's mama but his Aunt Bertha says is really hers, then he sliced the ham and put it in a skillet over a real low fire, and put the hard muffins in the four-slice toaster his mama won playing bingo only that one time in her life. Then he got the tray his mama used to carry the drinks last night. It was still on the washing machine, where his mama put everything when she was in a hurry. It had a swan on it, and it was just big enough for a plate and a glass and a cup and saucer. Then he broke four eggs into a little bowl, and when he'd got a thin layer of water boiling he slid in the eggs. He hated poaching this way, but he couldn't find that little aluminum poaching pan. He used a spatula with holes in it to scoop out the poached eggs and put them on toasted muffins he'd laid thin slices of the grilled smoked ham across, and then he poured the sauce over it all, and sprinkled a little paprika over the sauce. Then he poured some cranberry juice in a glass and hot water over a Lipton tea bag into a mug because his mama always had a cup of tea first and then coffee, and then he put the knife and fork on a paper towel he folded like a napkin.

As he carried the tray to his mama's room he remembered how he and his Uncle Teddy used to cook together, how much fun it used to be just hanging out with his Uncle Teddy in the kitchen when it wasn't football season and his uncle had more time. His Uncle Teddy had loved to cook almost as much as he'd loved to make dudes twitch like bugs on the football field. Cooking by himself just wasn't the same, except when it made his mama happy.

———————————

Lou was inconsolable all morning. She was livid that Nat had disposed of Poon's body without consulting her, to which Nat had responded by suggesting that the sight of the dead animal might have traumatized Edie; Lou had screamed that he'd been ready to have the child see a dead person stretched out in her own bed, to which Nat had had no answer until he'd simply told her the truth: he'd panicked. He was sorry, deeply sorry, he'd disposed of the animal's body, but he'd been so taken aback by the sight of the dead dog he'd not known what to do.

Lou'd settled down just as it struck Edie that Poon was gone. Marti had not much cared for Poon, early in her life experiencing a kind of sibling rivalry with a creature whose place in her mother's heart pre-dated her own. But Edie had always loved Poon, and even though the ugly little thing had been dying ever since she was born, Edie'd considered Poon a playmate, even if the only play it could rise to consisted of flopping on its side for Edie to rub its tiny, disgustingly distended tummy. Edie'd bawled for most of an hour following Nat's dropping Marti off at school.

And Lou had wanted to know where Poon's things were, his bowl and ball and mat and collar and leash. Why had Nat thrown them away?

He couldn't answer. He'd just felt the need not to have reminders of the animal around. He'd felt a strong compulsion to get rid of everything, its body and all its things.

He'd had to take care of Sandra's apartment because her family couldn't; they'd come over from Dallas to fetch the body then left. Nat had not wanted to go to her apartment, but he couldn't just leave the birds to starve, and something had to be done about her paintings.

Now she was out shopping in the French Market. She was buying Creole tomatoes, a rope of fresh garlic, ripe mangos and bananas, pistachios, red onions, young Brussels sprouts, a small perfect melon. She bought handmade Italian sausage and pasta. Now she was walking home, and Nat recalled how once they'd walked back to her place late one night, and George Benson's 'Masquerade' had been wafting from an open window over a balcony and down to them on the sidewalk of Ursuline, and suddenly the Button Lady, or the Bead Lady as some folks called her, appeared on an almost lightless stoop. She'd been gnawing something which, as they approached, Nat could see was raw bacon.

"Lucky Beads?" she'd squawked, as always, peering over the strips of white fat she'd held with both hands to her mouth like a squirrel. "Lucky Beads?" she'd squawked again.

"No thanks, Button Lady," Nat had said, which had usually been enough, but this time she'd leapt from the stoop, spilling the meat onto the pavement, and screeched horribly. Nat and Sandra had been terrified. The Button Lady had then begun to speak in tongues, as everyone who lived in the Quarter described it, flipping, it seemed, between several languages, cursing them, it seemed, in each, and she'd cursed Nat and Sandra mightily, then crouched having plucked something from her thickly-pleated flowing skirt, and began to sketch figures and symbols on the pavement with a knuckle of yellow chalk. They'd stood transfixed, then Nat had pulled at Sandra's elbow, but she wouldn't budge; she'd stood and watched and listened to the Button Lady's curses, by turns mumbled and screeched.

Now she was back at her apartment and must clean the birds' cages after she puts away her shopping and sets water to boil for pasta. She was a terrible cook, but she could do pasta.

He apologized to Lou, deeply and sincerely, and he apologized to Edie, and he explained how tired he was, and how much he wished he didn't have to speak at Bart's funeral. Lou never stayed angry long, but she couldn't stop quietly weeping all morning; all morning her eyes were filled with tears even as she went about her business around the house and then phoned her partner about another movie company that might buy up their stock of '50s summer clothes.

When Lou got off the phone, she said someone had tried to call while she was on, and he should check his messages.

Roberto Mancini wanted to talk to him. Nat sucked in and blew out three lungfuls of breath, then pecked the numbers.

"Nat! Thanks for getting back to me so quickly. How's the family?"

"Very well, sir," Nat said. The old gangster was sounding positively joyous. Nat felt a small thrill.

"Listen, things seem to be working out with Nick and his mother," he said.

"Hey, that's wonderful. He's been off a couple of days, so I hadn't heard anything from him. I did have that talk with him, Mr Mancini," Nat was quick to add.

"Yes, I know. He and I hashed over what you talked about. He was clearly impressed by what you said. And I have to say that I'm impressed by your powers of persuasion, Nat," he dangled the compliment like an expensive bauble to his mistress, and Nat in turn felt rather sluttish.

"Well, I don't know..."

"I need to talk to you, Nat. I've a proposition for you."

He *needed* to talk to Nat. He had a *proposition*. This could be very, very good, or disastrous to a Biblical degree. "I've always got time for you, sir," he said meekly.

"You're too kind. Listen, I've got a business meeting at the Lakefront Airport tonight, in that bar in the terminal? Ever been there?"

"Yeah, a long time ago," Nat answered, though he couldn't recall when or why he'd been there.

"Why don't you meet me for a drink, say around ten. I should be finished by then. After that we'll celebrate by doing a little gambling on the boat. You gamble?"

"I've gambled," Nat answered weakly.

Willie got the number for Morton Publishers in New York, and phoned the person who hooked you up with whomever you wanted to talk to in the company. Willie explained that a poet named Bart Linsey died and that Morton made his books, so Willie wanted to find out if Morton wanted the last one Bart Linsey wrote.

The woman was confused. She asked if Willie wanted to speak to an editor. Willie said he just wanted to talk to somebody about Bart Linsey. The woman asked if Willie'd said that this Bart Linsey was a poet, and Willie said yes, Bart Linsey was a poet, and she said hold please, then another woman came on and said she was Lynda Komensky and could she help him. Willie started all over and she acted puzzled when he'd finished, and she said one moment please, and funky old white people music started up, a bunch of them singing 'The Look of Love' with a lot of violins, and it made Willie want to puke. One of the times he just didn't like white people was when they made him listen to songs like 'The Look of Love' on the telephone while he waited.

Then another woman came on and he started all over and she said wait a minute please and put on that damned 'Look of Love' again, but then she came back on and said she'd found out who the editor was who'd handled Bart Linsey's work and gave Willie the number, saying the line was busy right now. So Willie went to the toilet and thought about Brandy, then hustled back feeling much calmer, and called the number.

A man answered saying his name was Lee Porter. Willie said he was William Singer, and he'd been Bart Linsey's muse and now Bart was dead; then Willie told him about *The Mystic Pig* and about how he'd get ten thousand dollars if he just told Bart's lawyer that he'd burned it.

Lee Porter didn't say anything for a long time, then he asked if someone was pulling his leg, and Willie said he wasn't joking, if that's what Lee Porter meant, and then Lee Porter sighed and said that ten thousand was better than he could do, and Willie said he didn't understand, and the man said Morton Publishers had never paid that much money for a book of poetry; some books had ended up earning that much or more, though those had been exceptions. Willie told him he wasn't trying to get any money; he just wanted to know if Morton wanted *The Mystic Pig* because Willie can lie and tell the lawyer he'd burned it; the situation was fixed up so he could lie to the lawyer and get the money.

Lee Porter said he was sorry about Bart, and Willie said nobody should be sorry about him now because he was dead but Willie had this plastic bag full of epic poem called *The Mystic Pig* and needed somebody to take it off his hands because it was driving him nuts having it around, so did Lee Porter want to see it.

Lee Porter said Morton had just published Bart's last book late last year, but before he could finish Willie blurted out, near tears, that Bart was dead, the poem was a piece of shit but it was important that somebody made it into a book.

Lee Porter paused again, then asked why it was important, but then before Willie could finish he asked if this was some kind of joke and Willie said no, dammit, Bart was dead and Willie was stuck with *The Mystic Pig*, an epic poem that was weird and that nobody could read or listen to and be happy about reading or hearing it but that Morton had to publish it anyway.

Lee Porter talked about the publishing business and before he got very far Willie asked if Morton made any money off of Bart's books, and Lee Porter said Bart's work had always been well received critically and before he could say anything else Willie interrupted and asked what that meant, and Lee Porter said it was when people wrote about your books in newspapers and magazines, and Willie said cool, like when they told you a movie was good or not, a review, like those in *The Gauntlet*; Uncle Teddy used to say he was going down to the *Gauntlet* office to smack the snot out of that puckerbutt dude who wrote them they made him so mad, and Lee Porter said he wasn't familiar with that publication, but yes, Bart Linsey's books had always been well received by reviewers, and they'd sold modestly well, and Willie asked what that meant, and Lee Porter said he didn't have the figures in front of him but he seemed to recall that Bart's books sold between six and seven thousand, though his first one sold over eleven thousand, and Willie asked if that was a lot, because it sounded like pretty much, and Lee Porter said it wasn't that bad for poetry. So why, Willie wanted to know, won't Lee Porter take *The Mystic Pig* off of Willie's hands.

When Lee Porter started talking about how more and more serious literature is being published by small presses, Willie had no idea what he was getting at, but figured serious literature meant what hardly anybody wanted to read, so Willie said what if he gave Lee Porter five thousand dollars, and Lee Porter shut up. Willie repeated that he'd give Lee Porter five thousand dollars if Lee Porter could talk Mr Morton into making a book out of *The Mystic Pig*.

Then Lee Porter started talking about editorial integrity, and Willie thought that meant five thousand just wasn't going to cut it for the hassle of getting Mr Morton to make it into a book, so Willie said he'd give him ten thousand but that was it, because that was all Willie was going to get for lying to the lawyer.

Then Lee Porter acted nicer, saying how impressed he was by Willie's concern for Bart Linsey's legacy, and asked Willie questions about himself. He got Willie to describe just what he meant by Willie having been Bart's "muse." And then he kept asking little questions to keep Willie talking, until finally Willie'd told him everything, about what it had been like listening everyday to that epic poem, about fetching Bart's liquor, about Uncle Teddy having been Bart's muse first, about Uncle Teddy being Teddy "Mad Dog" Singer, about Uncle Teddy getting killed in his car, even about Uncle Teddy and Bart being queer for each other, and how at the start of *The Mystic Pig* Bart had written that Uncle Teddy'd been the love of his life.

Then Lee Porter asked Willie why he was doing this, and if Willie didn't think Bart would have sent it himself if he'd wanted it published.

Willie said Bart had been just too messed up. All Bart had known was *The Mystic Pig* and a world of pain. Willie got a little choked up then, and mad at himself for getting that way, and said he wished he could just burn the damned thing, he hated that he couldn't, but he just couldn't.

Lee Porter was quiet a long time for being on the telephone. Then he said he wouldn't promise anything, but that Willie should send *The Mystic Pig* to him, and told Willie to get a pen and write down the address. Then he told Willie he should do something good for himself with the ten thousand dollars, put it in a college fund or something, and Willie said he had plenty in his college fund, and why didn't Lee Porter want the money. Lee Porter repeated that Willie should mail *The Mystic Pig* to him, and if Willie didn't need the money to go to college someday, Willie should do something good with it, give it to a charity Bart would have liked or to one of those small presses that do serious literature. Willie said no, he'd just give it to Dean Witter.

SECTION NINETEEN

NAT CROSSED THE Seabrook Bridge and curled into the parking lot of the Lakefront Airport. This was as close as he wished to get to New Orleans East except to blow by it on I-10 on his way through Slidell into Mississippi and all points east. He contrived a bounce to his step as he covered the brief distance from the sparsely occupied lot to the entrance, scanning the area near the hangars where corporate jets were parked, mostly Lears it seemed, and he glanced at the little fleet longingly. He'd always wanted to go up in a "tiny-jet" as he'd come to call them over the years, and riding in one was an experience which should have been easy enough to achieve, and yet it was also one a person could spend an entire lifetime managing not to.

Sandra loved to fly. She traveled often to other cities where her work showed. He had even accompanied her a few times, and it was wonderful to walk the streets of Chicago or San Diego or even Dallas, where her family lived, and not worry about being seen.

It was two weeks after the attack, and the cockatoos were dead, and the four fledgling mockers were dead, and the mating doves were dead, though the single egg they'd taken turns sitting on was beginning to hatch. The three fledgling jays were dead. The white owl's cage was empty, the door mangled. Nat found it under Sandra's bed, dead, beside a braided-leather sandal that had been horribly gnawed. Nat'd unlatched the door on the dove's cage, reached in, taken the cracked, warm egg from its nest, dropped it on the linoleum and stomped it.

"Nathan Moore, I'd like you to meet my lawyer, Cookie Bates." A pair of

192

legs, that Nat had thought might only be found in that realm where Socrates located Truth and Beauty, thrust up from her seat one of the most ridiculously gorgeous women Nat had ever seen in the flesh. As though he were seventeen, he popped an instant boner.

"Nice to meet you Ms Bates," Nat managed to say.

"Call me Cookie," she said, smiling, and shaking his hand. She was six-one, had pixie-cut brown hair and doe eyes. Her lips were full to distraction, cheeks high. She wore a short, tight-fitting cream skirt and a tight cream blouse through which olive-sized nipples of unencumbered, erect and bountiful breasts were traced.

"You're a lawyer?" Nat said, and realized immediately how stupid, and probably insulting, the question sounded. "Well, Mr Mancini just said so, didn't he?" he tried to cover before she could answer.

"Yeah, I handle Mr Mancini's interests in the service, entertainment and gaming industries. I have colleagues whose specialties are matched to Mr Mancini's other involvements," she answered.

"That's nice," Nat said, and smiled weakly. The bar was '50s funky, a charming, time-warped space at which no one Nat had ever known would seek refreshment more than once, no one but Roberto Mancini.

"It's good to see you, Nathan. How long's it been?"

"I think you and…" he stopped himself. "I think you dined with us in November, Mr Mancini," Nat answered.

"You were going to say me and Mrs Mancini, right?" he said laughing heartily. The waitress put a double-something, neat, with a glass of gassed water in front of Nat. He smelled it: Irish, probably Bushmills; the old gangster had ordered for him, and ordered well. "Thank God that after forty-seven years of marriage, the old girl really doesn't give a damn who's giving me legal advice!" he declared, and his laughter erupted again, and Cookie joined him, patting his arm. "And let us give thanks to those saintly makers of Viagra, darling, that you give such marvelous advice," he purred, and Nat was laughing despite himself.

Their champagne glasses were almost empty; the Dom Perignon bottle was turned neck down in the ice slosh of the silver ice bucket beside the shin-high table. That meant they'd had to pour their own to empty the bottle, because surely Roberto Mancini had told the waitress to keep the Dom rolling until he said stop. Nat was suddenly as furious as he would be in Newcastle's. No customer, much less a VIP, ever touched a bottle in Newcastle's. As their laughter ratcheted down to chuckles, Nat motioned for the cocktail waitress. She was maybe twenty-three, blond and nondescriptly pretty, made up severely for the dim light of the bar.

"Just out of curiosity," he began, "how many bottles of that stuff do you sell in a night?"

She froze. Puzzlement splashed her face.

"Look, here's a tip, and it's the only one you're getting from me tonight. Even if you don't know who this man is," he said, nodding toward Roberto Mancini, "and if you don't your bartender and/or manager should be fired – anytime somebody orders that stuff you treat him or her and anyone he or she is with like royalty, and royalty doesn't have to reach into a goddamned bucket to pull out a dripping bottle of expensive bubbles to pour for himself. You understand? You've got three tables, kid, and this ain't rocket science. Now, bring another bottle and put it on my tab. And you change the glasses and the bucket. Do you understand?"

She was scarlet, near tears. This was no show for Mancini and sexpot lawyer; Nat was simply performing a civic and professional duty. She mumbled yes, and backed away, then scurried, grabbing the silver bucket by its silver stand.

"Excuse me," Nat mumbled, averting his eyes a moment.

"No, that's fine," Cookie said. "I put myself through college and three years of law school waiting tables and serving cocktails. You told her exactly what she needed to hear. You understand how good service depends upon attention to detail. You own a classy establishment, Mr Moore. I'm from St Louis, and I know from experience that Newcastle's is one of two or three names that come to mind when people in other cities start naming New Orleans restaurants."

"Call me Nat, please, and yeah, I know that's true, but I don't have any delusions. The Newcastle family created the reputation. I've just managed not to damage it; not too much, anyway."

"You've done a great job, Nat. I've watched you," Roberto Mancini said. "In fact, I've watched you since Frank used to bring you by the house. You weren't like the others. I could tell even then. So when you came to me at Frank's wake and said you wanted to buy Newcastle's but the old man wouldn't sell, even in my grief," he touched the crucifix nested in his shirt hair; from across the low table in the dim bar light it seemed the crucifix lay in a white nest, "even as I mourned my dear, mischievous but good-hearted nephew, I knew I had to help you achieve your destiny, Nat. You know, there are times I feel I am only an agent of fate, son," he said somberly and, as far as Nat could tell, sincerely.

194

"Nat, what are your long-term goals?" Cookie asked as the mortified waitress uncorked the bottle, first putting down fresh long-stemmed glasses; Nat fought an urge to hold the glasses to the light.

"Career plans? They're pretty transparent, and obvious. I want to maintain what's quintessentially Newcastle's and change for the better what isn't."

"You don't plan to purchase other establishments, get into other endeavors? Usually men your age are itching for change," she smiled.

She was early thirties and Nat could read in her voice and her posture, her general striking appearance, that she was an expert on men Nat's age, probably in every respect, and was obviously doing postdoc work on men Mancini's age. This meant she'd progressed from men who kept things running to men who owned what required maintenance, including the men who kept things running.

"I'm a simple guy," Nat said; his hard-on withered. This woman fucked for power. Nat hated women who fucked for power. "I'm not Al Coplin. I'm not a kingdom builder. I'm a glorified shopkeeper. I know my place, and like it there."

"You sell yourself short," she said.

"She's right, son," Mancini said. "It took balls to approach me at my nephew's wake like you did. A shopkeeper doesn't do that. You saw what you wanted and you went after it."

"And you did what you had to to get it," Cookie added, and suddenly Nat noticed how powerful her perfume was; when he'd popped his boner for her, he'd lost his eye, and ear and nose, for detail, but now he noticed how incredibly aggressive Cookie's scent was, that indeed she was too smart, too calculating, too savvy not to know how aggressive it was to wear a scent that strong, and so much of it. Nat also noticed that she seemed not to blink, ever. He half expected any second her tongue would flick out the side of her mouth to wash her eyeballs, as he'd observed, watching the Discovery Channel with Marti, such behavior in desert reptiles.

"I just got lucky," he said.

"Men make their own luck," Cookie retorted.

"And women, too?" he said rather carelessly.

"Women make men," she said simply, and finally blinked, once, and Nat didn't doubt the fat, black depths to which that simple verb was meant to resonate.

"Mr Mancini, I do want to get one thing straight here. When I approached you at Frank's wake, I didn't have an agenda. I was just talking. I told you the truth about my life because you'd asked. I didn't request your assistance, though I remain deeply grateful for it."

There was a pregnant silence filled with forced smiles.

"Well," Roberto Mancini exclaimed, slapping his thigh, "let's head over to the boat and do a little gambling. We've got a lot to talk about, Nat, but I'm a man who believes mixing business with pleasure enhances both!" He pulled out his cell phone, tapped a number, mumbled for his car, and when they exited the time warp of the Lakefront Airport, the fresh bottle of pricey bubbles hardly dented, a gray stretch sparkled in the dim and residual light of the runway and loading zone. A tiny white Lear was taxiing; Nat wanted to pause to watch it loop skyward, but didn't want Cookie and Robert Mancini to see the longing in his eyes and find it charmingly pathetic, which of course they would. So he shuffled down the steps and stood by the door behind which a stoical, stout black driver held the handle, waiting for Cookie to get in first, but she paused, fixed Nat's unsteady gaze with her unblinking, reptilian one, and he crawled into the seat back-to-back with the driver's. She followed and faced him, and Roberto Mancini hunkered down beside her. A swarthy fellow Nat had not seen, until the very moment he slid into the passenger side next to the driver, materialized. He wore a dark suit, his hair was greased back and he stared straight ahead.

"That's Mick, my personal assistant," Roberto Mancini explained amiably. On the vehicle's exquisite sound system Jimmy "Crawfish" Krews was blowing 'When My Baby Needs a Toot', and it was less than half-finished before the stretch pulled up to the entrance of the waiting area where fresh batches of gamblers were supposed to line up for the boat to return from phony sojourns.

They entered the queuing space, Roberto Mancini's personal assistant hanging back but clearly shadowing them; there was glass all around. The space seemed similar to the small terminals of island airports, particularly the one on Samos, the Greek island less than a mile off the coast of Turkey. The creatures lined up, though, did not at all resemble the Euro trash, mostly Germans, Nat had found himself among there when, while touring Europe, he'd taken Bridget and four-year-old Nestor on a side trip to the beautiful and primitive island whose beaches were heavenly but whose food was wretched.

Nat drifted in and out of chatter with the graceful old gangster and the gorgeous reptile he was fucking thanks to modern science, and otherwise observed the humanity around him, of which Chubby Little Women seemed to comprise a significant percentage.

They were roughly half black and half white, though definitely comprising a group for which race was the least significant feature. They seemed, all of
them, bent on offending by their dress most reasonable standards of taste. Most
wore gaudy workout suits in which, by the look of them, none had even thought
to take a brisk five-minute walk. Chunks of fake gold and diamonds and pearls
dangled from or were clipped to their ears, and gold chains, some fake some not,
encircled their fleshy necks and wrists. All of them — at least fifty Nat reckoned
as the crowd swept him and his party, including the personal assistant a few
yards behind, to the boat — were chewing gum it seemed, and they were paired
or in clumps of four to seven unto themselves, manless and seemingly content
to remain so for the evening and beyond. From long straps they shouldered
enormous purses the main purpose of which no doubt was to haul huge profits
home to Chalmette, Jefferson, or the Bywater. They smoked, and fisted go-cups
with various cocktails in them. Whatever they were preparing to do on the boat
had about it an odd, romantic tinge, as though they were all singularly out on a
date with the same cad who promised, and largely delivered, equal pleasure and
exquisite heartbreak to each.

On the boat Nat, Roberto Mancini, Cookie Bates, and the personal assistant who followed them, wandered from deck to deck quietly observing the
rituals of gambling. The Chubby Little Women had established altars before
their chosen slots; from their enormous purses they'd pulled plastic Mardi Gras
cups — Comus, Proteus, Bacchus, Zulu, Bards of Bohemia, Isis, and so many
others, some tiny, that rolled in each season from all over the region — filled
with dull silvery coins, fake leather or frankly plastic cases in which they kept
their cigarettes (most seemed to smoke long, chocolate-colored Mores); some
even retrieved snacks from the depths of those purses, and their go-cups never
emptied. One actually fixed her make-up in a tiny compact mirror before slipping the first little silver wheel into the machine.

And the common emotion Nat sensed throughout the fields of silver slots,
from floor to floor on the great ugly floating casino, was one which did not have
a precise name like Joy or Despair or Indifference, but seemed an admixture of
all three. A small anticipatory joy accompanied the dropping of the coin and the
pulling of the handle, and was followed hard by yet another failure and therefore
small despair which melted quickly into the vast lake of indifference upon whose
mild swells the hopes of all true gamblers ride, minute to minute to minute.
Some people, who seemed to have been at their stations the longest, actually
appeared impatient to get the next disc into the slot before the flickering images

of the current spin had even revealed success or failure. Pinching the coins, their hands hovered near the slits into which they dropped, one after the other, slivers of their lives: grocery money, a new transmission, school clothes.

Nat recalled pitching pennies with Frank Mancini and the guys, how he'd gone along with such games, later even poker, simply for the camaraderie, not actually enjoying the wagers themselves, the transactions. Bart had gotten into the games from time to time, but got bored with them so quickly he eventually just stayed away. With Frank, everything had to escalate; pennies became nickels became dimes became quarters, and in their teens instead of pitching coins they sat around tables in the middle of which silver coins and dollar bills grew into piles, then got swept with a forearm heartward by one guy and then the next, and it had always been Frank who'd prodded friendly games toward serious affairs in which teenage boys lost significant portions of their total monetary worth. Frank Mancini, actually, had over the years clearly lost the most, and Nat, as fate and common sense would have it, got out of that two-year-long floating once-a-week game fairly well ahead, almost a thousand bucks he'd once roughly calculated. But to gamble at cards was at least sociable, unlike the private altars of slots.

Nat had always felt a strong inclination simply to redistribute his winnings, to give Frank and his other buddies back their money, but even to consider such an act, as Bart had early on suggested, would have been the most profound gender blasphemy, a yanking of the cosmic rug from under the already insecure footing of everyone's emerging manhood.

Nat chatted mindlessly with Cookie Bates and watched a blackjack table for several minutes. When a space opened up, a ruddy German tourist shaking his sweaty head and mumbling guttural incomprehensibles, Nat filled the breach. He got chips and antied, then doubled down on the first hand, winning one of them with nineteen. Then he busted, held seventeen and lost, then hit blackjack consecutively. Then he busted four times straight, won holding eighteen, busted, hit blackjack, and walked away from the table up forty-three dollars, feeling absolutely nothing, neither satisfaction nor regret, and certainly no desire to repeat the experience. In fact, in retrospect, he rather hated it. Why did those people spend so much time, so much of their lives in terms of time and resources, on these activities? No one smiled as she pulled the lever again and again, nor as he peeked at hole cards that added up nicely; there was no thrill, only raw, unmediated human compulsion.

Roberto Mancini and Cookie Bates drifted into a game at another blackjack table. The dealer obviously recognized Mancini, and seemed unnerved. A few paces behind Mancini stood his personal assistant, staring at the dealer, beyond emotionless, indeed zombie-like. Nat told them he was going to stroll out onto the deck for some air. Mancini turned at the waist and smiled back at him, acknowledging Nat's message over the unvarying din.

He eased out onto the deck of the great phony boat, the gaudily sparkling behemoth which, when local authorities forced it to actually follow the laws mandating that it ferry its commerce onto the shallow gray depths of Lake Pontchartrain, chugged occasionally across nervous chops of the lake a small distance, then returned. It was a floating casino that functioned in every way as a fixed one, a shiny testimony to the outrageous mendacities of Louisiana politics, a system of ritualized lying that the very victims of its lies had come to regard as charming, even entertaining. Across demographic and ideological spectrums, natives of the state, but particularly New Orleanians, had come to view politics as entertainment; having lost faith in the possibility of systemic change, blacks and whites, rich and poor, had hunkered down, over many generations but particularly the last four, to the only civic entertainment more outrageous than Carnival itself.

And as he gazed upon the water, and let his vision arc across the lights of New Orleans East, where kids were killing each other on any given night; and flicked back to the left of downtown and tried to distinguish the small lights of the Fauburgh-Marogny where, indeed, kids were killing each other on any given night of the week, Nat considered how walking to one's car after dark was pulling the handle; how, generally, being out among others, in the open, was to hit on fourteen.

"That gambling analogy's a bit worn out, sugar. Remember when we fucked in your Beamer over there?" Sandra was beside him, one arm laced with his on the railing, the other pointed out over the water toward Lakeshore Drive.

"Yeah," he said but didn't, and she knew he didn't and hit him lightly in the arm with her little fist. Then he kind of remembered when they'd driven down on a weekend when Sandra's sister had been visiting from Dallas and staying in the apartment on Ursuline. "Yeah," he said again, this time with conviction, smiling.

"Sugar, something's up with those two," she said, gesturing with her head back toward the entrance.

"I know," he said, placing his left hand over her right, pressing it into his right forearm. "The other shoe's going to drop soon enough, whenever Mancini feels like dropping it. What do you think's up?"

"You know what's up," she said, gazing out at the lights of the boat reflected upon the water.

"You tell me," he said.

"He wants Newcastle's. Don't you think that's pretty obvious?"

Nat was stunned.

"Baby, don't act so surprised. You know that's what it is. That's all it can be," she said firmly but soothingly.

"Do I have a choice?"

"Of course not, sugar. You've only been holding the joint for him, guarding it even, like a eunuch. But you've always known that, Nat. When he was under indictment and Frank'd just gotten baptised to death wasn't the best moment for a famous gangster to take over one of the French Quarter's hotsy-totsy eateries. You don't get where that guy is without impeccable timing."

"His face was in the papers everyday…"

"Well, sure. And on TV coming and going on the court-house steps in Baton Rouge. How long did all that drag on?"

"Jesus, I can't exactly say. In one form or another over a decade. Until last April, I think."

"And when did he lean on you to hire Penis Boy?"

Nat gazed east, into the darkness over the lake.

"He wants to turn soulless New Orleans East into a global glitz Mecca, a coonass Las Vegas," she said. "And that's no secret. Hell, he made that big show over the summer of buying up all the land under those trashy condos and town houses on Dowman. Got it for almost nothing."

"What's Newcastle's got to do with that?"

"He wants to anchor his family to some symbol of the New Orleans establishment even as he drags the Big Easy's gambling industry into the brave new world of globalisation. He doesn't give a flying frick about Joe Sixpack. He wants Don Juan Rodriguez, the pride of Chalupa to bring his pesos north to gamble. He's not looking to compete with the Redneck Riviera. He's going to get in a classic pissing contest with the real thing, and with his cousins in Vegas. High rollers. Global."

"But then why'd he bother developing the gulf coast?"

"Hey, the guy's made a bundle and sold most of his interest. Those wretched little tack palaces just prove the domestic business is there. And that anemic casino downtown just proves you can't do this stuff half-ass. You can't do gambling on the side. A city's got to bet everything or nothing. At least that's what Mancini wants everybody to think. But the bottom line, sugar, is you've got to sell your restaurant to him. He's as inexorable as the fucking weather," she concluded.

"What will I do?" he asked, sounding more pathetic than he'd wished.

"What *will* you do?" she shot back.

"I don't know," he said.

"Then you're not the man I fell in love with," she said, and pulled back her hand from between his hand and forearm.

"Please don't act like that," he said. "I don't deserve it."

"I didn't deserve what happened to me," she said. "Very few people in the world deserve the suffering that comes to them. And you'll hardly suffer. Your daddy left you pretty well fixed, babycakes, and Mancini's not just going to steal the place. He'll pay you what it's worth. Now, try again: what are you going to do?"

"With what?" he asked, agitated.

"Your life, sugar, your life! What are you going to do with your life?"

"I'll raise my family. I'll love you."

"Aaaaaaa!" she said, making the gesture of pushing a button. "Wrong answer, sugarpie. I'm gone. Kaput. I'm out of here!" she said resolutely and with wicked cheer.

"What do you mean?" he asked, distress soaking the question. She wore the red shift she'd had on the night they'd seen an old and puffy, but still beautiful, Peggy Lee in the Blue Room. The wind blew her hair off her shoulders; for someone who couldn't age, she was aging exceedingly well. Her figure, almost exactly like Bridget's – small pointed breasts, a graceful waist from which a small and gorgeous ass was suspended, legs that were thin and muscular – had only fleshed out a little, and, like Bridget's, to excellent effect. Her voice had grown a bit huskier over the years, also to excellent effect.

She stared out over the water, placid, almost sad. "You shouldn't need me anymore, Nat," she breathed.

"I'll always need you!" he shouted, and didn't care who saw and heard him talking to no one.

"I can exist as a secret, but not as a lie," she said. "Love your babies. Give them all of yourself. Hold back nothing from them. And give your passion to someone or something until it breaks your heart or yields a thing of beauty. If you don't take that risk you'll hate yourself as you lay dying, sugar."

"I've given my passion to you!" Nat protested.

"And I'm giving it back," she said, and smiled.

"Where will you be?" he was weeping.

"I've staked out a cosy little synapse in your left frontal lobe," she laughed, putting her arms around his neck, looking up into his eyes. Then she gently pulled his head down to her until her mouth was at his left ear. "Let me be dead, sugar."

Nat knocked on the door, then rang the bell, then realized his mother would hear neither from her bed at the far end on the sprawling house, his ur-home. He used his key, then quickly stabbed the deactivation code on the alarm system. He walked to the rear, down the long hall, past portraits of ancestors who were his and yet not; past porcelain stuff he'd broken as a child but that had reappeared, repaired; past the cabinet in which his father had kept his pistol, a Smith and Wesson something-or-other, in a black holster. It was the last thing he'd stuff into his briefcase before his weekly drives to Baton Rouge; past the bathroom that had been his father's and into which Nat had not been allowed to venture; past the cabinet crowded with crystal his mother used perhaps four times as he was growing up.

He opened the door to her room; she lay under the quilt she'd brought with her from England and which her mother had brought there from Czechoslovakia. He walked to the bed, casting a long shadow above her that arced across the ceiling. He pulled the quilt down from her shoulder. "Mama?" he whispered. She stirred, as Marti and Edie stirred, so deeply involved in the fact of sleep. "Mamink?" he said a little louder, and she opened her eyes. She saw him, wrinkled her brow, but then smiled. He'd never, as an adult, disturbed her sleep this way, slipping unannounced into the house and then her room and waking her, yet she smiled at him as she did when he was small and would wake her as he crawled beside her under that quilt, black and yellow squares, the yellow already turning gray when he was small enough to sleep with her.

He knelt down, as he would to his girls, and put his hand on her shoulder to keep her from raising her head from the pillow.

"Please don't get up, Mama. I'm only here for a moment," he whispered.

"Have you been drinking?" she asked through her haze, with no recrimination, or even concern, in her voice, just mild curiosity.

"Sure," he said, "but I'm not drunk. I want you to go back to sleep, but

202

first I want you to tell me about Jarka," he whispered. He glanced at the little whiskey-colored prescription bottle, white cap off, on her nightstand, and a glass of water more than half full. She was seeing him through the most delicate white feathers, he knew.

"Jarka?" she breathed.

"Yes, Mama, tell me about her."

She stared at the ceiling, her eyelids barely raised, then, with no emotion in her voice, "a doll."

"Daddy told me she was a doll," Nat rasped. They spoke as though there was someone in the room they might wake if they spoke too loudly. They spoke as though Nat's father were sleeping, facing away from them, on the other side of the bed, where he'd be on nights Nat was not allowed to crawl beside his mother.

His mother closed her eyes. "Your father told me he told you. I had a friend named Ludmila. She gave me her doll Jarka before she and her family were taken to Terezin. We were fourteen, too old for dolls, but it was a bad time. Children were frightened to be children, but more frightened to grow up." She opened her eyes, stared at the ceiling. "I slept with Jarka every night. When my mother and I left Prague, I couldn't carry Jarka with me. I was too old. I packed her in one of our trunks, but that trunk did not make the passage. Ludmila perished in Auschwitz."

"Mama, you're lying. You've lied all my life."

She closed her eyes. "What don't you believe?" she whispered.

"You didn't have a friend."

She said nothing. Nat could hear his father's breathing.

"You had an older sister. Your sister had a child. Your sister was married to a Jew. Jarka was the child's name."

She turned to face him. "How long have you known this?" She was placid.

"Only now. A long time ago Daddy told me he thought you'd had a sister, he'd seen some pictures or something, but that I should never mention it. The rest I just guessed. I'm also guessing you took care of the baby, that you were a good little sister."

"I took care of Jarka during the day while Ludmila and Mama worked in Prague 5," she whispered. "And most nights I slept with the baby because Ludmila was too weary from working to tend to her."

Nat smoothed back her hair, kissed her forehead. Her eyes fluttered, then closed again as she heaved the first heavy breaths of re-entry to a drugged sleep.

SECTION TWENTY

N AT HAD WRITTEN his eulogy from three-thirty to five, taking it through just two drafts. He realized it was entirely possible that what he held folded in the breast pocket of his black suit was sentimental gibberish that would mortify both his families unto that time he himself would require eulogizing. He'd not slept, and didn't doubt he looked like shit, and realized that his best hope may indeed be that this cross-section of New Orleans Old Money would be so concentrated upon how haggard he appeared they wouldn't actually hear what he was saying.

After the service he would go into the restaurant, for the last time, at least as its owner. He would tell everyone he was selling Newcastle's to Nick, that Jack would be running the place now. He would joke how every worker thinks the boss is a dick, and now...

It had been Jack's stipulation for going back to his mother's house, for not leaving her, for letting her think Nick was staying with her. During his protracted battle in court, Roberto Mancini had put a large chunk of his holdings under his sister/daughter's name. Now, with her future priest of the One True and Holy Church back in the bosom of her daily regard, she would release those assets back to her father/brother, little by little.

Nat wasn't angry with Jack; he even rather admired him, and felt that Jack's desire to follow in Nat's footsteps was a kind of compliment. Cookie Bates, who'd done most of the talking at the casino bar, had suggested that Nat see it as such. That Jack's desire to own Newcastle's corresponded with Mancini's wish to link his family with the respectability of the Newcastle name had sealed Nat's fate, of which Mancini was if not master, at least a major shareholder. Cookie Bates quoted a figure that was eight-hundred thousand more than what Nat had originally paid, and did not include what they would later negotiate for the property on Ursuline, which the restaurant would continue using for storage.

It seemed so soon after his father's memorial service to be attending yet another at Bolton Funeral Home. He knew he was at the age when such occasions would only accelerate in frequency toward that time when they would be routine. That was the price of the stability one enjoys growing up, then getting old in one place. So many of the connections that constitute a deep sense of home blink out, darken. Nat wondered if anyone was fully adult until tending to the dead became routine.

His father's funeral had been attended by so many of the luminaries of New Orleans, the Old Money who saw Nat as a not unpleasant curiosity; he'd always been a loner, at least among them, preferring as a young man the bohemian life of the Quarter to the complexities of rank determining their world: he'd married common twice, belonged to no social club or Carnival Krewes, and there had been gossip years ago about a terrible crime being committed against him, though details had varied as to what that had been. Some said he'd been kidnapped and held for ransom; others said he'd been beaten up and left for dead; one old school chum, a girl he'd dated thrice and fucked twice and who was now married to Greek shipping money, had insisted he'd been abducted by aliens. Such things do get back to one, especially Uptown. But now all gossip had fizzled; the vague and titillating stories had blown away years ago. There was only a mist of sadness through which his social peers observed him.

Nat's father had been mortified that so many of his clients and friends recognized Nat as a waiter at Newcastle's years after Nat had graduated from Tulane. He'd helped Nat put together the financing to purchase the restaurant, even though having a son who was a restaurant owner was only a little less mortifying than having one who was a waiter. Nat was actually glad his father's biological son turned out so much like the old man. The other family, the one he'd conducted in Baton Rouge, comprised of a forty-six-year-old woman, a twenty-four-year-old son in his second year of law school at Yale, and a nineteen-year-old daughter, had attended the funeral as discreetly as they could under the circumstances. Neither Nat nor his mother had contested their inclusion in the will; there was plenty to go around if one weren't greedy, and Nat had never been. He and his mother, wives and children had not addressed his father's other family; Nat would not even make eye contact with the woman when she glanced his way. He'd found her rather attractive, and had not wished to deal with such oddities of the heart as attraction to one's father's mistress. That Nat's father's mistress was the eldest daughter of his previous mistress, long deceased, was the kind of information he wished could be cleansed from memory. The simple fact was that Nat's father hadn't been around much. He'd been kind but distracted, and besides small, formal gestures of familial affection, which included nice chats at the dinner table on those increasingly rare occasions he'd been home, he'd shown Nat no strong feelings except embarrassment. In fact, Nat had been the gift of a faithless man to a shattered woman, a woman who'd had absolutely no connections to that most bizarre and most un-American of American cities she'd found herself in, a city she'd not even heard of before leaving Europe except from her young husband who'd assured her she'd be happy there. But she'd not been happy, and her American husband, a Southern Gentleman to the core, a man of honor, had compensated her with a flesh-and-blood doll, and for all intents and purposes, even as he provided for her and for that child of strangers, deserted her.

Nat couldn't recall what he'd written down just a few hours ago, and realized that since he'd scrawled it longhand he'd probably not be able to decipher some of it as he stood before the roughly one hundred and fifty people gathered for the service either, most of whom Bart had loathed and by whom he'd been loathed. Nat predicted a pathetic performance, but wasn't at all distressed. He'd take his best shot, but would probably sound like an overwrought drunken idiot, for he'd written it mostly drunk and was still a little drunk. Lou and the girls sat near the rear of the bank of neatly rowed folding chairs. When he'd told them a few hours ago that he was selling Newcastle's they'd been shocked, even Edie who hadn't been sure why she was shocked but followed her mother's and sister's leads. When he'd told them how much money he was being paid, shock, at least Lou's, shaded to joyful perplexity. What would he do? They could talk about that later. Four point six million, which was right around half a million over the restaurant's annual gross, was a pretty good grub stake. All Nat knew was that he had to get the fuck out of New Orleans, at least for a while. After the religious stuff, which Bart would have hated but had not in his instructions rejected, the mayor, a very well spoken black man with impeccable political instincts but who was otherwise a complete idiot, blathered charmingly for two minutes. Then a white writer in his sixties whose name was vaguely familiar spoke condescendingly for eight. Then Nat was called to the podium.

He cleared his throat, making a disgustingly wet hawking sound that got bounced about the large, open space by amplification. He glanced back at Lou and she was staring down, wincing.

"A person may have more than one mate over the course of a lifetime." The mike squawked, but Nat soldiered on. "He or she will likely have more than one job, even profession and, statistically, he or she is likely to participate in the creation of more than one child. In our society, many of us even have more than one mother or father. But there are two relationships, the exclusive province of youth, which may never be duplicated at mid-life or beyond."

Nat paused. His own handwriting was deteriorating before his eyes, and he'd forgotten to put on his glasses. He fished them clumsily out of his shirt pocket, and hung them on his nose, so now he did not have to hold the crinkled pages at arm's length. Where was he going with this? What the hell had he been thinking just a few hours ago when it was still dark outside and the bottle of Bushmills was still filled as high as the top of his fist.

"The first is that exclusive, usually but not always same-sex friendship which, if one is lucky, affords a soulmate to help one through the wonders and horrors of adolescence, unto that second relationship, that devastating and miraculous madness of young adulthood known as first love.

"Our gay brothers and lesbian sisters have always understood the deep-rooted psychic connection between these two life-defining, never-to-be-duplicated relationships. My guess is that most women, generally, also at least intuit the connection. It is straight males who fear, and repress as a result, the dynamism of that connection. We fear its homoerotic implications. We fear the connection between our best, usually male friend of adolescence and our first lover as young adults."

People began to fidget. The mayor was frowning. Several old timers who'd been back-slappingly close to Nat's father were just plain pissed. Everyone knew Bart had been queer, but it wasn't something you were supposed to talk about in his eulogy, for Christ's sake. And Nat felt them wondering if what he was getting at was that he, too, was a cocksucker.

"When we think we have found the love of our life, those of us capable of such feeling, we don't want to consider how that new, intense intimacy was in part determined by the one we had as kids with our best pals.

"Bart Linsey was my best friend through childhood and adolescence into young adulthood. We drifted apart, coming together with much delight but only occasionally into midlife. In a sense, when he died in my arms, he was a stranger, because so much of what he'd become after our lives had drifted one from the other was strange to me, so many of the details of his complex and emotionally rich life I simply could not know or even understand, and yet we were intimate strangers, because I knew his essence and he mine, I knew his boyhood dreams in as much detail as I knew my own, and had stood before the mysteries of life with him as only adolescents may, in that glory of radical innocence wherein resides the quintessence of hope, and which each of us must recover with all the midlife soulfulness we may manage if we are to have hope even as we are no longer innocent.

"What a blessing that my soulmate in adolescence was a poet, a singer of the mysteries of life, a soul as old as the farthest stars, and as inscrutable as the void beyond them! We would sit and talk for hours about aspects of life to which I am now numb but not entirely lost. Because my soul mate was a poet I had permission, as other boys did not, to express myself, my fears and my desires, my heart. I loved Bart Linsey, though I took that love so for granted I didn't give it the name of love. And when, as an adult but only a few years out of childhood, I gave my heart away, it was because my friend had taught me how, and I didn't even know it.

"With him died my youth, and yet with his passing, in the glow of the dignity with which he died, I found the courage to embrace the ghost of my youth, and tell her goodbye."

"I've never talked in front of a lot of people before, and I don't know why Bart Linsey told his lawyer he wanted me to talk to all you people about him, but he did and so I'm here talking to you, even though I don't know any of you, except the mayor from TV, and Mr Moore, I know him a little."

Willie dropped his head and closed his eyes. He took a deep breath. "Bart told me I was his muse, and that made me mad because the muses were girls, but then he told me it was okay because even my Uncle Teddy, who was Bart's friend, was his muse before me."

He looked around. Everyone stared at him. He wasn't scared and the longer he stood there the more not-scared he got. "There's not much to musing, I can tell you. All you've got to do is sit there and listen to what the poet says, and then tell the poet what you think. At least that's how it worked for Bart and

Uncle Teddy, but Uncle Teddy killed himself so Bart had to settle for me, and now I know why he made me his muse. I didn't know the whole time I was musing for him, but now I do." Willie got tears in his eyes, but he wasn't crying, not officially, because you couldn't hear the tears in his voice, and you're only crying if the tears are in your voice.

"He made me his muse because he knew how much my Uncle Teddy loved me."

Willie looked around and everybody was quiet as they could be and just looking at him. The flowers, their heavy sweet odor, filled his head as he breathed in to speak, and as he spoke he felt like the odor he'd breathed in was now talking.

"There are lots of things people don't know about my Uncle Teddy. They don't know he liked to read books and talk about them, and they don't know he loved jazz and would sometimes sit back with his eyes closed listening to the music and shake his head like it was talking to him. And people don't know he loved to cook. And he taught me how to put different things together just right, and treat them just right with the heat so they come together just right and taste as good as they can being one thing, one taste. And people don't know he loved to tell stories, and he loved to hear jokes, and he loved to go to the zoo, and people don't know he was in so much pain sometimes he would hold parts of himself, his arm or leg or neck and moan with tears in his eyes."

Willie looked around but everything was blurred, the faces of the people in the folding chairs, the ones who were standing on the sides and in the back. "And people don't know he loved Bart Linsey. And I guess that's the main thing I've got to say."

SECTION TWENTY-ONE

"You look like shit," said Bridget.

He slumped to the table. "Since I went on the wagon, I feel like shit."

"You smell like a distillery."

"Yeah, well, I just jumped on a few hours ago. Got some coffee?"

She filled the kettle with hot tap water, pulled down his blue mug, dumped in a spoonful of Community instant.

"How'd it go?" She'd liked Bart just fine, but hated any Uptown gatherings, especially if Lou was going to be there, so had begged out of going.

"I made an ass of myself, babbling about the connection between adolescent friendships and first love, and then a beautiful twelve-year-old kid got up after me and made me look like a phony asshole."

"Were you?"

"Some."

"You didn't go off on one of your jags, did you?"

"Yeah, kind of." He rubbed his eyes. He owed his body some sleep. "I sold the restaurant," he said.

"What?" She turned from the counter to face him, mouth open.

He explained.

"Well, I'll be damned," she said, putting the mug before him, smiling.

"You seem happy. Why?"

"Because I hated that fucking place. I knew you loved it more than you loved me."

"That isn't true. I never loved it more."

"There was something, Nat. From the time you knocked me up, you were distracted. Jesus, how many times have we been over this?"

"It wasn't Newcastle's."

"What was it then? Who was it? Who were you fucking? You can tell me now, Nathan."

A silence, the old silence, dead air between them, disconnectedness, an aggressive, even savage, silence. Then he told his first wife, the mother of their good and decent son, under the very roof he'd shared with her, under which he'd perpetrated so much savage silence, about a beautiful young woman savagely defiled and murdered, and about his own cowardice, how he'd witnessed the horror to save his own life, then watched and smelled her body decompose.

They were silent again for a full minute after he'd finished talking. Tears ran down her cheeks.

"You pathetic son of a bitch," she growled between clenched teeth. "You kept this from me our entire marriage? You've raised a son with me to adulthood and you're just now telling me about this? I could chew your balls off."

This was not the response he'd expected, but was somehow the one he was glad to be getting.

"I'm sorry. I couldn't. I can't tell you how it affected me," he mumbled.

"Nathan Moore, you self-centered prick, I *can* tell you how it affected *me*. I married a man I wanted to spend my life with, and had a child with him and would've had others, but though he was always sweet, always caring, he was never *with* me. And I never understood why. But now I find out it's because he was out of his fucking mind with grief. And she was the love of your life?"

Nat nodded.

"Horseshit. She became the love of your life after she died."

"You don't know that. You can't."

"Nat, it all falls into place, now. It all makes sense now."

"What makes sense?"

"My life with you!" she shouted. "You've seen two deaths in your days, right? I grant you the first one was a doozy, but do you have any idea how much death I've seen in twenty years? I've watched more babies die than I could begin to count. I've seen boys who thought they were men weep like babies as they bled to death inside. I've heard old people dying lucidly, weeping for their mamas. While you were helping customers decide which Sauternes to order with dessert I was trying to coax patients to sleep on their sides so their bedsores would heal." She pulled up the bottom of her blouse and wiped her face.

"I knew what you were going through. I listened, Bridget. I really did."

"But what did you hear?"

"I heard a woman lamenting all the pain she was witnessing and I heard her scream and held her hand as she pushed a beautiful child out of herself. Darling, I always respected you for your work. I always felt we were connected by the work we did. We tend to people, you and I. I've always been happiest making others happy, and so have you."

"Keeping people happy and keeping them alive are not necessarily the same thing."

"I know that. I'm not trying to say what I do is as important as what you do."

"And I'm not trying to say it isn't. I'm just saying that death keeps happening; life too. And there's got to be at least one person in the world at any given moment of your life who knows everything about you. I offered you that. I offered to take everything. I wanted all of you, and I knew there was something you kept from me and now I find out it's a corpse." New tears gathered and fell.

"It wasn't a corpse," he whispered, and touched her arm. She turned her head towards him.

"What was it, then?"

"You asked me the other day if I'd ever cheated on you. I'm telling you now I cheated on you every day of our marriage, as I've cheated on Lou every day of my marriage to her until today."

She said nothing. He swallowed hard. "Sandra lived in the apartment above the storage space over on Ursuline. I bought the building the year before you and I were married. Daddy knew the owners. I got a good deal."

He closed his eyes to see Sandra, and could only manage her dead, defiled body. This, he assumed, was progress. "The thing is, I kind of kept her there, in that apartment. She became my mistress. She insisted that I marry and have kids because she knew how desperately I wanted a family. I stayed at the restaurant waiting tables because it was close to her apartment. She lived a good life. Painted, tended to her birds. I told her everything, everything about you, about Nestor, and then about Lou and the girls. She knew everything about my life. She advised me, scolded me, teased me. I watched her age. But now she's gone."

"Where'd she go?" Bridget whispered.

He thought about it. "I'm not sure. All I know is it's like she died again, but this time with a little dignity. I have a history with her. Twenty years. I could tell you stories," he sighed.

"You told her everything?"

"Everything worth telling."

"You talked? I mean, you really talked?"

"Yeah. Every day, almost. Some days she was too busy, or I was. But there was nothing about my life she didn't know."

She wrinkled her brow in thought. "Nat, if she'd lived, are you sure she'd be what you made her?"

"It's funny, but I've never even considered that. I've just always assume..."

"I remember the name. You mentioned her. A girl named Sandra. You told me it didn't work out."

"That was the only lie I ever told you," he said.

"Besides our entire marriage?"

"Yeah, besides that."

"Ever since I met you, you've been involved, deeply and intimately, with a figment of your imagination?"

"So to speak."

"Well, I hate the bitch!"

"She's gone now, for good."

They sat in silence for a long time, but it was not like the silence they used to occupy together. It wasn't a void. It seemed charged.

"Katie found out," she finally whispered.

"About your new friend?"

"Yeah, I'm in love with her. Drop-dead in love."

"And she feels the same?"

"Yep."

"And Katie's probably, well, fucked up."

"Yep."

"What's she going to do?"

"She's moved back to her mother's. And she's given notice at the hospital. She's already got another job lined up."

"You guys staying friends?"

"Yeah, women do, most of the time."

"And your new love?"

"We don't know. She and her partner are getting untangled. They've got some property issues to deal with. But we're taking off to spend two weeks up in Provincetown. She's got a little bungalow on the beach her parents own. We're going to try to figure everything out."

"How's Nestor taking this?"

"He's sad. He loves Katie. He's with her right now. They're sailing."

"That's why he didn't make it to the service?"

"Yep. They need this time together. I leave at the end of the week. Will you come over and take care of the plants and do the lawn, check the mail, that kind of stuff?"

"Sure. Where's Nes going to be?"

"He and that kid he works with… what's his name? They're going to Chicago on the train. They're meeting some people about that Internet chess scheme they've got."

"Halle-fucking-lujah," Nat whispered and raised his hands and eyes to heaven.

"Well, we'll see what comes of it. But at least he's moving his ass." They were silent a moment; it was that good, new silence. "Nat I'm so sorry for what happened to you. All those years I knew you were damaged goods. I just didn't know how damaged."

"It's okay. I'm sorry for what I put you through. I did love you. I do love you."

"I know," she said, and put her hand over his on the table. That new silence; then, "Before you go, would you change the bulb in the hall?"

For five days, right through Fat Tuesday, Nat Moore thought himself the only sober man in the city of New Orleans; there may have been others, but they were either huddled together in AA meeting halls, hunkered down as for a hurricane, or ghosting the thinnest fringes of the crowds gathered to beg for trinkets. All the girls' lives he'd worked long hours each Carnival season, squeezing every dollar he could from the increased and randy clientele. This time he'd taken them to all the big parades, and even attended a party in Algiers Lou's oldest brother threw for the extended family, which included those fishy, toothless, eleven-fingered Cajun boys Bridget, Nestor and Katie loved to goof on. Lou's brother Pierre roasted a big pig, something of a religious ritual in Lou's family, and it yielded the most succulent, tasty flesh Nat could recall ever having eaten. Pierre had taken it as a personal insult that Nat wasn't drinking, and Lou had even asked him if he was quitting for good. He'd told her probably not, but that it was the right thing for right now. All and all, she'd seemed indifferent on the subject.

Eighty or so people had been at the gathering; Nat had come to think of them as the usual suspects, people he saw only on those occasions and usually only in that particular place, a blue shotgun with a huge back and side yard. As Edie had run with one tribe of cousins, and Marti with another, Nat had taken his wife aside and told her about his birth mother, and that on Wednesday, Ash Wednesday, he'd fetch her from the airport. Lou had seemed mildly pleased, but obviously didn't really give a damn. He'd considered telling her about his secret life, but knew that she wouldn't understand the way Bridget did, did not require such knowledge.

Nat parked a block up on Magazine and walked back to the shop, a bright-blue camelback with vanilla trim. He was surprised to see the red-letters-on-black CLOSED sign hanging on the door, especially given that the van was parked right in front. The usual drill was for Lou to watch the place while her partner Becky went to lunch and then at around one-forty picked up Edie and her own kid from preschool. Nat had hoped to coax Lou into closing the place for a couple of hours and going to lunch with him before he headed out to the air-port. He wanted to talk about the future.

He peered through the glass, pressing his face to it and making a little tent with his hands around his eyes to diminish the glare. The door to the rear was closed. She would not hear him if he rapped on the door.

He climbed clumsily over the low gate to the side of the store; the little alley between camelbacks was overgrown with weeds, and just on the other side of the gate Nat stepped on something soft he did not feel inclined to inspect.

He could make out her torso through the rear window, her bountiful, beautiful breasts hanging down as she was bent over and writhing. He heard the little hiccuppy staccato yelps she made in lovemaking, though they were inter-spersed with pleasure moans of such intensity as he had never heard issue from her. She was taking it from behind, and loving it, and though Nat could see the top half of her beautiful, voluptuous body in an ecstatic state, due to the angle and the play of shadow and glare, he could not see the agent of joy.

He backtracked, stunned. In front of the shop he noticed that the van behind their own belonged to Percy the bottled water guy. *Percy* was stenciled on the door of his vehicle, and Nat recalled that Percy indeed serviced his and Lou's house, and remembered only because he'd never known anyone named Percy, and *Percy* was even sewn on a patch over his pocket, and he was a large, very dark and lovely man who hauled a plastic jug filled with spring water on each muscular shoulder when he entered the house through the back door.

In heavy traffic on the way to the airport, Nat recalled his final attendance at Newcastle's. As he'd rounded the corner of Dauphine onto St Louis, he'd spotted just ahead of him Jack and Birdsong with their arms wrapped around each other. She'd seemed to walk rather gingerly. He'd shot back around the corner to await their going in first, then, after a couple of minutes, strode through the front door of Newcastle's for the last time in his life, for he was resolved never again to step foot in the place. The meeting had been brief and to the point. He gave hugs all around, went to his office and cleared out what he needed, mostly files, a few books and mementos. He'd dumped everything into a dark green trash bag, and hauled it Santa-like out the back door of the restaurant, glancing once at the silver dishwasher.

As he drove, he considered how except for his children he was utterly alone in the world. He realized, though, that if he shared such a revelation with Grace she'd laugh in his face, and appropriately so. Everyone knows he or she is alone, but feels the full weight of that condition but rarely. His one true love, the one woman to whom he'd been faithful, required nothing of him because she required nothing, being herself nothing. His first wife, whom he had loved but poorly, did not require him for anything but small domestic tasks. His "present" wife required him fiscally, but obviously had committed her deepest womanly desires to the able charge of someone other than himself.

That life is a series of gambles and accidents, crashed plans and blown bluffs, tore only at the father part of him; he feared for his children mightily but now regarded his own extinction less with terror or longing than wonder. Wherever death was, he figured he'd already been there, swimming among the stars, or lolling in the guts of a car radio in east Texas the night Billy Epstein charmed the panties off a sixteen-year-old girl named Grace.

The world careened toward complete annihilation; the very fact that there was a limit not just to human life but to species existence was the dreadful jackpot; that timeless void, and not eternal bliss, pours from the bowels of the ultimate One-Armed Bandit Nat was certain.

A light rain commenced, mixing with and loosening the permanent film of grease and oil on I-10, making it more treacherous than it would be completely soaked. Ahead of Nat in the middle lane was an eggshell white early-80s Chrysler with LICENSE APPLIED FOR scrawled on a ragged piece of paper and taped to the driver's side of the rear window. Only in Louisiana, Nat knew, could so many people be so cavalier about registering automobiles, and indeed it seemed that on any given day in New Orleans literally one out of thirty cars had LICENSE APPLIED FOR signs in their rear windows.

Nat did not like how LICENSE APPLIED FOR was hugging the bumper of the Chevy truck in front of it, so he gunned his tight light BMW into the fast lane even as the rain intensified, and sliced through what swiftly became torrential with the ease one should expect from a forty-seven thousand dollar automobile.

Hitting his lights and cranking the wipers up a notch, he settled back into the center lane, and just as he did witnessed in his rear-view mirror the Chrysler spinning out and getting plowed into.

Nat did not look again. He kept driving, in a sensible manner, past Williams Boulevard to the Airport Exit. He gripped the wheel to keep his hands from shaking, and coming out of the looping turn down from the overpass off-ramp onto the road running parallel with the north/south runway, Nat settled into the thirty-five mile an hour limit numerous signs threatened one must not exceed, and let the thwacking of the wipers calm him. Nat walked the long corridor to the gate and realized suddenly that he needed to indicate who he was. He begged a piece of paper from a fellow sitting just inside the waiting area, scribbling on a notepad. The guy quickly, distractedly lifted the sheet he was working figures on and tore a fresh sheet and passed it to Nat without looking at him.

Nat bummed a pen from an airline employee behind the gate counter, and wrote in big letters GRACE. As the passengers from the flight began to pour through the gate, he held the little sign to his heart.